Forgotten Florida

Forgotten Florida

An Engaging Story of the Building of Tallahassee, the Establishment of Key West, and the Settlement of Sanibel Island

Clarissa Thomasson

Pineapple
Press
Palm Beach, Florida

Pineapple Press
An imprint of Globe Pequot, the trade division of
The Rowman & Littlefield Publishing Group, Inc.
4501 Forbes Blvd., Ste. 200
Lanham, MD 20706
www.rowman.com

Distributed by NATIONAL BOOK NETWORK

British Library Cataloguing in Publication Information available

Library of Congress Cataloging-in-Publication Data
Names: Thomasson, Clarissa, author.
Title: Forgotten Florida : an engaging story of the building of Tallahassee, the establishment of
  Key West, and the settlement of Sanibel Island / Clarissa Thomasson.
Description: Lanham, MD : Pineapple Press, an imprint of Globe Pequot, the trade division
  of The Rowman & Littlefield Publishing Group, Inc., [2022] | Includes bibliographical
  references. | Summary: "Forgotten Florida tells the story of the Florida peninsula from the
  Adams-Onis Treaty in 1819 to the beginning of the Second Seminole War in 1835. The story
  is told from the perspective of well-documented men who took part in the development of
  the Gulf coastal areas from Pensacola to Key West and include Commodore David Porter,
  Colonel James Gadsden, Colonel George Brooke, Colonel Duncan Clinch, and Major Francis
  Dade as well as Captain William Bunce of the Aristocrat and Captain Fred Tresca of the
  Margaret Ann-both of whom sailed the Gulf coast from Key West to Pensacola and served to
  connect the various settlements"— Provided by publisher.
Identifiers: LCCN 2021061030 (print) | LCCN 2021061031 (ebook) | ISBN 9781683343172
  (paperback) | ISBN 9781683343189 (epub)
Subjects: LCSH: Florida—History—1821-1865. | Tallahassee (Fla.)—History—19th century. |
  Key West (Fla.)—History—19th century. | Sanibel Island (Fla.)—History—19th century. |
  Florida—Biography.
Classification: LCC F315 .T43 2022 (print) | LCC F315 (ebook) | DDC 975.9/04—dc23/
  eng/20220301
LC record available at https://lccn.loc.gov/2021061030
LC ebook record available at https://lccn.loc.gov/2021061031

This book is dedicated to the many men and women who devoted their lives to bringing the fragile and forbidding land of Florida into existence and to its many current sons and daughters—whose lives have been immeasurably enriched by the sacrifices of so many over the past two hundred years.

Contents

Introduction

$\mathcal{O}$n Ponce de Leon's first voyage to the Florida peninsula in 1513, he claimed "La Florida" for Spain—a claim vehemently disputed by the Calusa Indians on his subsequent visit to the southwest coast in 1521 when he was mortally wounded as he attempted to set up a colony near present Charlotte Harbor. From that point through the Third Seminole War, which did not end until 1858, two ideologies warred to claim possession of the land—often described as sweltering, swampy, overgrown, insect-ridden, and alligator-infested—albeit vastly important to the farming and fishing efforts of local Indian tribes—and to Spain, England, and the early United States as each sought to establish safe shipping lanes through a hotbed of notorious pirates and illegal slave traders.

The first Spanish settlement was located on the upper east coast of the peninsula and became the town of St. Augustine—established in 1565. Spanish missions were built along the northern border of the territory and attempts were made to educate and convert the natives to Christianity. From the beginning, however, the native ideology of existing from sunup to sundown and season to season with the land and the bounty of fish, game, and crops it produced was an anomaly to the European mind-set of land possession, colonization, and control.

Despite a brief period of English control from 1764–1783, Spain did little to populate the peninsula while they controlled it—even allowing General Andrew Jackson to pursue marauding Indian tribes into Spanish territory to keep them below U.S. borders during the First Seminole War, from 1817–1818.

By 1818, Spain's King Ferdinand was tired of dealing with Indian problems, Jackson's forays into northern Florida, and the heavy debt he had incurred to the United States. Wanting to rid himself of the problems of Spanish Florida, he divided the territory into three parcels and bestowed them as gifts to his three favorite noblemen—thereby passing the land and all its problems on to them.

Southwest Florida from the Suwannee River to Biscayne Bay in present Miami was given to Duke Alagon. While thrilled with the gift, Alagon had no intention of colonizing the area, but he did need money. So he offered to sell his new possession to his good friend Richard Hackley, the U.S. Consul at Cadiz, Spain. Planning to return home shortly, the wealthy New York lawyer decided on a lark to purchase the land—which might come in handy someday.

The date of the legal agreement Alagon and Hackley signed was disputed until 1905 when the U.S. Supreme Court finally ruled that the purchase was finalized before King Ferdinand eventually agreed to negate all purchases and give the entire peninsula to the United States for the forgiveness of his five-million-dollar debt.

The thirty-six years from the 1819 Adams-Onis Treaty until the end of the Third Seminole War in 1855 saw the constant confrontations as President Jackson sought to contain the Seminoles in a remote area of north-central Florida and then to remove all natives from the territory—to open the land to new U.S. settlers.

• *1* •

September 1823

 $\mathcal{J}$ unlight bounced from the white crests of the three-foot waves that assailed the flat, sandy beach as the large schooner rounded the point and headed to the makeshift dock at the port of "Thompson's Island"—originally called "Cayo Hueso"—a Spanish term meaning "Key West." Far from deserted as Robert Hackley had expected, the harbor was filled with a roiling flotilla of small, identical two-mast ships belonging to the U.S. Navy—and popularly called the "Mosquito Fleet," whose newly established purpose was to eradicate piracy in the Caribbean and Gulf of Mexico.

The cries of the crew as they hurried to lower and gather the billowing sails were drowned out by a cacophony of braying oxen, mooing cattle, protesting pigs, and disgruntled chickens penned beneath the hull and being thrown into one another as the ship turned against the prevailing wind and laboriously made its way to the long, wooden pier jutting into the churning current at the juncture of the Atlantic Ocean and Gulf of Mexico. It was a perilous feat in the best of times, and even more so today as the wind blowing east from the Atlantic threatened to impale the ship on the extended wooden structure. After much maneuvering, however, the schooner eventually was pulled alongside the long dock—where the crew was able to secure its moorings and bring it to a rest in the turbulent harbor.

Finally exiting the cabin and struggling for a foothold on the rolling deck, Robert Hackley attempted to secure his cap atop his wildly blowing light brown hair with one hand—while offering a clumsy salute with the other as he poised to jump onto the dock—amid a group of several armed guards, which had quickly materialized in front of a small, hastily erected building—rifles drawn. A crude sign above the door read "Customs House."

"Robert Hackley, New York," Robert called over the cacophony in a joyful attempt to break the chilling reception. "Heading up the Gulf Coast," he continued—pulling a rash of documents from his jacket pocket and waving them at the men as his crew continued to secure the rigging—while watching over their shoulders as the guards advanced.

"Sorry for the unfriendly welcome, but we can't be too careful," the lead officer called out. Lowering his rifle, he walked onto the dock and reached out to take the papers as Robert disembarked onto the rolling surface. Quickly perusing them, the officer then turned and carefully assessed the large schooner before him—with its cargo of wooden poles, logs, and agricultural instruments lashed to the deck—and the never-ending braying and mooing emanating from below.

Nodding, he handed the papers back to Robert and reached out his hand. "Received a message from one of our ships out of St. Augustine that you were en-route—but I'm not sure what it is you want down here. Planning to build a homestead with all that lumber? Or more importantly, are you interested in building our officers' mess for the U.S.'s Anti-Piracy Squadron? We can use all the help we can get," he laughed—as the other three men also lowered their weapons and returned to their station at the Custom House door.

"Building a homestead," Robert smiled—attempting to gain a foothold on the swaying dock. "Not here, though. Got me some land farther up the coast—at an area called 'Tampa.' It's at the juncture of Hillsborough Bay and the Hillsborough River," he added—gesturing to the north. "Good distance I believe. Hope to get there before the days get too short—got a lot of work to do. We just stopped for a few supplies before we head on."

"Hope you only need a few because that's all we have down here right now. Commodore David Porter," the slim, clean-shaven, darkly tanned middle-aged man offered—shoving an errant, curling lock of dark hair back under his officer's hat and holding out his hand. "Got some Cuban coffee inside, though," he offered—motioning toward the rude, wooden structure at the end of the pier.

"Far cry from New York," Robert muttered—replacing the papers in his pocket and removing his heavy jacket with a sigh. "Is it always this hot down here?" he asked—wiping his forehead as he followed Porter up the dock to the rude structure at the end.

"Even hotter," his escort answered. "Good thing is that summer's ended now—although the temperature won't prove it. At any rate, we had a pretty bad time with the yellow fever earlier this summer—endured a bout of it myself. Commodore Biddle even had to take his *Macedonia* back north with a shipload of pretty sick sailors on board. From what I heard, when they returned to Hampton Roads, seventy-six of the sailors had died and fifty-two were sick.

"And that fever's only the beginning for our ships out there," he added—pointing over his shoulder toward the west and the Gulf of Mexico. "If your crew is well, then just try heading out into the Straits on the lookout for Jean Lafitte, or the notorious Blackbeard, or one of the slave ships! No shade on deck when we go after them."

"But I was told that your 'Mosquito Fleet'—or your 'West Indies Squadron,' I think it's more properly called—had made the Gulf of Mexico safe for travel now," Robert answered—as Porter pushed open the door of the Custom House and ushered him inside. "My father has bought a fairly large plot of land up the west coast, and I'm planning to set up a homestead there. I was only expecting to take on some supplies here and move on. Are you saying we're not safe out there?" he continued—pointing toward the churning waters visible just beyond the open door.

"What exactly have you heard?" Porter asked, interested—as he removed his hat and hung it on the hat rack beside the door. "Not much news makes it down here." Turning to a nearby table, he picked up two cups and filled them with a very dark coffee. Handing one to Robert, he motioned to a nearby chair and sat down himself at his desk—while pushing a stack of papers to one side. "Just want to know how our fame has spread," he continued—offering a quizzical gaze at Robert.

"Well, the report my father, Richard Hackley, received before he sent me off here was that Lt. Commander Matthew Perry had taken Cayo Hueso from Cuba about a year and a half ago and named it 'Thompson's Island' to honor our Secretary of the Navy. I was told when I disembarked at St. Augustine that President Monroe had established you and your 'Mosquito Fleet' down here with sixteen vessels . . . ," Robert began hesitantly—pausing to take a drink of his coffee and trying to hide his distaste of the powerful brew.

"Correct," Porter nodded, settling down in his chair and enjoying his guest's discomfort. "So go on, what else are they saying about me?"

"Well, you see . . . ," Robert answered uncomfortably, "those in the know told my father that the Gulf was now safe for travel—as you and your fleet had removed all the piracy and slavers."

"You're just a young man—who obviously still believes in fairy tales," Porter laughed—smiling at Robert over his coffee cup.

"You . . . mean it's not safe to sail into the Gulf of Mexico? And I thought . . . I mean, my father said he had heard . . ."

"Tall tales travel far. The truth is that our Thompson's Island is the best harbor within the limits of the United States or its territories, south of the Chesapeake. It's protected in most directions—with the prevailing wind from the east. It's usually pretty tranquil down here, but can be powerful sometimes as you and your crew experienced today with the tropical gale that's blown up. September is noted for storms. The harbor, however, is deep enough to accommodate most of the navy's largest ships—which makes it ideal for our operations. With that said, I felt it well within the jurisdiction of the U.S. Navy to secure the port against the likes of Blackbeard and William Kidd, who've been using the Florida Keys for years as a base where they could prey on U.S. shipping interests.

"Oh, we've had our successes and have gotten rid of Jean Lafitte, Steve Bonnet, and Black Caesar as well, and even the lady pirates like Anne Bonny and Mary Read. Now there was a tough lady, I'll tell you!" he laughed. "The woman dressed as a man and terrorized ships all over the Caribbean. Yes, son, we've had our successes, and although I'd like to believe your father's claim, I won't say we've made the Caribbean and the Gulf entirely safe at this point."

"Then, what you're saying . . . ," Robert answered hesitantly.

"Is that you'll need all those crew members armed and ready to defend your shipment—if and when your cargo becomes apparent. Selling those oxen, cattle, hogs, and chickens in Cuba could bring a hefty profit for any of our pirates. And I daresay they won't treat the rest of you civilly, either. Many a body we've found washed up in the mangroves up the coast. If the crew is lucky enough to be left alive, we've heard many of the captured sailors are being sold into slavery themselves."

"Then, are you saying we should turn back?" Robert asked. "I promised my father . . ."

"Let's give you an escort," Porter smiled. Picking up a ledger and running his finger down the listing, he pushed himself away from his desk. Walking to the door, he motioned to one of the guards stationed outside. "Can you find Voorhees for me?" he asked. "I think he's taking the *Sea Gull* out one last time tomorrow."

"Right, Commodore Porter," the man answered—saluting as he ran off down the dock to a makeshift structure positioned on the mainland.

"Captain Ralph Voorhees is scheduled to patrol from Thompson's Island up the Gulf of Mexico tomorrow," Porter replied, returning to his desk. "He's going as far as the mainland—just above all those mangrove islands out there—which we judge to be the uppermost reaches of our Caribbean piracy. If you follow the *Sea Gull* and head on up the coast from there, you should be in safe waters. Only crafts up that far are some of the rancho fishing boats, and they only care about getting their catches to Cuba alive.

"Once you get adjacent to the actual coast, you will find several of those ranchos on the many islands—all the way up to the entrance to Bahia Tampa. Owners are mostly Spanish—but friendly—if you speak Spanish!" Porter laughed.

"Spent most of my childhood in Spain," Robert nodded. "My dad was a consul in Cadiz for many years."

"Then you should get along just fine with them—if the need should arise. Remember, fall is especially prone to heavy storms coming up from Cuba—so it's imperative that you seek cover when one approaches. Why don't I give you a list of the various settlements and their owners? Let's see—I've met several down here on their way back north. One you really ought to meet is Jose Caldez—elderly fellow all wizened with constant exposure to sun and sea, but pleasant enough. Has a rancho up at Useppa Island near Charlotte Harbor. He employs about twenty men, who have mostly married local Indian women and produced a veritable passel of mixed Spanish Indian children. Women and children live on the rancho year-round, while the men do the sailing and bargaining in Havana. Ranch should be in full swing right now.

"Accommodations are not what you will be used to, however. Bunch of small wooden homes about fifteen feet square roofed in palmetto thatch. Sparse furniture and beds designed to ruin even the toughest of backs. Since you have a pretty comfortable cabin on your own craft, I advise against accepting a room for the night. Still . . . you can't beat the meals they will serve you—fish of all varieties, potatoes, citrus fruits to your heart's content. Oh, and I forgot to mention their Cuban coffee! Some of our men down here swear by it, but I don't think you share their feelings!" he laughed—looking at Robert's full mug on the table in front of him.

"And then, let's see—if you venture farther up the coast, you will find the Caldez brothers, Joaquin and Jose, up at a place called Oyster River—near Sarazota Bay. Their two ranchos have over six hundred acres each. And then there's Andrew Gonzales a little farther north on the same bay. Let me tell you, if you like citrus fruit, you really should pay one of those ranchos a visit. Besides the fish, they have cultivated extensive groves of orange and lime trees. I think I heard that Gonzales has over fifteen acres planted in them!"

"Having learned to love oranges while in Spain, I might take a side trip to Sarazota Bay, then," Robert nodded.

"As for the area north of Sarazota Bay, I'd be a little wary of the Seminoles, who live in the area. Chief is called Neamathla—older man with dark, fierce visage. Very smart, I hear, and rules with a firm hand. His reservation is a little farther north and west—near the Apalachicola River, but that doesn't stop his tribe from venturing down the coast— lots of fishing and hunting near Hillsborough Bay. Good spot for them to barter with Cubans and Bahamians for arms and ammunition as well. The chief caused a lot of trouble in our first encounter when Spain was still in control of the territory.

"Good news, though, is that our territorial governor, William Duval, is negotiating with Neamathla this month in Moultrie Creek—south of St. Augustine. Proposal is to offer his five tribes a permanent reservation in the center of the state—where they will be protected and compensated for the loss of their land. Knowing the Seminoles, however, I don't expect it to be an easy sell," Porter laughed. "So I'd advise you to keep a lookout until you hear your area is safe."

"I heard about the Moultrie Creek meeting when I was in St. Augustine," Robert nodded. "Those with whom I spoke seemed to hold out great hope for ending the hostilities with the natives."

"No one hopes it ends peacefully more than I. Pirates give us enough trouble without another native uprising! At any rate, I expect you need to get moving," Porter said, rising and pushing back his chair. "I'll write the names of the rancho owners down and the general directions. Never know when you might need to drop in on one of them in a storm."

"I . . . I can't thank you enough, sir," Robert offered, breathing a sigh. "It's just that . . ."

"Don't thank me, son, thank President Monroe, who saw fit to send us down here to protect our U.S. shipping interests. At any rate, I'm going to be taking the *Sea Gull* back north for repairs in the next few days, and Voorhees needed to check out a few items before he gives me the command.

"But now—as to those supplies you need . . . don't know how many building supplies we can rustle up for you. It took an awful lot to erect the base down here. Makeshift though it may seem you will note there is little lumber available on these islands—unless you count the palm trees!"

"I actually think we have all the building materials we need. Mainly, though, we need food for the oxen and cattle we loaded in St. Augustine. My Lord, nobody told me how much they can eat," Robert laughed—relaxing a bit.

"Think that can be arranged. And what else?"

"Well, my crew is a good one, but they eat a lot, too, and I don't expect we can find much up the coast."

"Unless you buy a load of sheepshead or mullet from one of those ranchos up the way. But I warn you, their cargos don't come cheap! There's big money to be made in Cuba.

"Better yet, why don't I introduce you to our new neighbor down here, Captain William Bunce? Fellow recently arrived from Baltimore with get-rich-quick ideas of setting up a dry goods store down here—sometime after the New Year. He brought a whole ship load of supplies with him. Only problem is that our personal supplies are shipped down here by a naval supply ship—and the few other residents down here are used to Spanish food and the Cuban coffee—which I notice you loved, judging by your full cup. Still, I think you can find what you need at Bunce's mercantile, and I think you will make his day if you purchase all you mentioned. If you like, I'll walk you over. It's just beyond the barracks," Porter offered—standing and heading to the door.

"Give me a moment to alert the crew as to where I am going," Robert smiled—replacing his cap and following Porter to the door.

Beyond the harbor and the hastily erected naval yard, the small town of less than a hundred inhabitants was laid out in a diagonal fashion extending from the westward Gulf of Mexico and running southeast to end at the Atlantic Ocean's long, wide stretch of sun-bleached sand—littered today with piles of seaweed washed up by the churning tide. As the former "North Havana," most of the residents were still of Spanish descent—their homes simple, light-colored, wood frame one- to two-story structures—generally set on foundation piers about three feet above the ground to allow for occasional flooding from storms. Several had covered porches or balconies fronting on the street, and a few sported picket fences bordering the property. Landscaping was achieved mainly by several lone palm trees set along the dirt road. Interspersed along the main street were a few commercial establishments—such as a fish monger, a small lawyer's office, and a hastily erected town office.

As Porter led Robert eastward off naval property—and into the continuing gale—he stopped at a construction site at the end of the street adjacent to the churning Atlantic. "Not usually this windy," he apologized—struggling to hold on to his hat. "But without much shipping today, I daresay Bunce will be happy to have a customer!"

The small shop was indeed still under construction—with a team of local Cuban carpenters on the roof of the single-story structure busily conversing in Spanish and laughing at a comrade who was struggling to hold on to a wide plank—that threatened to take him with it off the roof.

"Dónde está, Señor Bunce?" Porter called up to the men on the roof.

"Dentro," the closest man answered—pointing below to the main door.

"We're in luck," Porter smiled. "Didn't know if he'd be on his ship or not. Guess—finished or not—it's better to be on terra firma in today's gale. Come on, I'll introduce you, and then, I'm afraid I'll need to head back," he added, opening the small door and ushering Robert inside.

The small establishment appeared to be an open storeroom with only a tiny, unpainted wooden counter in place by the front door.

Noticing no one about inside, Porter headed to the back of the room—peering around a large stack of cartons. "Bunce?" he called. "Brought you a customer!"

"Porter? Just the man I want to see," a booming voice bellowed as a large, burly Irishman with an unruly, bushy red beard called—materializing from the dark interior. "And what does our fearless leader want this time? Have I violated any naval restrictions?"

"No violations, I'm happy to say. Just thought you might want a little company—a man who speaks your language and needs some of the many supplies you brought with you! Captain William Bunce, may I introduce you to Captain Robert Hackley—from New York. I daresay he's even more adventurous than you—as he's heading up the Gulf to set up a homestead and is in need of some food—for his livestock—as well as his crew."

"Welcome, Captain Hackley," Bunce called, wiping his hand on his stained apron before offering it to Robert.

"Expecting to head up the coast tomorrow," Robert smiled, "and Commodore Porter assures me you can supply what I need."

"Leaving you two to discuss business. Need to get back for an afternoon briefing to the *Sea Gull*'s crew before they set out tomorrow," Porter explained as he turned and left the store.

"I'd offer you a chair—if I had one," Bunce laughed. "But let's just pull up a box or two and get acquainted. I can't tell you how good it is to find someone from home who speaks my language. Tough dealing with all the hierarchy over at the base—as well as practicing my Spanish for the locals," he laughed, swinging a large wooden crate into the room, perching on top of it, and motioning to an adjoining one for Robert. "So tell me what you're doing way down here and what it is you need."

"Heading up the coast," Robert offered as he ran his hand over the suggested crate to check for any errant nails before taking a seat.

"Planning on establishing a rancho? Good fishing in the Gulf and profitable market in Cuba. A lot of them must be vacant now that Spain has pulled out of Florida, though. Think a lot of the owners have gone back to Cuba. Got an idea where you want to locate?"

"Fishing's not in my plans. I'm really looking to build a homestead. Actually, my father bought a large swath of property on the territory's west coast. Hear there's a bay up there that DeSoto explored. Lots of lumber and good grazing land . . . I've got my own team of oxen and cattle—not to mention hogs and chickens—so we'll at least have some food until we get the land cleared and planted."

"Shouldn't have any lack of fish as well—if what I hear is true. Both fish and shellfish are so common up the Gulf they practically jump into the boats, the locals say. Those coastal ranchos are so close to Cuba they can run a boat across in one day. That is if one of the pirates or slavers doesn't get you first," Bunce added with a loud guffaw. "Thought about starting one myself but listening to the men down at the naval yard, I figure I'd do better to save my own scalp until their Mosquito Fleet gets rid of all the pirates. I have a particular aversion to my red scalp being sought as a prize among all the dark ones!

"But you're so young. Why is it you want to venture out alone up the coast? I mean, do you have plans to start a colony up there, or what?"

"Have you heard of a man named S. S. Seymour?"

"Just got down here myself," Bunce replied—shaking his head. "Does he own one of the ranchos?"

"I think he's more of a vagabond explorer. Works up the coast near the large inlet the Spanish called 'Bahia Tampa.'"

"Got a love for the natives, does he? That's an old Tocobaga area. I think it was initially called 'Tanpa'—meaning 'sticks of fire'—I heard from one of the rancho owners who stopped here a few weeks ago. And does this Seymour still have his scalp?"

"According to my father, he's still very much alive. At any rate, my father, Richard Hackley, hired him to look over his property. Seymour said the area was pretty much virgin land—and he didn't see any natives if that answers your question. At any rate, he gave the area such glowing reviews that we decided it was a good idea for me to look at the area, set up a homestead, and hope others see the same possibilities. Besides, it was a diversion for me to get away from my dad's law office for a while.

"Right now, I have all the lumber and fencing I need for a home and barns on board my father's new schooner. As green as I am as a sailor, however, I'm afraid I didn't count on the appetites of the men I hired in St. Augustine and the two yoke of oxen and eight cattle I secured there. Mainly need food stuffs for both, and Commodore Porter assured me you could provide them. I can send some of my crew over here if you've got what I need. We plan to leave in the morning—when the USS *Sea Gull* is set on a reconnaissance mission. Porter assures me we should be safe following them," he continued—removing a folded list from his pocket.

"Why not give me your list," Bunce nodded, nimbly jumping from the box and taking the paper, "and we'll see what we can do. Is your ship over at the naval yard?" he asked, waiting for Robert's nod. "Then I'll need you with me when we deliver. Seems those navy guys don't trust the locals I have working for me. But rest assured, we can get you whatever you need.

"Nice to have made your acquaintance," he continued—pocketing the list and reaching out to shake hands. "Who knows, when I get tired down here and things quiet down in the Gulf, I may decide to head up your way to take over one of those ranchos. My *Associate* is just waiting to pull anchor, and—truth is—after so many years of sailing in Baltimore, I'm itching to get back on the sea myself!"

• *2* •

September 1823

$\mathcal{A}$ bright sunray sneaking through the tiny east-facing porthole brought Robert suddenly upright in his bunk and onto his feet. The *Sea Gull* was sailing at sunrise, he remembered. Stepping quickly into the britches lying haphazardly at the end of his bunk, shrugging into his jacket, and running a hand through his disheveled hair as he pulled on his cap, he quickly made his way to the cabin door. Throwing it open, he was met by the cacophony of mooing, braying, and cackling—as well as the unmistakable odor emanating from the ship's hold—coupled by the yelling of his crew and the flapping of the sails as they were hoisted into the warm, humid air. Exiting onto the deck, he was pleased to see that the entire waterfront was now alive with activity—as the schooner slowly began to move—ready for the next leg of its voyage.

Surely, this was not the same harbor in which he had fallen asleep—to the music of clanging ropes, the moaning of gale-force winds, and the uneasy rhythm of the rolling waves—Robert mused. Turning to the port side as the vessel slowly executed its turn, he marveled at the eastern sky as the sunrise now glowed with brilliant gold and orange swirls against a cloudless, bright blue sky.

"Under control, Robert," the very tan middle-aged man dressed in work clothes smiled as he watched the sailor climb down the mast. "All in place and awaiting your order," he answered—removing his ever-present cap, which covered his almost bald pate—and affecting a clumsy salute. "Now that we've come this far, I think everyone's ready to be off."

"Not as much as I, Rhodes," Robert laughed—motioning toward the ship's hold. "Happy to be out here where I can breathe! Can't wait to get rid of those beasts you insisted we bring on board."

"And you'll be singing a different story when we unload them and have instant eggs and milk in the wilderness. Don't think we'll find anyone there like that man Bunce who brought the supplies yesterday," Rhodes answered—turning back to the shipboard activity.

"Beautiful, isn't it?" Lorenzo Thomas, a recent West Point graduate who had begged passage to join Colonel George Brooke in Pensacola, called as he exited the open door of the cabin. "Don't get weather like this in New York! Think I got lucky in being assigned to Florida—unless this bright sun manages to cook my skin," he added—pulling his cap closer over his light hair and fair skin. "Great-grandfather's name couldn't counteract my mom's British ancestry! But want some coffee?" he asked amiably—displaying a steamy large tin mug.

Turning in surprise at encountering his passenger, Robert answered, "Not if it's that Cuban stuff Porter tried to pass off on me yesterday."

"Think it's some of the new stock that man Bunce off-loaded yesterday," Lorenzo grinned—his blue eyes shining. "Chef's got it in the kitchen. I could get you a mug . . ."

"Thanks, but I think we'd best get on with our journey first. I've gotta check with the captain and look out for the *Sea Gull*. We're supposed to . . ."

"Do you mean that two-mast ship up ahead?" Lorenzo asked—gesturing with his mug at the small vessel already waiting at the harbor entrance.

Looking more closely, Robert was surprised to see the name "Sea Gull" emblazoned on its side—as Voorhees's vessel signaled before heading south into the open water beyond the harbor.

"My God, it looks like we're underway already!" Robert announced—struggling to keep his balance as his own deck began to roll on encountering the *Sea Gull*'s wake. Watching as his crew jumped into action, he turned quickly and assumed control—anxious to continue the last part of his journey.

Once in the turbulent Florida Straits at the base of the island, the *Sea Gull* turned westward—heading from the Atlantic into the more placid waters of the Gulf of Mexico—with Hackley's schooner close behind. As they rounded the island and headed north, the waves quieted to a gentle roll, which brought the quiet turquoise sea to life with a brilliant border of fine sand and seashells. A flock of pure white ibis emerged from the distant mangroves to settle on the nearby beach near a large colony of bright coral flamingos picking along the tide line. The morning's quiet was interrupted by a noisy flock of gray and white seagulls, which surrounded the schooner and called out a noisy cry from the animals confined in its hold.

"Couldn't be more beautiful," Robert remarked—as Lorenzo leaned over the side in awe—watching several pelicans swoop at the large school of silver fish in the clear water. This was how the sailors he had spoken with in St. Augustine had described the Gulf of Mexico—although he surely hadn't believed it yesterday.

"Too beautiful to go below," Lorenzo remarked, "but the smell of breakfast is compelling as well."

"Hopefully, it will all still be out here when we're finished. And I'm famished," Robert answered—heading to the cabin.

Finally settling in with the cook's eggs and a cup of Bunce's coffee—as opposed to the vile concoction Porter had served yesterday—Robert determined to try to enjoy the rest of the cruise. He could only hope that they would encounter no pirates and that today's weather would stay with them until they reached Bahia Tampa—although Porter had advised him of the sudden Gulf squalls in the early fall and had given him a crude map depicting the various inlets up the coast where he might wait out a storm.

A far cry from the rocky coral islands on the east side of Florida, the western coastline was interspersed with intermittent swampy islands filled with layers of low-growing trees—their slim roots arching above the dark, murky mud. Since his dad had told him his eleven million acre purchase included the land on this lower side of Florida as well, he began to imagine draining this land and creating towns down here as well as up in the Tampa area. Yes, it was hot and prone to the many tropical storms like the one he had experienced yesterday, and Porter had also warned him of the devastating "yellow fever" with which his men had been infected. Yet wouldn't the beauty and lack of winter attract many Americans now that Florida was a part of the United States? And thanks to the West Indies squadron, the seas were now free from piracy—allowing shipping to supply the settlement's wants. The possibilities were endless, he decided, settling back in his chair.

A sudden shout from one of his crew suddenly drew him away from his daydream. As he turned in his chair, Lorenzo entered—calling out, "Robert, this is what the men at the base told us about. But I never believed I'd see . . . ," he added—as Robert jumped up to follow him up the stairs.

Once on deck, the two noticed several of the men leaning over the side of the ship to view the clear wreckage of a large schooner resting on its side in one of the shallow inlets—its masts broken with the useless sails undulating in the sudden swell caused by the *Sea Gull*'s passage. On closer inspection, a large crater was visible on the upturned port side of the craft. Canteens, pots, clothing, and even maps swirled in the low tide beside the hole—as inquisitive fish explored the wreckage looking for anything resembling food. So as much as he had preferred to disbelieve Porter's warning, Robert was now alerted to the ever-present danger of venturing up this coast unattended—as a chill ran up his back. Hanging over the side, both Robert and Lorenzo tried to ascertain any present danger as the wreckage slowly disappeared behind them in the darkened lagoon.

As they proceeded onward a short way, however, the men noticed the *Sea Gull* pulling over to a small island—where three tattered men in a small rowboat, which was almost hidden in the heavy overgrowth, were signaling wildly. As Voorhees approached the starboard side of his ship, the men began paddling toward the *Sea Gull* yelling. Finally, with much unintelligible gesturing and motioning toward the sunken ship, the men indicated that they were the only survivors of the attack. Looking around himself, Voorhees eventually nodded and allowed the men to pull up to the ship. Taking them on board, the *Sea Gull* once again pulled out into the open Gulf of Mexico—having completed yet another rescue mission in the area.

It was midafternoon when his man Rhodes entered the cabin. Looking from one to the other of the two young men, he shook his head before announcing, "Looks like we're on our own now."

"What do you mean?" Robert asked, turning around. "I thought Porter said that Voorhees was going to lead us . . ."

"To the mainland coast," Rhodes nodded. "That's it up ahead—at least I think it must be because the *Sea Gull* has just banked and is turning around in the open water to the port side."

"Let me see!" Robert said—running onto the deck. Shielding his eyes with his hand, he walked to the port railing—just in time to see the salute from Captain Voorhees as his ship slipped behind them in the open water.

"Happy hunting!" Voorhees called.

"My God, Rhodes," Robert called. "I didn't realize our escort would leave us this soon! I mean, I don't even know where we can put in for the night."

"I talked to some of those sailors at the naval yard yesterday. They told me once we got away from these accursed islands, down here it was mostly sandy beaches up the rest of the way. Lots of inlets and deepwater harbors to pull into. Don't worry. It's a beautiful day. By my estimation, we should get up near a place called San Carlos near nightfall. Let's wait until then and just see what we find. We've survived so far, haven't we?"

Watching from the port side cabin window as the afternoon sun blazed across the turquoise water and sank lower in the sky, Robert marveled at seeing an actual sunset from the sea. As accustomed as he was to Atlantic sunrises when the gray morning haze suddenly gave way to the golden dawning of a new day, he was totally unprepared for this slow transition as sky, water, and nearby land masses turned golden and then burst into a blazing, orange fire that seemed to encompass both land and sea. He marveled at the lone seagull highlighted against the blazing sun—as he turned at the splash beside them of a group of porpoises—hoping to find a morsel of last night's dinner—or other delicacy tossed overboard to them.

"Never gets old watching the sea, does it?" Lorenzo called—taking the seat beside him. "As beautiful as it is, though, do you have any idea where we can pull in for the night?"

"Rhodes assured me he had heard there were several inlets up the coast where we could shelter. But I'm not sure what he has in mind. Perhaps I should find out . . . ," Robert answered, turning as the cabin door was suddenly thrust open.

"Captain Hackley, we've spotted a fairly wide inlet up ahead," Rhodes called—removing his cap and running his fingers through his thinning hair. "You asked to be informed if we found a safe harbor for tonight. The charts we got at the base seem to indicate that the island to its west is called the Isle of San Marco—named for St. Mark, I assume. I remember Porter telling me it was an open harbor once we got past all the shallow waters down south, but I wasn't clear exactly where it was. Area looks clear. No other ships in sight."

"Let's see," Robert called. "We really need to determine the depth before we venture in. Don't want to be stranded down here—or to be fair game for any leftover pirates," he remarked as he jumped up to follow Rhodes to the door.

"Are you sure it's safe?" Rhodes asked. "I mean we all saw that wrecked schooner down south, and we had just left the pirate-infested area when the *Sea Gull* headed back. I remember hearing the tale about Ponce de Leon when he came ashore a little farther north," Rhodes offered.

"If it's deep enough, I'm willing to chance it—and get into a safe harbor for a while. I'm sure the crew will be willing to take the same chance," Robert answered. "Let's head in. It's been a long day!"

• 3 •

September 1823

Although it was mid-September, the heat had not abated, and the large room had grown unbearably hot as the five Seminole chiefs and the U.S. Treaty commissioners finally shared a pen to sign the new "Treaty of Moultrie Creek." The treaty had been a long time coming—and although it had not covered all the necessary stipulations, it was a welcome start, Colonel James Gadsden, the U.S. government's head commissioner, decided—breathing a deep sigh of relief as he accepted the pen and signed his own name at the bottom of the paper. Running his fingers through his mass of dark curls and pausing to wipe his face on his damp sleeve, he proceeded to place the treaty into his leather valise.

Offering their hands to each of the five assembled chiefs, the commissioners waited patiently until each one had left with his contingency. It had been a lengthy procedure with over four hundred natives awaiting the outcome in the swampy area surrounding the small town of Moultrie Creek—located several miles west of St. Augustine. The treaty was a first step, Gadsden knew, but former treaties had proven the unreliable nature of the several Seminole tribes. As head of the U.S. delegation, it was his duty to close any loopholes that might arise—the chief one being outside interference—such as the clandestine shipping of both arms and ammunition from both Cuba and the Bahamas—which had plagued Andrew Jackson during the previous Seminole conflict. With so many of the ranchos in the upper Gulf now closed as the owners had moved on to Cuba, Hillsborough Bay, which was at the eastern edge of Neamathla's territory, was now a perfect transfer spot for the natives to receive contraband supplies.

Waiting until each of the commissioners had stretched and poured a mug of water, Gadsden slid the waning candle closer, pulled up the nearest chair, and motioned for the delegate to resume their seats to many groans—as it was late and uncomfortably hot. Gadsden had the signed treaty—what else could he need, they wondered? Pulling a sheet of paper from his valise and picking up the pen he had dropped on the desk, he tapped the pen for quiet before addressing the room. "We all remember the trouble General Jackson had in the last conflict when the Seminoles obtained both arms and ammunition from Cuban mercenaries. How much easier will it be this time when our western borders are still open and easily accessible from Cuba or the other islands?"

As a flurry of assents erupted, he raised his hand for quiet, continuing, "As I see it, the most vulnerable place with access to both Seminole reservations and the new Seminole territory west of here is the area of Hillsborough Bay. With easy access from Cuba and no permanent settlements or ports to block the transport of goods or ammunition, I see it as our weakest link in the treaty."

Waiting for the din to die down, he continued, "My proposal then is a letter to Secretary of War, John Calhoun, suggesting we establish a military post at the head of Hillsborough Bay. If we establish it at the mouth of the Hillsborough River, it could prevent goods from being transferred either in the bay—or up the river—agreed?"

"Do we have troops in the area?" one delegate interrupted.

"Knowing our military presence in the territory is still quite limited, I checked that out before proposing it," Gadsden smiled. "As it turns out, Colonel George Brooke is now in Pensacola with four companies of men from the U.S. Fourth Infantry . . ."

"Pensacola! Have you any idea how far away that is from Hillsborough Bay?" another delegate interrupted.

"Brooke's assignment," Gadsden continued unabashed, "is to move his troops to the area just north of St. Marks—where Neamathla's reservation is located—to ensure Neamathla makes good on his promise to move his tribe eastward to the new territory. Our naval ships at Pensacola can provide the five ships necessary for the travel to St. Marks—and from there on to the new location—probably near the first of the year if all goes well. The sooner the better, as far as I'm concerned. It will take time for my letter to reach Washington, so time is of the essence.

"Now, I know it's late, but in the essence of brevity, I have written a letter to Secretary Calhoun proposing exactly what I just discussed," he added, pushing the sheet of paper in front of him and the ink well into the center of the table and laying the pen beside them. If you all are willing to sign it, I'd like to have permission to propose the area at Hillsborough Bay as a new fort called Cantonment Brooke—with one Colonel George Mercer Brooke in charge."

Anxious to be done for the evening, all the men quickly took the pen, signed the letter, and departed—happy to be relieved of their unpleasant duties of the past several days.

Carefully replacing the letter in the valise next to the signed treaty, Colonel Gadsden breathed a lengthy sigh, blew out the candle, and closed the door behind him—on a treaty that would, hopefully, ensure the safety of the many settlers that would now flock to the new Florida territory!

• 4 •

September 1823

At the first hint of dawn, the quiet harbor suddenly seemed alive with raucous cries as a myriad of seagulls assailed the schooner. Dressing quickly, Robert left the cabin and ran up the steps—to see Lorenzo perched along the starboard bow—gaily throwing bits of last night's leftover bread to the ravenous birds. As his attention was diverted, Lorenzo suddenly dodged as one of the larger birds refused to wait for the morsel to be tossed and swooped at the ship, taking the piece of bread from his hand.

Trying to control his laughter, Robert shook his head. "After spending so many years on the Virginia coast, I could have told you to beware of seagull invasions! But what a beautiful sunrise!" he added, looking across at the mainland shore where thin turquoise fingers crept silently among the dark mangrove roots, just appearing in the early morning haze. Alternately reaching and retreating, the tiny waves deposited small piles of seaweed and scallop shells on the fine white sand.

"It's definitely not New York!" Lorenzo added—turning to throw the rest of his bread over the side of the ship and checking his hand. "I do recognize the seagulls and the pelicans that have been about, but I'm curious about those dark elephant-sized animals that are lurking about down there," he said, gesturing to a pod of manatees that seemed to be circling the ship.

"Manatees," Robert confirmed. "They are quite numerous down here—as well as a gold mine in the Cuban market."

"What? Don't tell me the Cubans eat those ugly creatures? Remind me not to taste any delicacies if we stop at one of the ranchos."

"I think it's their oil that is most valuable," Robert laughed. "Seems the Spanish use it to grease the hulls of their ships Porter told me. Although with that much flesh, their meat might be profitable in Cuba as well."

"Ugh. Stupendous greeting by all the wildlife down here, though. Do you think it's the same all the way up the coast?"

"From what I've heard, we'll see the same birds and fish, but we should leave the full mangrove areas once we get farther north. At least I hope so—as Father wants to market his land as homesites, and—lovely as it is—I can't see anyone wanting to settle in this swamp. Seymour said the rest of the coastal islands are mostly sand and the area where we are going is supposed to have stands of hardwood trees."

"How far does your father's land grant extend? I don't think you ever said," Lorenzo asked, leaning companionably against the railing.

"Eleven million acres—all the way down here—if what I understood is correct. At any rate, he wants us to check out the island a little north of here called Sanybel. Best feature of that area, Seymour told him, is that the island juts out at right angles from the west coast, which protects it somewhat from tidal action and storms. A flat, tropical island should be perfect for crops. We should reach it by noon if our plans and compass hold. I'd planned to take some time to check it out, but we'll need to get moving," he remarked, as several crew members emerged to set the sails.

"Aha! Right on time," Robert remarked as he watched the procedure for a moment. "Now that we're getting underway, I think I'll go to the galley for a cup of coffee—Bunce's brand. Want to join me?"

Robert recognized Sanybel from Seymour's description when the sandy coast loomed out at them in the distance. Pulling into the large, flat stretch of water to the east of the island, Robert decided to take Rhodes with him on an excursion of this side of the island. Flat and sandy it might be on the west side, but this side was a jungle, as far as he could tell, and covered with large, dark-green mangroves whose many bare, protruding roots prohibited landing.

Cruising along the coast in the small rowboat as they looked for a landing spot, Robert was astounded at the number of herons, egrets, and lovely pink water birds with a flattened bill he could not identify. Looking upward, he pointed out a soaring eagle that landed in a large nest within a grove of pine trees farther back on the island. Warm weather and tropical beauty were definite selling points, he mused, as he and his father looked to create settlements and towns on their newfound land. He'd have to send home information for future exploration.

As the two finally beached the small craft in an open, marshy cove and attempted to climb out, they were immediately attacked by a large crowd of small, buzzing insects flying in droves out of the nearby swamp and attacking any unexposed skin. Swatting and running toward the water to ward off the bugs, Rhodes ran headfirst into a monster alligator that was sunning itself on the only dry spot of land. Hissing and snorting, the alligator turned its head, thrashed its tail, and began to move forward quickly, despite its ungainly appearance. "My God," Rhodes called as he turned back and ran headfirst into Robert, "I say it's worth your life to try to develop this area. I'm heading back to the ship!"

"Guess we should have investigated the west side of the island instead," Robert admitted, taking a cautious glance at the monstrous alligator, which was now lumbering forward toward the men. "Not sure either of us wants to be dinner for that monster," he added, running back to their craft and jumping in as Rhodes quickly pushed off. "If he's still interested in developing at Sanybel, my dad can send some-one else down here!" Robert replied as they returned to the ship.

With the crude map Porter had supplied in hand, Robert entered several of the inlets listed farther north determined to look over the extent of his father's property and send home a detailed report. Although the sandy coast itself was generally flat and mostly free of vegetation, it did harbor the real possibility of the severe storms the many captains with whom he had spoken had warned—some of them with little enough warning to move residents to higher ground. Beautiful though the various beaches might be, a permanent development on any of them would be risky—especially for a first endeavor. The inland sides of the coastal islands then seemed more desirable for habitation; however, the need for removing the heavy vegetation of mangroves and cypress trees would be a large deterrent for a development. A bonus, though, was the extensive local stand of pine, which could prove a godsend in providing building materials.

His father would be glad he had taken the time to check out the property; however, the constant stink and noises of the animals in the hold, the restlessness of his men, and his desire to build his plantation in the area proposed by Seymour—up at Hillsborough Bay—and be settled by the end of the year spurred him north. He had also taken on the responsibility of delivering Lorenzo to his army post in Pensacola by the end of the year. Further exploration would have to wait for another visit.

• 5 •

October 1823

$\mathcal{D}$espite his vow to move forward to Hillsborough Bay, Robert knew that it would be some time before he could get back down the coast to investigate the many islands and coves in his father's immense tract. The weather for the most part was pleasant—if hot—so after leaving Sanybel, he directed the schooner into the area his crude map had identified as San Carlos Bay. Moving north in the bay, he was impressed with the protected coastal mainland. Wonderful, protected port, he decided at the entrance to the river identified as the Caloosahatchee. Protected from the Gulf by a combination of two islands, the area would be perfect for a development. With no idea of the river's depth, however, he decided exploring it would best be left for another time—with a smaller draft vessel.

As they traveled north in the area Porter had identified as Matlacha Pass, gathering dark clouds to the west soon promised a late afternoon storm. Not wanting to return to the Gulf and the full fury of the approaching storm, Robert decided to remain in the protected bay for the night. Ordering the crew to take down the sails and close the hatches to the animal area below, he retired to the cabin, where Lorenzo was poring over the map that had been laid out on the desk. "Where exactly do you think we are?" Lorenzo asked as Robert entered.

"I think right about here," Robert answered, pointing to the area Porter had identified as Bokeelia—an area on the north end of the island north of Sanybel. "Don't want to go out into the open Gulf with all that's going on out there," he confirmed, nodding to his left. "Think we'll anchor here for the night. Should be smooth sailing tomorrow when we hit the area Porter called Charlotte Harbor."

"Isn't that where Porter said there was a pretty big rancho?"

"As I remember," Robert nodded. "Owner's name is Jose Caldez. Elderly Spaniard Porter said. Lives out on a place called Useppa Island. Employs about twenty men, I understand, and has several acres of citrus and other crops—besides his fish drying and exporting. Why do you ask? I hadn't planned to stop there—unless you are tired of our shipboard fare and have a hankering for a fish fry."

"Actually, I was thinking of that storm out there," Lorenzo answered—pointing out the window on the port side, where the dark, menacing clouds were gathering. "Looks to be rather a big one. We may need to find a safe harbor for a while."

"Oh, it will blow by overnight. I wouldn't worry."

By morning, however, everyone on board was worried. The howling of the relentless wind had made sleeping almost impossible, and the volume of rain had turned the deck into a dangerous slipping hazard—with deck hands in constant fear of being swept overboard. To top it off, the braying of the cattle and oxen and the terrified cackle of the chickens in the hold had been nonstop all night.

"What do you think, Rhodes?" Robert asked—as the poor man swung into the cabin—drenched to the skin. "Any chance of heading north today?"

"Just checked with the captain, and we both think we can't take a chance of putting out into the open Gulf at this point," Rhodes answered, shaking his head. "Weather's taken a turn for the worst, I'm afraid. Got any idea where we might put in before we leave the pass?"

"Lorenzo asked last night about a local rancho up here. I thought he just wanted to be invited in for a fish fry."

"So there is one?" Rhodes asked hopefully.

"Apparently just a few miles north of us—at a place called Useppa Island. Think we should try to get over there?"

"I don't think we're safe staying here for the duration—however long that might be."

"Then I think you and Lorenzo are on the same page. And to make it unanimous, I'm with you. Go tell the men we're going to try to find a safe haven—if possible—and get the boats ready. We'll have to leave the animals on board, but the rest of us should be able to reach safety on land."

"Hey, Robert," Lorenzo called, running into the cabin. "Looks like we've found our saviors."

"What do you mean? I was just issuing orders to abandon ship and make it onto the island over there," Robert answered, annoyed at the interruption.

"No, I mean there are several men over there on the beach."

"In this weather?"

"They're motioning to us to come over," Lorenzo nodded.

"Careful. They could be pirates," Rhodes worried.

"If you'll pardon me," Lorenzo countered, "I don't think these men intend any harm. I don't see that they are armed. They are waving and calling to us, but I don't know what they are saying."

"Cover me," Robert answered, pulling a small gun off the shelf and handing it to Rhodes as he picked up a matching weapon. I'll see what they want. Porter told me the Cuban ranchos up this way were friendly. He said they often supplied his crews with fresh fish."

"Now you're talking," Rhodes whispered.

Donning the wet slicker he had hung by the door, Robert left the cabin and headed for the deck. Walking to the rail—with the drenched Rhodes right beside him—gun aimed, Robert called, "Hola, amigos! Que deseas?"

"You . . . you speak their language?" Rhodes called.

"Grew up in Spain, remember," Robert laughed, not turning around.

"Señor Caldez dijo que bajara a tierra!" the lead man yelled, motioning for them to come to the beach.

"They seem to be a greeting party for the local rancho. As I guessed, they said Caldez sent them. Said he has invited us to stay with them until the storm abates," Robert confirmed. "Think that must be his compound up the way," he added, pointing to the small collection of rude one-story, wooden structures covered with palmetto fronds that were situated along the coast.

"Muchas gracias, amigos," Robert yelled, nodding to them. "Hay diecinueve hombres," he continued, waving his arm to indicate the additional sixteen men on board.

"Señor Caldez dijo traer a todos!" the leader answered, motioning frantically as lightning popped on the beach behind him.

"Get the men, Rhodes. They say we're all welcome. Need to get those sails down and then the rowboat. The weather's getting worse, and we'll need at least three trips," Robert called, wincing as the next bolt of lightning hit behind the nearby beach.

"Are you sure it's safe?" Rhodes asked, still fingering his pistol. "I mean, we all saw that wrecked ship."

"Oh, come on!" Robert answered. "These men were nice enough to offer us a shelter, and I say we go for it—far preferable to visiting Davy Jones' Locker if this storm continues."

After the deckhands had lowered the small rowboat from the side of the ship, Robert, Rhodes, Lorenzo, and three of the other men boarded and quickly made their way to the nearby beach, landing beside a small, wooden frame structure with a peaked roof made of dried palmetto leaves—which did little to protect the interior from the storm's fury. The interior revealed several rows of wooden planks covered in drying fish, now drenched from the storm. In the churning water beneath, the men noticed cages of small fish awaiting shipment to Havana. A young manatee pup was also corralled nearby, straining against the rope netting attempting to break free.

"Hola, amigos!" the nearest man yelled above the thunder's roar. Smiling through a dark mat of wet hair, he frantically gestured to the men to head up the beach.

"Roberto!" Robert nodded, patting his breast and motioning to his fellow shipmates to follow him as one lone deckhand turned the boat around and headed back to the ship.

Following the three men as they led the way up the beach, Robert was amazed at the small, cleared compound—which consisted of one good-sized, single-story tabby structure covered—as was the fish shack, they had observed on the beach—with layered palmetto leaves. The rest of the compound was rather small, consisting of eight small raised and open wooden structures also covered in the ever-present palmetto leaves.

Stopping at the opening of the tabby structure, their guide ushered them inside with a frantic gesture—as more lightning popped just behind the building. Glancing into the darkened interior, Robert saw a small firepit surrounded by a few crude wooden stools—now filled with the many workers and their families. Several dozen naked children were playing a game on the dirt floor backed by a pile of rolled mats stored in the far corner.

"Bienvenidos!" called a bent, wizened, and darkly tanned older man—seated on a stool at the back side of the firepit. "Me llamo José Caldez."

"Roberto Hackley," Robert answered. "Muchas gracias para su hospitalidad," he continued—carefully removing his slicker at the door and laying it by the wall—as his men did the same and followed him into the crowded room.

"Mi familia," José continued, waving to encompass the whole room. Pointing to two dark-skinned young men seated to his left, he continued, "Mis hijos," as both smiled under a shock of long, straight, dark hair.

"His sons," Robert translated.

The surprise was evident on Lorenzo's face as he looked from father to sons. These two men were clearly not Spanish but seemed to be Native American. The connection was clear when José continued, "Mi esposa y mis hijas," as he pointed to the Native American woman seated on his right and several young girls dressed in two layers of flowing, colorful skirts, who were seated on the floor nearest to the door. As they were acknowledged, the girls moved back into the room to clear the area for Robert and his men.

After a short conversation with the woman, coupled with several gestures toward the newcomers, José turned with a smile. "Mi esposa dice, Bienvenidos! Pescado frito para la cena. Pero, despues de la tormenta!" he laughed, waving his hand to encompass the full room.

"She's his wife," Robert whispered, turning to Lorenzo and the rest of the men. "And she's invited us to a dinner of fried fish after the storm!"

"I don't care who she is, but count me in if she's serving fried fish—whenever!" Lorenzo called, looking back at his companions.

As each of the crew's other men entered the room, José motioned to the crowd of children to move farther back into the room. Then, smiling, he gestured to the men to find a spot to stand along the back wall. As Robert was the only one of the men who could speak Spanish, it was left to him to introduce himself and his crew. Realizing the mistake it would be to reveal to José that his compound was essentially situated on land that now belonged to Robert and his family. Robert related only the fact that he was headed farther up the coast to set up a homestead. It might be that José and his compound would be of service once his father decided to sell the land on the nearby mainland. Surely wouldn't do to make enemies down here!

The heat and humidity—as well as the odors of the many bodies crowded together and the inability to converse—were beginning to wear on the shipmates when the rain suddenly ended and a bright ray of late afternoon sun found its way into the door of the crowded tabby retreat. Noticing the change, all those in the room suddenly looked at José to ascertain the next step. After a short conversation, he nodded to his wife and stood, straightening his back and grabbing at one leg in obvious pain. Clearly, the sitting had not been kind to his age and physical stamina, yet he smiled and gestured to all those present that they were now free to leave.

"Ven con migo," José offered. Gesturing to Robert and his men, he walked to the door and motioned for them to follow him. The sand was covered with puddles and downed branches from nearby oak trees, yet José led the men up the nearby sand dune and pointed to the vast laid-out acreage—now flooded—with sodden leaves floating in the many puddles. "Mi Jardin," he acknowledged with a large grin as he pointed to the extensive garden, which consisted of countless rows of beans, squash, melons, and pumpkins—backed by a number of orange and key lime trees covered in small, green undeveloped fruit. Naming each vegetable and fruit with obvious pride, he led the men along row after row on the sodden sand.

"Impresionante!" Robert smiled. "Who would have thought," he whispered to Lorenzo. "These should all grow well in my new compound as well. I'll have to ask him to give me some seeds or shoots to take north with us."

Finally, responding to a call from his wife back in the compound, José turned, waving at the men as he descended the sandy bank. "Ahora, cena!" he called, rubbing his stomach and smiling.

The dinner consisted of fried fish, which Robert gleaned were called pompano and were one of the most prized fish sold in Havana. Clearly, José and family had rolled out the red carpet—as his stepmother in Virginia would have stated. Side dishes of beans and squash accompanied the meal, and Robert was amused at the antics of the several Indian children waiting as the watermelons were cut and passed out.

As the meal ended, one of the sons ran into the tabby structure and returned with a small drum. Perching near the door, he began a slow beat, which increased as the two young girls Robert had seen earlier ran back inside returning with several strands of shells, which they affixed to their ankles. Then, as their brother continued his slow beat, the girls began to dance—swirling in a mass of color as the sun—finally released from hiding—silhouetted them with its own bursts of red and gold.

Rising sadly as the dance was ended, Robert motioned to his men to return to the ship and turned to bid farewell to his host—who invited him to return "en cualquier momento," or at any time. José also gave him the name of his brother, Juan Caldez, whose compound was at Sarazota Bay—near José's other rancho. He also mentioned his friend, Andrew Gonzales, whose rancho he said was situated a little north of the Caldez properties. With a smile—accompanied with a smacking of his lips—José announced that Andrew could supply Hackley's ship with his numerous citrus products from his orchard of orange and lime trees—as well as offer a shelter should the fall weather give another need to "abandon ship."

Returning to the ship, Robert turned for one last look at the blazing West Florida sunset. Life couldn't get any better than this, he decided—as he looked at his companions, who seemed as mesmerized as he.

• 6 •

November 1823

$\mathscr{D}$espite his hopes for smooth sailing now that the storm had cleared, Robert soon found fall in Florida was unpredictable at best. As they moved northward, new afternoon storms caused Robert and his crew to wait out for a short time in Charlotte Harbor. Finally, moving northward, they were eventually forced to accept the invitation given by Caldez's friend, Andrew Gonzales, at North Sarazota Bay to wait out a lengthy storm at his compound.

As the sun finally appeared, Robert and Rhodes returned to check the schooner. Finding it pretty much intact in the protected harbor where Gonzales had directed them, they accepted his gifts of oranges and limes and again set sail for their final push.

With no further weather delays, they eventually approached the island Bunce had mentioned as Egmont Key—the area in which Hernando DeSoto was reported to have landed and the entrance to the bay the Spanish called Bahia de Esperitu Santo. It was now November, and Rhodes had warned him the home he wanted—even with the preliminary framework he had brought along—would take up to eight weeks to construct.

Actually, Robert had hoped to get home to Virginia to celebrate the holidays with his family—and he still had to take Lorenzo up to Pensacola to meet his army unit before the New Year. Amazing how slow the ship travel had been—which made him a bit apprehensive about anyone deciding to move to Florida permanently—no matter the beauty of both the land and the temperature. Still, the house he had planned was perfect, and it wouldn't be too bad to sit out the winter in it!

Sailing into the sunlit bay, Robert was encouraged to find the more northern hardwoods of pine and oak that Seymour had reported—perfect for building the homes in the development he and his father had envisioned. Could not have been a more perfect spot, he smiled. Noting at once the tall, sandy hill Seymour had reported on the east bank at the entrance to the wide Hillsborough River, he slowed the ship and instructed the crew as they threw the anchor and cheered. Over two months of travel had finally come to an end!

The first orders of business—and long overdue—were to build a dock, clear the land, fence it, and get the oxen and cattle on land. Surprisingly, all had survived their lengthy confinement, but Robert was sure his ship would never lose the odor in its hold! The pigs would need a pen, and the chickens would need a coop—as they, too, had been confined.

Motioning to Rhodes, Robert ushered the older man into one of the rowboats the crew had taken down. Watching as the small craft approached the beach, Robert perused the nearby shoreline. Small white birds he had learned were called ibis were rooting in the grass near the river—accompanied by a stately blue heron—as raucous seagulls called overhead. A large splash just behind them caught his attention as a large pelican—much bigger than those he was accustomed to in Virginia—rose from the gentle waves with a huge fish in its mouth—surprising two small dolphins, which dove beneath the waves in perfect unison. Looking into the water, Robert was amazed to see Seymour's vision of the swarms of fish just off the beach. While not a fisherman, he could not identify even one of the varieties, yet he recognized the value the fishing would bring to the land.

Turning, he made his way up the beach above the tide line—where large live oaks spread their limbs covered in Spanish moss amid a veritable forest of virgin pine trees vying to outdo their neighbors by reaching into the cloudless blue sky above. "Well worth the trip, don't you think?" Rhodes called—smiling as he joined Robert at the entrance to the woods.

"I never imagined . . . ," Robert answered—dumbfounded as he looked around. Clearing the land for homesteads would take work. However, outside of the high mound at the bay's entrance—topped by a strange, large, gnarled tree with red bark Porter had called a "gumbo limbo," the terrain was flat as far as he could see and should need little grading to create both homesteads and farmland. "We didn't believe Seymour's description—which is why my father sent me down here," Robert said at last. "Just wait until I tell him what he owns!"

"Sorry to interrupt your evaluation, but we've waited long enough to get started, and there's still a good bit of daylight left. After so long on shipboard, the men are anxious to get started on the dock—as well as your compound. Just tell me where to start, and I'll give the order," Rhodes said.

Turning and looking toward the ship, Robert could see the men storing the sails, stretching and pausing to look at the placid river behind them. "This area is perfect. Just look at that view of the water," Robert asserted—waving his arm to encompass the wide mouth of the Hillsborough River, which stretched northward.

Turning, then, he pointed into the surrounding woods behind him. "I think with those magnificent trees to surround the house—as well as give a bit of shade in this heat—we can erect the house right over there. Preserve the view as long as we situate it well above the tide line. I do remember seasonal flooding on the Virginia coast, so we'll need to be careful.

"But first of all, I think we'll need to clear enough space for the livestock," he answered, looking around. Then, pointing inland a bit to a sunny spot farther east, he gestured. "Over there in the grassy area beyond these trees. I know you brought fencing. Let's get the dock built first so we can unload our supplies and then get those oxen, cattle, and pigs over here for a breath of fresh air! I'm sure they will be as glad as we are to leave that stinking hold. And with their help, they may clear much of the underbrush as well—and save us that task. I'd eventually like to build a ranch farther inland—but for now, this will do."

Nodding, Rhodes hurried back down the beach where several men had already loaded a rowboat and taken it ashore and were already busy unloading pilings and wood. The house could wait, he agreed—as he, too, would be glad to be rid of the constant odor of both animals and feces!

As Robert had predicted, the animals were obviously thrilled with their newfound freedom—when they were finally turned loose on the beach. What little grass had found its way on the sand was soon devoured by both oxen and cattle, and the pigs found a boggy area near the oaks—where they were able to root to their hearts' content—as the men hastily erected an enclosure beyond the planned homestead. By nightfall—which came early this time of year—an acceptable enclosure had been made for the cattle—with an attached area for the pigs. As the sun sank behind the trees, however, Robert decided the chickens would have to wait another day. Despite their constant chatter, they were not as smelly as had been their cabin mates, he decided as he sat down on board the anchored ship to a simple meal—composed of local fried bass the cook had prepared.

"If every meal is like this," Rhodes commented—spearing another bite—"I think we're all going to enjoy this adventure!"

"Not to mention the weather," Lorenzo answered, taking the seat beside him. "Do you know what the temperature probably is right now in New York? It seems I drew the best possible assignment of my classmates in being stationed down here!"

"Which brings to mind," Robert interjected, "I will need to know just when to take you to your unit. As the weather this time of year can be unpredictable, we'll need to be sure we allow enough time for the trip."

"My assignment doesn't start until early January," Lorenzo answered. "As I spent many hours in my father's workshop, I'd really like to help out here—if that's all right. I'm in no hurry to head any farther north, and I'm sure now that you've found your location you are also in no hurry to sail further."

"I was hoping you would say that," Robert smiled—"as I have a real hankering to watch this homestead take root—right here on my father's own property. I can't believe the pre-assembled pieces we had prepared. Two stories with a covered front porch—complete with large floor-length windows and ten columns—wasn't it, Rhodes?"

"And don't forget the upstairs with its dormer windows—to overlook that spectacular view out there," Rhodes interjected—waving his arms toward the port side of the ship and the river view from the porthole.

"You mean you brought all that on board?" Lorenzo asked. "I knew you had building materials down in the hold, but I never believed you had something so elaborate in mind."

"What did you expect—one of those tabby structures at the ranchos we stayed in?"

"I meant . . . I just thought you had a cabin in mind," Lorenzo
continued—embarrassed.

"If that was what he planned, I never would have agreed on this
gosh-awful expedition," Rhodes answered—downing his tankard with
the ale they had saved for their arrival. Wiping his mouth, he smiled.
"Obviously, you don't know Richard Hackley—or his family. Where
any of them are concerned, only the best will do. Daddy Richard
personally designed this homestead with the architect. It's a real low-
country plantation house—rather like one you would find in Savannah
or Charleston. Richard even had some sketches he had brought back
from his time in St. Augustine. 'Gotta have the best,' I remember him
saying, 'if we hope to draw new settlers to our various Florida developments. If it all works out well, I'm prepared for the long shot—as we
draw new landowners down here.'"

"Suits me as well," Robert smiled, downing his own tankard.
"Despite the travel turmoil, it surely beats stuffy New York, snow and
ice, and the legal field!"

"Well, I never imagined," Lorenzo smiled. "I can't wait to see it
all finished. How long do you expect it will take to put it together?"

"If what Rhodes says is true," Robert answered, "you should get
your wish. We're hoping to move me in by Christmas!"

• 7 •

November 1823

$\mathcal{A}$wakened by the raucous cry of a myriad of seagulls assailing the ship, Robert quickly donned the work clothes he had left on the nearby chair when heading to bed. His new home awaited he remembered. Quickly making his way up on deck, he was surprised to see Lorenzo once again up and about early. Mug in hand, the young man smiled and gestured toward the nearby tree line. "Beautiful!" he offered. "I'd say you're the luckiest man alive to spend the rest of your days with this backdrop!"

Nodding, Robert turned to watch as the early sunlight blazed orange and red—filtering through the Spanish moss, which entwined each large live oak, and silhouetting the taller cabbage palms vying for their chance at the open sky above. "If we can clear some of the smaller trees and vegetation, I think . . . right there will be the perfect spot for the house," he pointed—indicating the two large oak trees at the edge of the forest.

"My thoughts, exactly," Rhodes offered—walking to the rail beside him. "Give the order, and my men are ready to clear the land today. Saw a lot of rabbits, two deer, and a wild turkey or two in the clearing between those two trees when I got up. Might be wise to supplement our meat supply. I could send one or two men out to hunt—if you'd like."

"Not a bad idea," Robert answered. "Although the fish last night were great, some red meat would be a welcome change—if you can spare some of your workforce."

"Done," Rhodes smiled. "After all the fish, I think we are all ready for a change. Question for you, though, before I send anyone out—did your man Seymour say anything about natives in this area? Need to know if we need to be aware."

"From what he told my father, there had been an encampment near here—as well as a group of relocated slaves who had come down from Georgia—seeking freedom with the Spanish officials," Robert offered. "Near as he could tell, though, both groups had vanished. He said one of the rancho owners said most of the former slaves had gone to Cuba to escape being returned to their former owners. He wasn't sure about the natives. He said he found a mound nearby—probably that one out there at the river's edge," he added—pointing across the bow. "He did say, however, that he saw no evidence of current settlement nearby."

"Probably the Seminoles have all headed east toward the new settlement the Moultrie Creek meeting was setting up in September," Lorenzo interjected. "One of the men I met when we were loading the livestock in St. Augustine was heading there. When I told him I was heading to meet Colonel Brooke at Pensacola, he assumed our division would be assigned to move the Seminoles out of the western part of the territory. He said the new Treaty of Moultrie Creek has set up a four million acre settlement in the middle of the territory—where they hoped the Seminole leaders would agree to relocate."

"Assuming they all agree to move," Rhodes put in. "With this backdrop," he continued—waving his hand toward the distant tree line, "I don't think I would be convinced to move."

"As long as they are not armed," Robert smiled, "I wouldn't mind a small settlement. We could probably use a few on our compound. Remember all the natives who worked with Caldez on his rancho."

"I'd suggest we all just be observant right now," Lorenzo continued, shaking his head. "I've studied enough about the first Seminole War to know how unpredictable our interactions with the natives can be!"

"Well, until we see any, that's just one less thing to worry about," Robert countered. "Right now, I'm ready to find some chow and start building my dream home. Ready, Rhodes?" he asked—heading to the galley.

Clear skies and mild temperatures were a boon as Rhodes assigned four of his men to clear the land farthest from the beach—where it was protected from saltwater intrusion. Although clearing the dense undergrowth was a challenge, the oxen and the two plows Rhodes had insisted they put on board soon produced a decent plot for the vegetables and the lime and orange seeds Caldez had given Robert—with instructions to plant them as soon as possible—to assure at least a small crop by next winter.

Rhodes also assigned four men to construct the barn they had brought with them to house the oxen and cattle, which had already proved their worth in both clearing the underbrush and eating the long grasses along the tree line. The pigs were fenced in an area near the proposed barn. Finally, a small chicken coop was established next to the barn, and the chickens were at long last removed from the ship's hold—providing a welcome respite from their constant cackle.

The final eight men were the crew Robert had assembled to construct the large plantation home—whose framework his father had ordered in New York. After several attempts to off-load both the foundation pieces and joists—not to mention the large windows and dormers—onto the hastily constructed dock, however, Rhodes realized the futility of attempting any further activity until the men could construct a much larger, proper one. Delaying the home construction for five days then, it was clear that the new structure would be a benefit for any further importing of goods—as well as passengers when the nearby plots would be offered for sale. A necessary addition, Robert had to agree—after he had followed his father to his various assignments in virtually unapproachable places in Europe.

Finally, about a week after landing, the new wharf was completed. By dinnertime, Rhodes announced plans to begin the house construction the following morning. "Sorry it couldn't have been sooner," he apologized, "but you chose the time of year with the shortest daylight. Last summer we could have had another two hours or so to work."

"Then I suggest an early bedtime and up at dawn," Robert answered. "Still have to get Lorenzo up to Pensacola by late December—and I'd really like to spend a night or two in my new surroundings before I have to squeeze back onto my cot on board."

"I think you speak for all of us," Rhodes asserted. "I—for one—would love nothing better than a real bed myself. I never expected all the delays when we started out last summer. The end is in sight now, though, so take heart!" he smiled as he waved and disappeared below deck.

The following morning—thankfully—dawned bright and clear. Heading to the galley for a mug of the good coffee that still remained from Bunce's stock, Robert noted that the men had already left the ship and were busily off-loading lumber and fully made sections of walls.

"Good to see it all coming together. I know you're glad after all this time. Just going to take a look myself—and see if I can be of any assistance," Lorenzo called—heading back up the galley steps with his own full mug. "Want to join me?"

"Thanks, but I'll be along shortly. Just want to consult my list of supplies and make sure they're unloading the right sets of pieces," Robert answered, heading back up the stairs with his list in hand.

Encouraged as he watched each pre-assembled piece being off-loaded and noted that—despite the ordeal—they each seemed to have weathered the journey, Robert was lost in his own thoughts as he checked off one structure after another.

"Robert," Lorenzo called loudly running up the ramp onto the ship. "You need to come down here—right now!"

"What?" Robert called—laying down his clip board.

"Visitors!" Lorenzo called—visibly out of breath as he motioned toward the beach.

"No one's come up the river," Robert answered—confused as he looked off the bow at the river.

"Seminoles!" Lorenzo gasped—pointing toward the beach where three of the young men whose dark braids protruded from brightly colored turbans had assembled to inspect both the schooner and the cleared land where the men were carrying the lumber.

"Oh, my Lord," Robert answered, hurrying to the ramp. "My pistol's in my cabin," he whispered. "Do you have yours?"

"Didn't think to bring it," Lorenzo whispered—shaking his head. "But I think they're friendly. Don't see any weapons—unless they are concealed inside those long shirts."

"Did they say what they want?" Robert asked—following Lorenzo to the beach.

"They're speaking Spanish," Lorenzo continued—shaking his head. "Must think we're from one of those ranchos out there on the coast. You're the only one around here who can speak with them," he continued—pointing to the obvious man in charge and waving toward Robert.

"Buenos dios, amigo," Robert called—motioning to the lead Seminole. "Me llamo, Roberto," he answered—pointing to his own chest.

"Amigos," the lead man replied—pointing to his companions. "Bienvenidos a Tanpa!" he continued—motioning to one of his companions who held out a dead rabbit. Two other natives soon emerged from the nearby woods carrying the carcass of a small doe, which they laid on the beach. "Regalos," the first man added with a gesture at the doe.

"He says they've brought presents, and is offering the rabbit and doe to us," Robert said in an aside to Lorenzo. "What can we give them in return?" he whispered.

"What about some of the oranges and limes Andrew Gonzales gave you at Sarazota?" Lorenzo answered. "I think cook could part with a bag or two."

"Wait here, and I'll go get them," Robert nodded—holding his hand up to indicate he would return.

"Looks like you've made new friends," Lorenzo smiled as Robert returned with two burlap bags of citrus. Examining the bags, the lead man nodded his thanks. Then, affecting a clumsy salute, he shouldered the bags and motioned to the others to head on up the beach—leaving the rabbit and doe on the sand beside Robert and Lorenzo.

"Whew," Robert uttered as the last man disappeared around the mouth of the river. "Good idea. I never would have thought . . ."

"Sorry for depleting our stock. Cook may have it in for me," Lorenzo laughed. "But it worked."

· 8 ·

December 1823

*W*aiting anxiously in St. Augustine for official word affirming his request for Colonel George Brooke and his four companies of men from the Fourth Infantry in Pensacola to be reassigned to the area on Hillsborough Bay, Colonel James Gadsden was relieved when he received orders from the Adjutant General's Office sent on November 5 officially establishing a military post at the juncture of Hillsborough Bay and the Hillsborough River.

As the mail had been delayed in its transport from Washington, Gadsden did not receive the order until December 1. Fearing too much time had been lost already, Gadsden was quick to take up his pen and write Colonel Brooke in Pensacola relaying the news and proposing to meet him by the middle of January at the area he had proposed. Time was of the essence, he communicated as he wrote: "I feel the more anxious on the subject as the Indians to the south have of late exhibited something like an unfriendly feeling."

Handing the letter off to a courier bound for Pensacola, Gadsden quickly called together a small detachment and—as Indian Commissioner—hurried off to survey the new Indian Nation north and west of St. Augustine—before heading on across the territory to meet Brooke at the new area to be designated as "Cantonment Brooke."

True to his promise to have the new homestead completed before the end of the year, Rhodes excitedly ran up the ship's ramp. Finding Robert at his office on board—he approached the desk with a flourish. As Robert looked up confused at the intrusion, Rhodes reached out a set of keys—which he dropped unceremoniously on the sheet of paper on which Robert had been writing. "It's yours, Robert," he smiled. "We have finished in time for the Christmas Eve ceremony we had planned on shipboard for tonight. What do you say we move the celebration to your front porch?"

"Rhodes, you said it would be finished," Robert smiled—eagerly picking up the small set of keys—"but I'll admit, I have been so busy planning this trip to Pensacola—I guess the time rather got away from me. Tell me, is it really ready for occupancy—or is there still more to do before we can use the inside?"

"All finished, Robert. As a matter of fact, your bedroom is even completed. If you like, you can spend Christmas Eve in your own bed."

"Wow, what a concept! You mean no more bunk down here?"

"Until you swap your bedroom back here for that trip to Pensacola you've been talking about," Rhodes smiled. "I did promise you the work would be finished before the end of the year. What about a tour—if you can spend the time, that is," he continued—indicating the stack of papers on which Robert had been working.

"Are you kidding? Nothing could keep me away right now!" Robert added—laying his pen down on the desk and rising. "Imagine, my own home—way off here in Southwest Florida—only the first of many, I pray, once we spread the beauty of our new home to all those frozen northerners. Perfect timing, too for advertising the beauty, warmth, and availability of homesteads and farms down here. I'll send the report to my father once I get to Pensacola and have him begin the advertisements. A perfect Christmas gift!" he continued—following Rhodes out of the office.

Stopping on deck, Robert perused the lovely new homestead directly ahead of him at the edge of the woods. "Perfect, I would say," he smiled at Rhodes. "That large gumbo limbo tree on the Indian mound near the beach is a great target for us in future trips up the coast—as well as a lookout to assess any visitors! And the oaks you retained are the perfect frame for the whole structure. Just look at those branches—with those beautiful air plants and all that Spanish moss! Who says there's nothing left of Spain's occupancy," he laughed—waving his hand at the festooned branches shading the west-facing porch. "And the front porch not only gives a full view of any traffic coming into the wharf, but also will be a great spot on which to watch those magnificent sunsets we've all been raving about."

"I think it was Lorenzo who first pointed out the setting at the edge of the woods," Rhodes confessed—as he led the way up the small hill, "but—with the need for protection from intruders—it couldn't be situated at a better spot."

"Oh, come on, Rhodes. There you go being paranoid again. Outside of those five Seminoles we saw a few weeks ago, there hasn't been a soul near here since we arrived. Nor is there likely to be—until we see some buyers. Now, go on. I want the grand tour!" Robert added as they reached the front steps.

"Although the structure is elevated above the beach," Rhodes began, "we have no actual reports on the wave action down here. We do know that hurricanes are common in the late summer and fall—although after that last squall in Sarazota—we luckily haven't seen one so far. Nevertheless, to be on the safe side, we have elevated the whole structure on small pilings above the ground—allowing what we call a 'crawl space' to allow water to drain off without entering the house. The three steps here to the porch will keep your whole home safe from flooding," he continued—kicking at the nearest step as he led the way to the porch. "Frankly, I suggest that all the property you develop down here be elevated—with crawl spaces beneath."

"Noted!" Robert smiled—taking a moment to look beneath the steps as he climbed to the porch. "Oh, Rhodes," he called—suddenly noticing the white, wooden swing hung on the side of the wide front porch. "You know how to treat a homeowner," he continued, taking a seat and swinging it slowly. "Perfect spot to watch the sunset!"

"Or an enemy approaching," Rhodes countered—with a smile. "But I gave you the keys. Don't you want to see the inside?"

"Able to see a lot through these windows we brought along," Robert joked, standing up and peering through the glass panes of the nearest window. "But if you insist, after you!" he laughed—following Rhodes to the wide front door situated at the center of the front porch—between the eight floor-length windows flanked by green wooden shutters. "Just for 'show' I suppose," he smiled—fingering one of the open shutters.

"Oh, I expect you will be glad to have them in place once a storm comes. We've been lucky so far, you know," Rhodes continued—pushing open the front door and ushering Robert inside with a wave of his hand. "Parlor to the left—with a view of the river—and a study on the right for you. Not much furniture right now—as we had enough to bring with all the building lumber—as well as the livestock. A couple of my men are pretty handy, though. Given the task, I'm sure they can create what you want."

"Bed's the main thing," Robert laughed. "I suppose it's up this flight of stairs," he added—gesturing to the wide flight of wooden stairs. "Can we go up?"

"Several bedrooms. You can take your pick—although I thought you might want the larger one on the front of the house—over the parlor. Perfect view of the river."

"In case I want to watch for those intruders you keep imagining," Robert laughed—heading down the hall. "Oh, Rhodes, I'm sorry," he apologized—looking into the room. "It's—I mean—it's even more beautiful than my bedroom in Virginia. I couldn't even have imagined . . ."

"Funny you should mention your family's Virginia home—as I believe your father told me your stepmother ordered the furniture. Wanted the new 'lord of the manor' to live in style, your father joked. It is the only room we brought with us intact. But be assured, there is plenty of pine and oak out there to make whatever else you want. You can order fabric when you are in Pensacola—and have room to bring back any other furniture you'd like to purchase there."

"The kitchen?" Robert asked.

"Behind the house," Rhodes answered—leading the way back down the stairs. "We can go out there when we finish here, but I'll warn you, it's still pretty bare."

"As long as I'm in port, we still have the galley," Robert laughed. "And the firepit and spit are still perfect for the big Christmas meal we have planned for tomorrow," he added—heading back to the front door.

"Robert!" a frantic Lorenzo called, running up the front steps. "Oh, I see you've had a chance to visit the house."

"Just now, Lorenzo," Robert answered—noticing Lorenzo's anxiety. "What's wrong? You look like you've seen one of those intruders Rhodes is so worried about," he continued—turning to Rhodes with a smile.

"If you mean Seminoles," Lorenzo nodded, "those same three we sent off with the citrus are down by the ship. I . . . I can't talk with

them, but they are carrying two large wild turkeys, and they were gesturing at me."

"Oh, heavens, what a housewarming," Robert called, running
down the front steps and heading to the ship with Lorenzo just behind.
"I hope they've come in peace."

"Buenos dias," Robert managed as he approached the three Seminoles with a smile.

"Regalos," the lead man called—holding out the dead turkey and
indicating the second one the man beside him was holding, "para tu
nuevo hogar," he continued—gesturing toward the new house.

"Muchas gracias!" Robert answered—clearly moved by the gesture. "Lorenzo, they have brought us turkeys for our celebration," he
called. "What . . . I mean, what can we give them in return?"

"Oysters," Lorenzo smiled. "I was down by the wharf, and you
wouldn't believe the catch the men brought in. Give me a minute, and
I can get them a whole bag," he called running off down the beach.

"What a feast!" Lorenzo called—placing a large platter of food on the
long table the men had assembled on the front lawn of the new plantation
house. "Don't think I've ever had a Christmas celebration like this," he
added—taking his seat. Sorry to have to leave all of this. It's for certain I'll
just be having to dream of this roast turkey," he continued—motioned to
the large slices of meat on his plate—"and all the delicious fried fish . . ."

"Oh, I expect you can have target practice on the many wild animals you will find farther west, and the army should be able to find you
some fish at least," Robert laughed—taking a swig from his tankard of
the last wine left from Bunce's supply and saved for this occasion.

"Not the Gulf varieties," Lorenzo added—shaking his head.
"Think we're massing for a land excursion. Last I heard we were to be
assigned to move the Seminoles further into the center of the territory.
Of course, all that may have changed by the time I get to Pensacola.
Haven't been able to keep in touch out here."

"Inland suits me," Rhodes interjected. "Never want to repeat that
trip over here from St. Augustine. Prepared to meet my maker right
here—if it meets your approval, Robert," he added, turning to his host
as he gnawed on a turkey leg.

"That's why I brought you along," Robert nodded. "I need you
to keep an eye on things while I'm away. 'Master of the house' so to
speak for the time being."

"Any idea how long that might be?" Rhodes asked.

"Sadly, it might be two months or more," Robert answered. "Only two nights in my new bed and I have to go back to that accursed bunk."

"Robert, I'm sorry," Lorenzo apologized. "It's all because of me having to join Colonel Brooke's unit over in Pensacola. I shouldn't have asked . . ."

"Nonsense," Robert interrupted. "Now that the house is finished, there are several supplies we need—things we didn't have room to bring from St. Augustine. And then, there are the several men we brought along to build this beautiful mansion," he continued—waving his hand to encompass the glowing, white structure beside him with its long front windows reflecting the setting sun. "Since they are no longer needed, I have offered to take them on to Pensacola as well—where they can get overland passage back to New York. Being landlubbers, too, I don't think any of them would welcome another trip around the territory," he laughed. "So your transport is only part of the reason for the trip. But we are all going to miss you!" he added.

"As I will miss all of you," Lorenzo sighed—taking a drink from his tankard. "But believe me, I will never forget the past several months—despite all the problems."

"Expect you will be ready to leave at sunrise," Rhodes added, "and I daresay, once we have finished that stock you brought from Bunce, we may not be able to hold an intelligent conversation. So do you have any last-minute requests for me?"

"Mainly to protect this lovely estate you and your men have created from all those intruders you keep looking for out there on the river!" Robert laughed.

"Understood," Rhodes chuckled. "We'll be on the lookout."

"And—lest the men you have remaining get too bored with fishing, catching oysters, and entertaining our Seminole friends," Robert added—waving toward the woods behind the house, "I'm hoping you will be able to start on the ranch—out there where we've already cleared the land. Judging by the size of a few of those cows we brought along, we should be looking at a new calf or two this spring—and our first crops should be appearing by the time I get back. Once I get to Pensacola, I will alert my father to put his advertisement for homesites in the newspaper so that we can look for our first buyers by next fall!"

· 9 ·

December 1823

The sun was just visible beyond the large oak trees behind the house—as the chickens cackled their welcome—followed by the low mooing of the cows as they were led out to pasture in the broad field. As if on cue, the front door opened onto the wide front porch as Robert emerged carrying his small valise. Pausing a moment to pull his jacket more closely about him, he told himself that it was—after all—late December. So if he had to pull out some of the clothing he had brought from New York—so be it. From what Porter had told him, though, the cold fronts were short-lived—and would be over by the time he returned.

Carefully pulling the door closed behind him, he turned to look back inside the nearest front window and to set the wooden swing moving before descending the three front stairs and turning toward the wharf. The chatter of two small squirrels chasing each other down the nearest oak caused him to stop. Noticing a red-bellied woodpecker attempting to drill into a nearby cabbage palm, he smiled. This was home! His father had sent him down here to establish his new property, which he had dutifully accomplished. But if his father—or any of his family—had any thoughts of him returning to either New York or Virginia, they were sadly mistaken. He was the lord of his new manor—and loving every minute of it, he smiled as he turned with one last look at the sparse grass lawn—backed by the large, white house, whose tall west-facing windows had not yet found the morning light. "I shall remember you this way," he whispered—giving a final wave to his home.

"We're ready to set off, Robert—unless you want to wish your new home another goodbye," Lorenzo laughed as he crossed the wharf and ran up to take Robert's valise and follow him on board.

"I never thought I could become so attached in so short a time," Robert admitted. Perhaps getting underway was best now—while Rhodes and the men he had left behind did the final finishing work. He had done a full appraisal of the things they still needed and had a list of the items he would buy in Pensacola. If the weather held, he should be able to return by spring, he decided as the ship made an about-face and headed back down the bay to the Gulf.

Although the day grew brighter, the colder wind on the Gulf required windbreakers on the deck. "Hadn't realized we'd be heading north," Lorenzo called out as he entered the cabin—pulling his jacket closer before putting his hands in his pockets. "And I'd been berating myself for bringing along my winter uniform," he laughed.

"If this is all the winter we will get," Robert laughed, "I'm not complaining."

"How long do you think it will take to get to Pensacola?" Lorenzo asked—pausing to glance at the map spread out on the table.

"First stop is a small port dating back to early Spanish occupation. It's called St. Marks and is on Apalachee Bay—where we can get off the Gulf for a while. We can pick up a few supplies there. Lot of history connected with the place I hear. It was part of Florida's Spanish mission chain and sported a good-sized fort. Indian village just to the north called 'Anhaica' was attacked and burned by Andrew Jackson in the First Seminole War, Porter told me when I mentioned where we were heading. Apparently, Porter had been here several times on his way to and from Pensacola. Said the chief, Neamathla—I think it was—has already agreed to move his tribe eastward, though, so we should have no trouble if we have to lay over awhile in the bay."

"Which I hope doesn't happen—as I am due in Pensacola by early January."

"And we'll get you there. I think—except for a few showers, the heavy storms are behind us for the New Year. I only plan on stopping for the night. Actually, though small, little St. Marks might come into its own eventually, Porter said, as it lies almost halfway between Pensacola and St. Augustine and might pull East and West Florida together some-day—once the many territory representatives tire of the long journey between the two towns. He was laughing as he told me of the trip the St. Augustine representatives took last year by sea to get to the first territorial meeting in Pensacola. Said it took them almost two months—and they swore on their return trip that they would never take that route again. Apparently, the delegation from Pensacola was to travel overland this year to meet in St. Augustine. At least they had the benefit of the several mission roads and Indian trails, but I don't expect they were any more pleased with the long journey. Guess we may hear more once we get to St. Marks or Pensacola."

"Lots of news we've missed," Lorenzo admitted. "Although I'm afraid I'll hear more than I want to once I check in to help move the Seminoles! Not an easy task, I assure you. Makes me question my decision to go into the military. Seems there is always a skirmish—or out and out war going on. Wish I had a father like yours who gave me half a new territory," he laughed. "Wouldn't mind building a home in the Tampa area."

"Finish your military requirement and come on back! Say the word, and I'll save you the choicest lot."

It was late afternoon when Robert and crew pulled into Apalachee Bay. Heading to the long dock at St. Marks, he chose a spot within walking distance of the several small shops. Signaling Lorenzo and the crew to wait until he returned, Robert pulled his jacket closer about him—as the air was much cooler than what he had experienced at Hillsborough Bay—secured his lengthy list in his pocket and headed off—enjoying the pleasant sunlit wharf with all its activity. His first stop was—necessarily—at the harbor master's small office at the end of the dock—to secure permission to tie up for the night. As he approached, he was surprised to see a small group of men gathered near the door—conversing in Spanish. Many of them appeared to be Cuban dock hands—just being relieved of duty and awaiting their pay envelopes for the week's work.

As he waited, Robert perused the few establishments down the street—planning a compact shopping trip before returning to his cook's evening meal of some of the fish they had brought with them and stored in the hold for meals. Lost in thought, he was surprised when he saw that the men were all leaving and the dock master was beckoning to him. "Sorry," he muttered—approaching the office. "Heading to Pensacola and just need to tie up for the night," he offered—heading to the door.

"Glad to hear some English," the dock master laughed. "Come on in, and we'll fill out your papers. Not much business today, but those hands wanted their pay before they left. Little chilly today," he added, "but the coffee pot is on—if you'd like a cup."

"Only if it's American," Robert smiled, "and not that vile Cuban brew Porter tried to pawn off on me down in Key West."

"Oh, so you've been to Key West. Long voyage, I expect," the dock master answered—holding the door for Robert to enter. "But what brings you all the way up here?"

"Settling new territory—down south at Hillsborough Bay. Built myself a house, but we couldn't bring everything we need, so I'm heading to Pensacola. Got an army recruit I need to deliver, too. I think he's supposed to help with moving the Seminoles eastward, but we haven't heard much more since leaving Key West," Robert answered, taking the offered chair.

Removing his hat, the dock master hung it on the hat tree behind his desk, and—running his fingers through his graying hair sat down at his desk preparing for a leisurely visit with one who spoke his language. "Think they're moving that Anhaica settlement that's just north of us," he nodded. "Somehow our new governor Duval got Chief Neamathla to agree to move—peacefully—last October at their meeting over at Moultrie Creek.

"While I understand our country's need to secure the natives so the territory can be opened for settlement, I still can't help feeling sorry for the tribes who have made it their home for so long. And the word I've heard is that the new land in the center of the territory is swampy and very different from the rolling farmland up here," he added, shaking his head. "Could be trouble once the move is official."

"But an overland route between Pensacola and St. Augustine is really a necessity. Porter told me the St. Augustine delegation swore no more ship voyages when they came back through Key West. I can echo their thoughts," Robert laughed—enjoying hearing some news after so many months.

"Well, the Pensacola delegation didn't fare much better on their overland trip. The gist was that the legislature sent John Williams and William Simmons on an expedition to find a central location for the territory's capital. Met right here—as a halfway point. News I've heard is that they will be converting Anhaica to our new capital. Gonna call it

'Tallahassee.' Name means 'old town.' Guess it fits—if you consider it was an old Muskogean settlement—before Andrew Jackson burned it to the ground about five years ago. Killed a lot of the natives there as well.

"Neamathla's tried hard to reconstruct the settlement, but it seems he's now given up. Guess with the army's determination to move the natives east, he had no choice," he continued—pushing a paper and pen across the table to Robert.

"Now, how about some of that coffee?" he added when Robert signed and slid the paper back to him. "I promise it's an American brew. Small grocer down the street keeps me supplied. Can get you some as well," he laughed. "Those Cuban dock workers swear by their stiff concoction—but I'm of your opinion."

"Sounds good," Robert nodded. "And if you have time, I could use some information on the rest of my trip. I took several trips back and forth from New York to St. Augustine while my father was acting as a U.S. revenue collector down there, but I never ventured farther down the coast—and certainly never to this side of the territory. All of it has been a real eye-opener—what with the pirating activity down in the keys—and then those Cuban ranchos up the coast. I mean—it's a far cry from the ports in Boston, New York, Norfolk—or even Charleston!"

"I think the east coast has had about a two-hundred-year jump on us. Will take some time to catch up," the dock master smiled—handing Robert a smoking mug of black coffee. "Give us time, though, and the Florida ports will surpass all those northern ones. Lots of rivers and bays, flat land, sandy soil—won't take much to make them ready—once our settlers start arriving."

"My sentiments exactly. Hoping to start a full settlement at Hillsborough Bay. Already have a home there and left a team to finish grading and planting. Actually, while I'm in Pensacola I'm planning on contacting my father to start advertising in the northern papers. Seems with winter up there right now, there might be many willing to trade shoveling their walks for sweeping sand off the front porch."

"Gotta be hardy souls right now, though. As you and those St. Augustine delegates have already attested, it's no vacation cruise! And—despite the Moultrie Creek agreement—I predict the natives are going to prove difficult to move."

"All the more reason to check out alternative routes to Hillsborough Bay. If the shipping lanes around the territory are so lengthy, and the routes across the territory go through the Seminole lands, I want to check out possible transport from the west. Might recommend new owners come south by riverboat and then travel eastward by ship. Seems like a much more acceptable route," Robert nodded.

"That's one of the reasons for my trip to Pensacola. I really know nothing about that area. But first, I need to know how long my next leg will be—as my recruit is rather anxious about meeting his regiment in time. Got any information on docking there—or where we might find his unit?"

"You'll find the town much more developed than our little St. Marks—as its history goes back over two hundred years. It's been under Spanish, French, English, and now U.S. control," the dock master answered—picking up his own mug as he pushed back in his chair. "As I heard it, the powers that be over there felt themselves much closer to the upper gulf communities and wanted no part of being annexed to the Florida territory. Think we are too primitive down here," he laughed. "In fact, the residents all voted to become a part of Alabama and were rather unhappy when President Monroe annexed it to Florida and sent Andrew Jackson there to become our first American governor two years ago."

"If the town is spread out, will I need to go up the river to dock? I mean, I'm not sure what the depth might be."

"No problem. You'll find Fort Barrancas right on the coast—at the entrance to Pensacola Bay. The fort's been in existence for years. I'm sure you remember reading about Andrew Jackson's victory there in the first Seminole War," the dock master smiled at Robert's blank expression. Obviously, New Yorkers hadn't paid much attention to events down here with the natives! Never mind, he decided. If he did make Florida his home over in the Tampa area, Robert would hear more than enough of the Seminole engagements. It could only be hoped that he would keep his scalp if things got testy!

"At any rate, our country has now established a naval base at the fort," the dock master explained. "I expect that is where your recruit will meet his unit. After you deliver him, you can cross the bay and find a good harbor and facilities for docking. Think you can find whatever you need in town there."

"Thank you so much," Robert answered. "I'll stop back on my way home." Embarrassed that he was so ignorant of local history, he rose, laid his empty mug on the table, and turned to leave. With the whole of the new territory formerly in Spanish hands, it had not seemed necessary to follow its history—and now he was afraid he would be living it!

January 1824

After his balmy fall and early winter on Hillsborough Bay, Robert was surprised as he and his crew headed farther west and found not only a jacket but also gloves and head coverings were necessary in the winter weather of Florida's Panhandle. "Wish I'd thought to bring warmer clothes along," Robert admitted—pulling his cap down farther and sliding his hands into his jacket sleeves as he stepped on deck.

"At least you will have a cabin in which to bed down at night—while you think of me in a small tent—somewhere in Seminole territory—listening for every sound to be sure I'll still have a scalp by morning on which to rest my army cap!" Lorenzo laughed—sitting down on his large duffel bag as the ship approached the Fort Barrancas naval dock.

"Hey, it's been a long trip. And I can't thank you enough for all the help you gave us in setting up my homestead," Robert said, turning to Lorenzo.

"Despite the long trek, I wouldn't have missed it for the world. And I thank you for providing my transportation over here to Pensacola—when I know you wanted to stay at your new place."

"Had to come over here anyway for supplies and to contact my father," Robert shrugged. "Closest town for now."

"Sounds like the new capital is going to be much closer at that new town they're calling Tallahassee. Probably where our unit will start our trek eastward."

"If that's where you're heading, why didn't I just leave you there?" Robert laughed. "Would have been a lot easier all around."

"Would've been a possibility. Who knew the capital was being moved when we started out five months ago? Still, I'm grateful for all the time we had together. It's been fun, amigo! You know I never had a brother," Lorenzo added—turning away to hide the tears in his eyes.

"Well, all I can say is . . . you know where I am—and you're welcome any time you're in the area," Robert offered—grabbing Lorenzo in a hug as both stood to watch the ship slide into the dock.

Watching Lorenzo in full uniform walk down the plank with his duffel on his back, Robert felt his first stab of homesickness—as he finally realized he was all alone now in this venture. Granted, he actually did have a brother—yet William seemed so far away. Perhaps, though, their father would send him down as well—once the land was settled, he thought—as he raised his hand in a final salute as Lorenzo turned at the dock and raised his cap in farewell.

Once Robert had left Lorenzo at the base, he directed the ship on into the harbor—anchoring at the edge of the prosperous town situated at the mouth of the Escambia River. Securing his hat as he stepped on the windy dock, Robert quickly checked his pocket for his lengthy list of supplies—determined now to complete his shopping trip and the contact with his father and get back to his new home. Checking in with the dock master, he secured a space for the following week and released the crew to explore the new town at will.

Turning back down the dock, he looked for a ship that might be heading up the river where they could deliver his message to his father to an overland carrier, which would get it to him much more quickly than the lengthy sea voyage around the coast.

"Just arrived from St. Marks," I hear, a rotund, partially balding man called—running up to him on the dock.

"What?" Robert called—startled at being approached.

"Sorry!" the man apologized. "Just had a chance to talk to one of your men, who told me you had just been in St. Marks."

"Well . . . as a matter of fact, we stopped at the port on our way west from Hillsborough Bay," Robert nodded—happy to find someone in this strange town with whom he could converse. As the dock master seemed completely inundated checking in shipments from the various boats, he hadn't wanted to bother him by asking directions.

"Sorry," the man replied. "Guess I should introduce myself. "William Wyatt," he replied—reaching out to shake Robert's hand.

"Robert Hackley," Robert answered—returning the handshake and taking a seat on a bench near the pier's entrance. "What is it you want to know about St. Marks?"

"Thinking of moving over there—to the new capital," Wyatt answered—taking the seat beside him. "I hear it's going to be named Tallahassee—although St. Marks is the closest port, and I was wondering what to expect once I get there."

"We were only there a short while. Harbor is easily approachable, and the dock is clean and safe. I found the dock master very personable—and knowledgeable. Mostly Cuban dock workers, but there are a few stores—enough to supply basic needs. We didn't venture inland, however, as I understood the area designated for the new capital is still a Seminole settlement. As I understand it, though, the army is now heading to the area to facilitate moving the natives eastward. Why would you give up Pensacola to move out there? Are you with the army—or the legislature?"

"Looking to get an early start on business in the area," Wyatt smiled—shaking his head. "Once the capital is settled there, the legislators will need a place to stay. Hoping to find myself some property—and build a hotel. Being the first in the area should be an advantage. But—not having any idea about the area—I need to know what I'll be undertaking."

"Looks like we are two of a kind," Robert laughed. "My father bought a large stretch of territory from Hillsborough Bay south, and I've been attempting to settle that area. Perhaps we can work together in identifying new residents—either coming from Pensacola or up the coast. I'm over here to purchase supplies for the new home I have built."

"Been here a few years," Wyatt nodded. "Tell me where you need to go, and I'll direct you. I'd love to see your new place as well. Perhaps once I get over to St. Marks, I will take a trip over to Hillsborough Bay. I hear it's beautiful!"

"I've got a wharf at the entrance to the river—and a guest room—once I find furniture for it while I'm in town."

"You're on," Wyatt smiled. "Now, you're looking to buy furniture?"

"Kitchen supplies, hardware items, food stuffs—you name it! But first of all, I need to find a way to send a message to my father about the progress on the property. I don't want to wait another five months to send it southward. Do you have any idea about local water transportation possible up the river and then overland?"

"Probably the way I came down here—and most of the other residents as well," Wyatt nodded. "Best way is via Mobile. To be honest, the residents here really consider themselves more a part of Alabama than Florida."

"Easy to understand—after the voyage I've had. Can you tell me where to find a boat heading upriver? I'm anxious to get on with it and find my way back home as soon as possible."

"Understood," Wyatt answered. "I'll take you down the dock a bit—where you can find a boat or two, and then—as I'm heading back through town, I'll give you a tour!"

• *11* •

January 1824

$\mathcal{H}$is mother always said hindsight was better than foresight, and Lorenzo couldn't agree more as he shifted his pack to his other shoulder and tried to ignore the pain in his back. Oh, why hadn't he joined the U.S. Navy instead of the army? While sailing with Robert had had its scary moments with the possibilities of pirates and the several storms—at least he had been afforded a decent bed on board ship and not a rough forest floor covered with pinecones on which to set up his small tent.

The only acceptable part was that at this time of year, the days were short enough to afford an early end to the day's march, a welcome campfire on which to cook the unit's sparse army fare and warm its frozen feet, and a chance to wrap its weary limbs in the thin blanket rolls as they bedded down for yet another uncomfortable night. Lorenzo remembered the small port at St. Marks—where Robert had put in on their way to Pensacola. He had understood that the new capital was to be just inland—as the troops disembarked with orders to advance to the Seminole settlement to facilitate moving the natives to the new area in the center of the state. As he figured it, however, "just inland" was several miles of hiking over hilly, oak- and pine-covered terrain with vines to entrap even the most careful hiker and herds of wild boars snorting and rushing from the hammocks as the troops crashed through the underbrush. His only job for the moment, however, was to follow the other recruits—led by one Colonel George Mercer Brooke, the thirty-nine-year-old, slim, dark-haired commander of the Fourth Infantry from Pensacola.

At last, when the shadows before him finally seemed to be lengthening, he was relieved to see the lead patrol laying down their packs and forming a circle on the damp pine needles in the clearing—ready for a word from Colonel Brooke before constructing the campfire and pitching their tents. As he gratefully laid down his own pack and took a seat on the ground, Lorenzo was surprised to see a small contingent of soldiers approaching through a clearing to the south. Hailing the foremost group, the new men signaled to Colonel Brooke, who broke rank and retreated to meet the newcomers. Exhausted did not even begin to describe the men, who took the chance to stretch, remove tight boots, and rub swollen feet or even lie down on the damp ground—awaiting Brooke's return.

It was dusk before Brooke finally signaled to the retreating patrol and returned to his men, who immediately snapped to attention to hear his information. "As it seems," Brooke began, "Chief Neamathla has voluntarily moved his tribe eastward to the new territory—so our stay here is unnecessary."

At the cheers that quickly erupted, Brooke held up his hand to quiet the men. "That does not mean our journey is completed, however," he added—to a chorus of groans. "I am sure you will all be glad to note, though, that the only marching we are now required to do is the twenty-five-mile jaunt in the morning back to St. Marks—where our ships will now transport us to the confluence of Hillsborough Bay and the Hillsborough River to set up a fort—at the western border of the Seminole land. Our new order is to keep the natives away and allow settlement in this western part of the territory.

"I've never been there, but I was told it is much more temperate than this area, is filled with abundant fish and game, and—best of all—totally uninhabited at the moment. Couldn't be a better assignment," he added with a smile—accompanied by a loud shout from those present.

"Excuse me, Colonel Brooke," Lorenzo called—surprising himself at daring to speak as a raw recruit.

"Excuse me? Is there dissension in the ranks?" Brooke bellowed—looking around to see who had dared to speak.

"I think the men with whom you spoke are mistaken about the area," Lorenzo began timidly.

"And do you personally know this area?" Brooke asked—turning to Lorenzo as he determined who was speaking.

"I've just spent several months in that area," Lorenzo nodded. "And I must tell you, it is owned by a man named Robert Hackley. Apparently, his father, Richard Hackley, purchased the whole area from the Hillsborough Bay to the Florida Straits from Spain several years ago and owns that whole side of the territory."

"Not as far as the U.S. Army is concerned," Brooke replied. "The word I received is that the whole area around Hillsborough Bay has now been confiscated as the site of a new army base. As it will be occupied by my infantry, it is to be called Cantonment Brooke in my honor," he added with a smile. "So the fact remains—no matter who claims ownership—as Florida is now a U.S. territory, the U.S. Army now has full rights to the property."

"But Hackley has built a new home and is setting up a plantation on the property," Lorenzo continued. "He is in Pensacola at the moment furnishing the home and buying supplies for the kitchen and the ranch he intends to establish several miles inland. . . ."

"So, our officers' quarters are already built!" Brooke smiled—running a finger down his long sideburns. "Who could ask for more? We are pleased that this Hackley has done us the favor of establishing our new home. And if he has cleared the land, even better for us in erecting barracks, store houses, and parade grounds."

As far as Brooke was concerned, the topic was closed. "It's 1,800 men," he concluded. Offering a salute to the men assembled, he motioned to his assistant and moved off into the nearby clearing.

"Is there really a settlement in that area?" the man nearest to Lorenzo asked.

"Left there just after Christmas," Lorenzo nodded. "Oh, my Lord, what is Robert going to say?"

"Is he a friend?" the nearby recruit asked.

"Rather—he was!" Lorenzo sighed.

The day dawned bright with puffy white clouds skirting in and out among the pine and oak forest behind the barn—accompanied by a chorus of raucous mockingbirds. Couldn't have picked a better place to spend January, Rhodes chuckled as he ambled slowly to the makeshift barn and swung the large door open, preparing to release the cows. Glancing quickly at the tranquil river view Robert so loved and anticipating his return with the other furniture and supplies needed to finish the house and ranch, he stopped—rubbing his eyes.

That wasn't Robert's schooner at the wharf! Remembering his fears of pirate attacks, he retreated into the barn—closing the door. Then, removing the gun he kept in the corner, he returned to the door and carefully swung it inward. Robert had left him in charge after all, and—like it or not—it now fell to him to address the invaders—whoever they might be. He could only hope they were friendly and only stopping on their way west to St. Marks or Pensacola.

Having spent the night anchored at the entrance to Hillsborough Bay, the men were up early—in uniform and ready for a view of their new home at Fort Brooke as the ships made their way north in the bay and approached the picturesque oak forest bordering the confluence of the Hillsborough River. In full dress uniform, Colonel Brooke approached the starboard railing of his command ship. Raising a small telescope to his eye, he scanned the nearby beach and forest—suddenly calling out, "There it is. That's the mound—with the red-barked tree Gadsden mentioned as our landmark. And would you believe it, we even have a wharf out here! What a Godsend! And what a palatial new fort is awaiting us on that dune over there," he continued—scanning the nearby beach and settling on the large plantation house. "I daresay not even our U.S. Army could have envisioned such an establishment!"

Lowering the telescope, he perused the several recruits gathered on the rail. "Now who is it who knows the chap who built this place?" he asked—having forgotten Lorenzo's name.

"The whole property belongs to Robert Hackley—from New York," Lorenzo spoke up—approaching the colonel. "I was actually his guest on my way to meet your unit. I watched him and his crew build the house with a foundation they brought all the way from New York. He swears he owns the property—as his father bought it from a Spanish Duke—and I hate to think what he will do when he finds . . ."

"He will homestead elsewhere. This whole area is now U.S. Army property . . ." Brooke interrupted—stopping in mid-sentence as he observed Rhodes approaching from the nearby barn—rifle in hand. "Is that Hackley?" Brooke asked—turning to Lorenzo.

"I told you, Hackley is in Pensacola. That is his caretaker—named Rhodes."

"Call to him," Brooke ordered. "Have him put down that rifle before someone gets hurt. Tell him the U.S. Army is now taking possession of this whole area for our new fort."

"Yes, sir. He's pretty cautious, though, and he takes his job pretty seriously, so I don't know how he will react."

"Then go ashore, meet him, and explain," Brooke ordered—stepping back from the entrance as the deck hands tied up the ship and lowered the plank to the wharf. As Lorenzo hesitated, Brooke commanded, "That's an order, son."

Walking slowly onto the wharf, Lorenzo attempted to wave to Rhodes—who stood steadfast on the pathway to the large house looming behind him. His job was to protect Robert's property, and—quaking as he was at the very threat he had so worried about since the stay in Key West, he was ready to defend the property at all costs.

"Rhodes, it's me, Lorenzo," Lorenzo yelled—advancing toward him. "If you'll put down that rifle, I'll tell you why we're here."

Shielding his eyes from the sunlight bouncing from the river, Rhodes finally noted Lorenzo's blond hair and recognized him. Nodding, he lowered the rifle and headed toward the wharf and its impressive naval vessel—while still keeping his finger on the trigger. "I don't understand the meaning of this," he yelled as he approached Lorenzo. "What do you mean bringing the whole U.S. Navy down on us? I thought you were joining the army and were in Pensacola, Lorenzo."

"Change of plans, Rhodes," Lorenzo yelled back. "Navy just brought our infantry over here from Pensacola. Seems the U.S. government has now declared Hackley's whole property army territory and has designated it as a new fort to keep the Seminoles east of this area. The fort is now named for our leader, Colonel George Mercer Brooke. He's right up there on board," Lorenzo continued—motioning to the ship's deck in hopes of turning the whole encounter over to Colonel Brooke.

"The government has done what?" Rhodes asked—heading to Lorenzo—while ignoring the colonel perched on the deck to observe the confrontation. "This property belongs to Richard Hackley—and to his son, Robert. You know that, Lorenzo. I even saw the deed Richard received from that Spanish duke. There's no way the army can take over Robert's property. He left me in charge, and I simply won't permit it. We've all invested too much in this venture. You will just have to tell that colonel up there—" he waved at the deck with his free hand— "that you men will have to build your fort elsewhere."

"I'm afraid that's not possible," Brooke yelled—finally taking over the introduction to Lorenzo's relief. Heading down the plank

and approaching the two men, Brooke held out his hand in greeting—
before laying it at his side when Rhodes refused to accept it. "Colonel
George Brooke," the colonel began. "I understand the shock this must
bring, but the truth is—although I am the new commander of Cantonment Brooke, the U.S. Army now owns this property. It is their choice
for a new fort on the western front of the territory, and I have four
additional ships on the way with the rest of my regiment. That said,
I'm afraid, sir, you have no choice but to accept the order. As of this
moment, I—and my infantry—are now in control of this property. That
lovely home will be our officers' quarters, and the barns and storehouses
will serve our needs as well. For the time being, my men will pitch their
tents here on the beach—until barracks can be built."

"But, what about . . . ? I mean, where am I and the rest of my men
to go? And I can only imagine what Robert will say when he returns,"
Rhodes spluttered.

"I assume he will be pleased that you have not attempted to stop
us," Brooke answered. "I can see there is plenty of land on this peninsula. We will cordon off the property we need—and you may build
another homestead. Please alert your men that they have an hour to
remove any personal items from the premises. And—as we have no
need for it, you may take your livestock with you."

"But . . . I mean . . . ," Rhodes attempted—watching in total dis-
belief as Brooke turned and walked back to the ship. "Lorenzo, is this
some sort of nightmare?" Rhodes asked, turning back to the young
man.

"I wish I could tell you that it is," Lorenzo answered sorrow-
fully. "And I especially wish I was not involved. I have grown so very
fond of all of you—and even thought of Robert as the brother I never
had. Now, he will hate me for bringing all of this on him—although I
promise I had nothing to do with it," he continued—reaching out to
grab Rhodes's free hand. "Will you tell Robert that when he returns?"

"Son, I expect Robert will want no part of either of us when he
returns. He so loved his new home—and he trusted me to protect it
for him."

"To your unit, Private," Brooke yelled back as he reboarded the
ship and motioned to Lorenzo—who squeezed the hand he was holding and turned back to the wharf—wiping his eyes on his sleeve as he
retreated.

• 12 •

February 1824

"Robert! You need to see this!" the frantic voice called from the open door.

"Spotted home yet?" Robert called. "Been waiting for this day," he added—sliding out of the chair. Hurrying onto the deck, he stopped as George, his first mate—still out of breath—handed him the telescope without another word.

"Should be approaching the turn to the river—if I guess right," Robert smiled—placing the telescope to his eye and angling it to the northwest. "My God, George, what am I seeing?" he yelled—lowering the telescope.

"Looks like someone else has found your complex!" George answered. "I couldn't believe it when I saw those ships out there—just about at your dock—if I guess right. Think it might be some Cubans from one of the ranchos down south?"

Raising the telescope again, Robert studied the two ships moored at the mouth of Hillsborough Bay. "Looks like U.S. Navy ships—unless I miss my guess. Saw some just like them in Pensacola. Lorenzo said his army unit had been commissioned to move the Seminoles east from the new capital at Tallahassee to the reservation the government had set up north of St. Augustine. Maybe they've tracked them this far. At any rate, I'm sure Rhodes has had a time dealing with the number of men who must have come in those ships. Hope they're moving on. We can't afford to feed them all!"

"More importantly, your harbor can't support too many ships," George answered. "We've never checked the depth farther up the river.

Think we're better off mooring south of the complex in the bay? We could lower the rowboat and make it to shore by the fishing shack."

"Looks like our only alternative," Robert answered. "And I was planning to spend the afternoon on my new front porch—waiting for a fish dinner! Best laid plans . . . ," he muttered—turning to head back to the control room.

"Who's the fellow who knows this Hackley?" Colonel Brooke bellowed—entering the large white tent where the men were finishing lunch.

"That would be me, Colonel Brooke," Lorenzo answered—rising and saluting. "Although I wish I'd had nothing to do with this."

"New assignment," Brooke interrupted—motioning for Lorenzo to follow him out of the tent.

"Our lookout just spotted a ship mooring to the south—down the beach. Launched a small boat already. Need to find out if it's that Hackley's vessel and him in the boat—or if we need to send out the patrol," Brooke answered. "Sending Baker and Jacobs with you for backup."

"If it's Robert, I won't need backup," Lorenzo answered. "He's going to have enough of a shock as it is—without sending armed guards to meet him."

"This is a U.S. military establishment, Private. Can't have anyone unauthorized entering the compound," Brooke concluded—nodding to the two guards waiting at the dock, who advanced to Lorenzo—as Brooke turned and headed back to the house.

"My God, Lorenzo, is that you?" Robert called—heading up the beach to meet the trio. "What are you doing here? Is that your unit camped down at the house?"

"I wish I could say it wasn't," Lorenzo answered—hurrying to meet Robert and George—as Baker and Jacobs laid back—hands on their weapons in case they were necessary.

"Didn't think we'd meet again when I left you in Pensacola. Glad to see you've made it this far," Robert smiled—reaching out to shake Lorenzo's hand. "I heard the Seminoles were moving east. Is your unit following them?"

"Stationed here," Lorenzo answered, shaking his head.

"Stationed where?" Robert asked—looking around the area and spotting the army tents and supplies spread out on his front lawn.

"Area has been designated as Cantonment Brooke—commanded by Colonel George M. Brooke," Lorenzo replied. "I'm afraid, Robert, that your home and plantation are now the property of the U.S. government. I know how much you love the area and all the work you and your team put in to making it a home, but I'm afraid you have no recourse. Rhodes and the rest of your team have moved farther south— to the area where you had started the ranch. Took your livestock—as the army had no need of them. I think they're building new quarters over there. Rhodes asked me to tell you he had no choice and would await you down there."

"The nerve of the army taking over my property!" Robert shouted angrily—as Baker and Jacobs advanced with their pistols raised. "My father bought this property fair and square—from Duke Alagon of Spain. We have the deed. The army has no right . . ." Backing off as the guards advanced, Robert checked his temper and asked, "Will you take me to this Colonel Brooke, Lorenzo? There are some things we need to iron out here—and I don't want to do it with pistols aimed at me!"

As Robert entered his own front porch, he reached out to give a light push to the suspended wooden swing he had so lovingly left on his departure—before turning to his front door—now labeled with a crude wooden sign reading "Officers' Quarters."

"'Officers' Quarters,' my foot!" he sputtered. Swatting at the offending sign—he succeeded only in knocking it sideways to hang at an angle as the door opened and a uniformed officer motioned him inside. His lovely living room, which had—on his departure—held only a desk and two chairs awaiting his return from Pensacola, was now filled with several desks and army-issued desk chairs. A rude counter rested on the back wall—housing a coffee pot and a stack of chipped cups.

Ushering Robert into the room, his guide pointed to a chair in front of the nearest desk. "Colonel Brooke will be with you shortly. Can I get you some coffee while you wait?" the man asked. "Good stock. I understand it came from Key West."

"Which I purchased and brought all the way up here—for what— the U.S. Army's brass to enjoy?" Robert replied angrily.

Assuming that to be a no, the man backed off—heading back to the front door and his desk by the entrance.

Across the front room, the windows were wide open—highlighting a view of the two spreading live oak trees—under which a series of small, white army tents had been erected on the carefully manicured lawn he had left—completely blocking any view of the lovely Hillsborough River at the end of the walk. How dare they take my property without asking, turn it into an army base, and accost me as a common criminal when I attempt to repossess it? Robert wondered. And who is now using my beautiful bed that I brought from New York, he continued—his blood boiling as he turned toward the stairs to see a tall man in full army uniform descending and heading toward him. Why this impostor was not much older than he, Robert observed—taking in the clean face with the dark, carefully groomed sideburns. How was it that he had the audacity to usurp a man's property?

"Colonel George Brooke," the man offered with a contrived smile as he approached Robert—hand out in greeting. "And you must be . . ."

"Robert Hackley, the rightful owner of this plantation—which your unit has proceeded to invade in my absence—evicting my caretaker and staff as well," Robert replied hotly—refusing to offer his hand in return. "And now, I'm afraid I must ask you all to leave and establish your base somewhere else. As I'm sure you have noticed the area is not exactly populated—so there should be room enough for your base without appropriating someone's own private residence."

"Begging your pardon, Mr. Hackley," Brooke replied—dropping his hand to his side, rounding the desk, and taking the chair across from Robert—"but this property was designated by Secretary of War, John C. Calhoun, as a military post on November 5 of last year. After the treaty with the Seminoles was signed, Colonel James Gadsden, who was one of the treaty commissioners, surveyed this area and designated it as the westernmost boundary of the Seminole territory to prevent them from receiving any help from outside influences. My four companies of the Fourth Infantry were ordered that same day to proceed immediately from Cantonment Clinch at Pensacola to set up Cantonment Brooke— named for me," he added proudly. "As you can understand after viewing the terrain from Pensacola to Hillsborough Bay, it took several weeks to move my troops to the proposed area. Yet here we are prepared to fulfill our duty as the westernmost outpost of the Seminole territory."

"Nonetheless, this whole area is part of the purchase my father, Richard Hackley, made from Duke Alagon of Spain—before Florida became a part of the United States. I have a copy of the sale in my possession and am prepared to show it to whomever is necessary to remove your men from my property—immediately," Robert remarked—trying to hold his temper in check—as he realized it would do no good to make an enemy of the U.S. Army—as it was clear they were in the area to stay.

"In speaking with your foreman, Rhodes," Brooke countered, "I learned that you and your crew did not arrive in this area until mid-November of last year. As the orders to establish Cantonment Brooke had been cut on November 5, it is clear that you and your crew were trespassing on U.S. Army property at the outset. We do, however, thank you and your men for this lovely establishment that has now become our headquarters.

"I understand your man, Rhodes, has now moved himself and your men to your ranch, which is south of our property and—as such—not needed for our operation. We shall be happy to have you as a neighbor," Brooke concluded—pushing back his chair and rising as a signal that the interview was ended.

"As a neighborly gesture, I will offer your friend—Lorenzo, I believe it is—and the two guards who accompanied him to meet you as a special duty assignment to help you unload your ship and transport your goods to your new home."

"Robert! You can't imagine how glad I am to see you," Rhodes called—rushing out of the newly fenced enclosure beyond the hastily established barn as the wagon drew up and Robert alighted—looking around. "I couldn't believe . . . but I mean, what a surprise you had waiting for you! I am so sorry. I tried . . ."

"Rhodes, I certainly can't blame you. If I had needed to stand down over two hundred members of the U.S. Army, I would have been able to do no more," Robert offered— taking his foreman's hand. "Yet I don't understand . . ."

"Lorenzo said their base here was already decided before you even arrived. If we had only known . . ."

"I only wish I had known our final destination," Lorenzo offered—unloading a large valise from the wagon. "Army protocol requires that troops are always the last to know their destination. Still, I could have prevented you from doing all that work—and losing your beautiful home. I know how much it meant to you."

"I don't blame you, Lorenzo. We all know how slow the news travels down here. I suppose if I had asked the right questions in Pensacola—yet what good is hindsight at this point? I see, Rhodes, that you and your men have salvaged our livestock and begun our new barn."

"Thank heaven you asked us to begin on the ranch when you left," Rhodes answered, "or we would have been sleeping on the ground. As it is, I'm not sure where you'll be able to live right now."

"I'd like to look over what you've accomplished in my absence and then get a list from you of supplies you still need—while Lorenzo and his fellows bring up the rest of my ship load."

"Do you want the full load?" Lorenzo asked—dropping the table he was carrying at Robert's feet. "I mean—is there a safe place to store it all?"

"Not sure the deer and turkey would steal it," Robert retorted. "Is there room in the barn?"

"If we leave the cows out for now, we can accommodate a good bit," Rhodes answered.

"Then, yes. Let's bring the whole shipment out here while I still have your wagon at my command. I have already alerted my father of our supposed progress so that he can advertise the property in New York. Since the message has been sent, I will need to be sure there is a house and plantation out here to welcome future landowners—and I'm sure I'm not prepared to stare down the whole of Brooke's regiment!

"So, Rhodes, let's sit down and decide what we will need, and I will head back to St. Marks. When the time is right, I will present my papers to the powers that be in the new capital and start the process for the army to pay me for the land they have unceremoniously taken from me. I'm sure my father's deed will surpass the government's unlawful appropriation of his land."

· *13* ·

March 1824

$\mathcal{S}$eething with the latent anger that had followed him all the way from Tampa Bay, Robert watched as the schooner slid into an empty birth at the small port at St. Marks. Watching as his crew lowered the sails and secured the ropes, he grabbed the list from his desk, jumped onto the dock, and headed to the port office to sign in—for an undetermined stay. Although he had not done much shopping in the small port on his two previous trips through there, he was hoping he could fill the list he and Rhodes had assembled before his departure—without the need for another trip to Pensacola. Certainly, if the new capital was indeed to be just twenty-five miles inland, the port should have experienced a recent resurgence of activity, he reasoned.

Finding the same dock master on duty, Robert extended his hand on entering the small building. "Welcome, Mr. Hackley," the master offered. "Never expected to see you again so soon. Thought you were ready to spend the rest of your life at your new plantation. Find something you still need?"

"Almost everything," Robert offered—exasperated—taking the chair in front of the desk.

"Must be quite a plantation you've set up," the dock master laughed—turning to pull a set of papers from the file behind him.

"It's now Cantonment Brooke—and home to over two hundred army members," Robert answered angrily.

"Cantonment Brooke? Wait, that's the new army base Colonel Gadsden was setting up over there near Hillsborough Bay. Don't tell me . . . ?"

"My new home is now the officers' quarters."

"But I don't . . ."

"Neither do I, but apparently the die was cast with the base being decided on before I even attempted to build on my father's own land. Nevertheless, I intend to wrest payment for the land our government so willingly took—without asking I may add."

"So what can we do for you here?"

"I have a copy of the deed," Robert added—pulling the document from his coat pocket. "Think I need to present it to someone in the new capital."

"Not much over there yet," the dock master said—shaking his head. "Only one fellow has dared to settle on that old Seminole reservation so far—name of Wyatt."

"Wait, would that be William Wyatt—from Pensacola?"

"One and the same," a voice answered as the door swung open to reveal the same rotund man who had toured Robert around Pensacola. "Never thought to see you again, Robert."

"Nor I you," Robert answered—rising and offering his hand.

"I believe I told you I was moving to this new Tallahassee. I'm hoping to build the first hotel over there. Legislators will all need a place to stay while the sessions are taking place. I also plan to set up a homestead and bring the family over—once Tallahassee is built up enough for them. But what brings you all the way back here?"

"Long story," Robert answered, shaking his head. "But if you're in town for a while, I could use your help in locating a few businesses."

"Got the whole day," Wyatt smiled. "And I know just the spot to top off your shopping with an old friend."

"So tell me what you know of the Seminole settlements up here," Robert said—as he and Wyatt sat down in the canteen at the end of the dock for a late lunch. "Heard Chief Neamathla had agreed to move eastward to the land set aside in the new treaty—yet the men at the base still seem to be worried that the natives are not willing to move."

"It's probably good to be on the lookout," Wyatt answered. "News I have heard is that the Seminoles are saying they're sorry they agreed to the treaty—and the pittance our government has agreed to give them—as the land up here is so much better for farming. Saying they can't get crops to grow over there in the new territory. I wouldn't be surprised to see an uprising—despite the treaty—if they decide to move back here."

"Are you worried about your property?" Robert asked, concerned.

"With my small property, I'm not much of a threat. And with the area becoming the new capital, I doubt they'll present much of a problem here."

"Any word on activity out my direction?"

"Newest rumor I've heard is that the natives think the U.S. will have a new war with England—and they're ready to side with them."

"Good Lord, with the reported number of Seminoles in the territory, there's no way we could hope to subdue them! The whole area around Hillsborough Bay is now in the heart of the Indian territory," Robert sighed. "According to new laws, no white settlers are allowed in the area except on official business. Looks like we'll all be sitting ducks!"

"Yet . . . you . . ."

"I'm not worried—although my foreman, Rhodes, thinks every deer or boar that comes near the property is a Seminole hunting party."

"Still, you said you are located in their territory."

"And that's where I intend to stay. I continue to remind Brooke that I have the deed—and I was here first. I guess he is still a little embarrassed at having deposed me—and so far has done nothing to move me further on."

"But living out beyond the fort—as you said—aren't you afraid of the natives?"

"Met a few when we were building my first home, but they were friendly—and even brought us gifts. Didn't see any this last time—and my foreman didn't report anything."

"Wouldn't trust them, though, if they feel threatened," Wyatt cautioned.

"I'll take that into account," Robert answered—folding his napkin and summoning the waitress. "Right now, I have many more immediate needs. Gotta finish my list and find out where I can register my father's deed. Thought with Tallahassee being the new capital I might find the proper office there."

"Not unless you want me to hold it until someone official gets over here," Wyatt laughed. "Got no idea when that might be, though."

"Thanks. Just think I'll post a letter from here to my father. Ask him to clear the deed in New York. Thanks for all your information.

I'd invite you over our way, but there's not much in the way of a new house until I get these supplies back there," he laughed. "Thanks for your help, and good luck with that hotel. May come back for a visit sometime."

• *14* •

April 1824

*T*urning into the Hillsborough River from the Bay, Robert directed George to head toward the eastern bank—intending to anchor south of his original wharf—where his men had built a temporary dock from downed pine trees and effected a temporary road to his new home—which he hoped they at least had under roof by now. Watching the shoreline for the new dock, he was surprised when George, his mate, called out, "Robert, looks like you've got more company!"

"What?" Robert asked, turning to look at the opposite shore where George was now pointing. "More army? I swear I'm not sure how much more this area can take. And there really isn't room for more ships."

"Don't think that one is much of a problem," George laughed. "Not much more than a rowboat, if you ask me," he continued—pointing to the small boat that was beached on the opposite shore—on the western side of the river. "Want to head over and take a look?"

"Can't hurt," Robert answered. "After all—despite the army's claim, I still own all the land they haven't confiscated. So whoever is over there is clearly trespassing—on my property."

Waiting until the ship was tied up at the new dock, Robert nodded to George, who helped him lower the rowboat. Heading across the narrow channel, Robert rowed into the reeds surrounding the beach. Reaching into the small duffel he had brought with him, he removed a pair of pistols. Throwing one to George, he ordered, "Cover me," as he secured the second pistol in his coat pocket, jumped out to beach the small boat in the murky, seaweed-covered water, and stepped out.

The beach here was not as clean as the one across the channel at the cantonment, but then it was at the mouth of the river—where it was littered with debris swept down by the many spring rains that had persisted for several days and delayed Robert's trip home. Skirting several downed branches and a few dead fish floating in the seaweed, he made his way to the nearby beach—keeping alert for any unforeseen activity.

As on his side of the river, the oak trees at the crest of the beach provided an almost impenetrable forest—save for a recently cut trail heading up from the beached boat he had seen on the shore. Certainly not Seminoles, he told himself—fingering his pistol in his pocket as he made his way up the incline and through the trees. Quickly approaching a small clearing, he was startled to find a new partially completed log cabin in the center. Stumps of what had been several pine trees surrounded the cabin, and pine sap still seeped from many of the logs. A group of children were playing in the nearby woods, a baby was in a tiny swing hanging from a tree, and a woman in a tattered dress was hanging out laundry on a line strung from the house to a nearby oak branch.

"My Lord," the woman screamed upon glimpsing Robert as he entered the clearing—dropping the shirt she had been hanging as she rushed to pick up the baby.

"I'm not a threat," Robert answered—while still keeping his hand on the hidden pistol. "Name's Robert Hackley. I own this property, however, and need to find out what you are doing here."

"Thought no one owned it," the woman answered—shaking with fear as she cuddled the tiny child, who was now crying lustily, and tried unsuccessfully to replace a long brown lock into the net behind her head. "Least of all, the men over at the fort said it was free game on this side of the river," she added, as the children ceased their game and came to assess the newcomer.

"Well, I'm here to tell you they're mistaken. My father, Richard Hackley, bought all this property from Duke Alagon—before Spain gave the territory to the United States. The army managed to appropriate the area where I had built my house and turn it into their base. I had no recourse there—as they definitely outnumbered me. You . . . however," he continued—as they all turned to a loud crashing in the underbrush as a brawny, dark-haired man in torn overalls with one shoulder strap hanging loose suddenly appeared—gun in hand and pointing it at Robert.

"Levi," the woman called—relieved at seeing the man. "This man says . . ."

"I know what he's told you," the man answered—lowering the gun. "You must be Robert Hackley," he continued—holding out his hand. "Colonel Brooke told me you had built that beautiful home he and his men have confiscated across the river. I'm Levi Coller, and this dear woman is Nancy, my wife. The five little heathens out there all belong to us. Too many mouths to feed while we're setting up our compound," he laughed.

"You see, I had found that same area across the river about six months ago. I went back to get the family up by the Suwannee River, but by the time we came overland, we found the oxcart was too big for the trail and had to resort to strapping our possessions onto our mules for the journey. Long trip—not one I'd want to repeat! At any rate, when we finally got back here, we saw the new base—and your beautiful house, which it seems Colonel Brooke has now appropriated. Can't tell you how sorry I am for you. Understood you have moved further inland. Guess you didn't have much choice."

"You have the story right—so far," Robert answered. "I have moved away from the base—had no option when the army moved in! The truth is, however, that I own this property as well," he continued—as he caught Levi and Nancy exchanging unbelieving glances. "I just sent a letter to my father to verify our claim in New York. Obviously, though, it's no more use to me than Cantonment Brooke—as the U.S. government has declared all this area Indian land. As I understand it—no Anglo-Americans are allowed to settle in the area."

"Levi," Nancy began—as she shifted the squalling infant to her other shoulder—"you never told me . . ."

"Oh, Brooke mentioned it, but when you think of all the time it took us to get here and the fact that we haven't seen one Seminole since we've been here, I'm not worried."

"As far as I can see, the cantonment doesn't have the power to do anything about squatters in the area right now," Robert nodded. "So for the time being, I suspect you're okay over here—as long as the Seminoles don't decide it's the perfect spot for their reservation. If so, we'll all be holding on to our scalps! Actually, I'm happy to have new neighbors—and will be willing to share our bounty once my fruit trees and crops come in."

• _15_ •

September 1824

The days were still unbearably hot, Robert mused—as he grabbed an idle moment to recline in the swing Rhodes had just hung on the front porch of his new home. Although he missed the view of the Hillsborough River the swing at the plantation house had afforded, he was now content to bask in the stillness the nearby oak hammock offered—with any views of the surrounding area obscured by a Spanish moss blanket hung from each of the nearby enormous gray trees. Watching the late afternoon sun sneak an errant ray onto the leaf-strewn path—still glistening from a quick afternoon shower—he turned at last to the papers he had brought out with him.

Although still quite content in his new surroundings—without a moment of missing the hustle and bustle of New York—he was, nonetheless, still anxious to receive word from his father about the possible sale of property in the area. With winter coming up north, he could well imagine the number of folks who would welcome a visit to Florida now—with the possibility of settling here—yet there had been no word since he had sent his letter from St. Marks in late April. His new home was now completed—with virgin pine cut from the many stands of local trees—and would serve as a prototype of the structures his men could build for new settlers.

Granted, the whole area near Hillsborough Bay had now been designated as Seminole territory and was currently off limits for any Anglo-American settlers. However, even though Brooke was aware of the Collers, their arrival had so far not even caused a stir as they were building their homestead across the river. Obviously, the army really had no intent in observing the restrictions. And frankly, no Seminoles had shown up nearby to claim the area as far as he had heard.

Nonetheless—although he had as yet made no attempt to retrace his former trip to the south—outside of the federal land appropriated by the cantonment, his family did still own all the land down the coast to the Caloosahatchee River. Perhaps now that the threat of severe storms was almost over, it would be a good idea to venture back down and look at the possibility of settling property on the mainland—or even at Sanybel—once the oppressive summer heat had abated.

Flipping through the papers in his lap, he pulled out the crude map of the southern peninsula Porter had given him at Key West. Sanybel, he laughed, remembering the horde of mosquitoes and the ravenous alligator that had chased him and Rhodes back to the ship. Best to look at the Gulf side of the island—or even better, the mainland area near the Caloosahatchee. Granted, he had seen firsthand the ranchos already established in the area, but that land was his right now. So if his father had managed to confirm his deed, there should be no trouble dislocating the Cuban fishermen. After all, their ranchos were not permanent settlements, he reasoned—closing his eyes and imagining the several villages he could build down there!

A sudden rustling on the hammock path—accompanied by a cracking branch—caused him to sit up quickly. Seminoles—he wondered. Although he had seen few since building his first house, this was still designated as their territory. Cocky! It had been foolish of him to leave his gun inside, he decided, as he laid the papers on the swing and headed for the front door.

"Robert!" a voice called, and he turned to see Lorenzo emerge from under the nearest oak—smiling under the cascade of blond curls that belied the stark army uniform. "You aren't still worried about Seminoles, are you?" Lorenzo laughed—shaking his boots off before stepping onto the porch. "Been on recon duty out this way all afternoon and haven't seen nary a one!"

"Got time for a visit?" Robert asked—indicating a chair by the door. "Sun tea is ready if you'd like a cup."

"Music to my ears," Lorenzo nodded. "Canteen ran dry over an hour ago," he continued—shaking the empty vessel as he took the offered seat. "Been too long, amigo!"

"Out here, one day runs into another," Robert smiled—taking two cups from the table, filling them from the large jug beside the stack, and handing one to Lorenzo. "Sorry it can't be cold down here," he apologized as he resumed his seat on the swing. "Missed seeing you. Rhodes and the crew keep busy, but we seldom have time to talk—especially now that they're all ensconced in their new bunkhouse. What's the news from the base?"

"Seems despite your cushy accommodations at the officers' quarters, the brass up there are planning to build their own homes. Bringing the families in—if you can believe it."

"But I thought only Seminoles were allowed in the area," Robert remarked.

"Not so you could tell it, if what I hear is correct. Law calls them 'tenants of the fort,' and they get permission to live on the federal property if they are in some way connected with the military.

"Colonel Brooke is having a house built for his family. Seems his wife has been quite ill. Apparently, she gave birth to a little boy, their third child, last January in Pensacola—just about the time he was over here setting up the fort. He's never even gotten to see the little tyke. It's no secret on base that he's been worried about all of them. Waits for the mail boat every week for a letter from Lucy. Now that everything is under control out here, he received permission to go for his family in Pensacola. He's leaving this afternoon on the mail boat and is hoping to bring them over by Christmas—if he can obtain return passage for all of them. I expect several of the other officers will decide to do the same. Rather lonely over here right now. We're all feeling it. No action, if you get my drift, so the brass thinks it will be safe enough for families. We unattached men can only hope one or more of the officers have a daughter or two," he laughed.

"But this is my father's land!" Robert objected. "Are they extending the base acreage? If so, we need to be notified. I'm sure my father will have something to say about that! I haven't heard a word from my father, though, after I asked him to verify our claim so we could begin to advertise."

"Is this what you've been waiting for?" Lorenzo smiled—pulling a letter from his pocket. "Came in this morning's mail. Since I was heading out this way, I thought I would bring it by."

"Dad's handwriting," Robert commented—turning the envelope over in his hand.

"Mind if I hang around a bit and hear what the news is from home? All the talk on base is just about the Seminole movements. Been too long since I've heard anything from the rest of the country."

Nodding, Robert slid his finger under the flap. Pulling out a fairly long letter, he smiled. "Brevity never had a hold on Dad," he said—running his eyes down the letter. "I remember his long epistles from Spain and then St. Augustine when he was there!"

"So—any news on your deed?"

"Says he's turned it over to a magistrate he often does business with in New York. He admits it may take a while, but he doesn't think we'll have any trouble proving its authenticity."

"Then it's all hands on deck out here?"

"Looks to be," Robert nodded. "He's looking at advertising our new holdings this winter in the New York papers.

"New news, though, is that my baby brother, William, is now attending William and Mary College and wants to go into law."

"Stands to reason," Lorenzo laughed, "a la Dad and big brother. But why did he choose William and Mary? Thought your father would have wanted him to stay in New York."

"Long family connection with William and Mary via my step mother, Harriet Randolph, whose family helped establish the college."

"Then, do you think he'll want to stay in Virginia?"

"Interestingly, no," Robert answered, shaking his head. "Dad says once he graduates, he wants to follow me to Florida, set up a practice here, and look after the southern end of our tract. Says our capital in Tallahassee should be set up by the time he graduates in two years, so he'll send him down there to take his bar exam and be licensed in Florida."

"Hope it will have grown some by then," Lorenzo laughed. "Worst night of my life—setting up my tent in that godforsaken wilderness and praying the howling coyotes and snorting boars would stay at bay until morning!"

"Man I met over in Pensacola—named Wyatt—has moved to Tallahassee to set up a plantation and build a hotel. I spent some time with him when I was in St. Marks recently. He seems to think things will be building up rather soon—as all the legislators are tired of traveling across the territory."

"We can both attest to that, I believe!"

"I guess I'll wait to hear further and then plan a trip over to St. Marks once William gets there. Oh, we had our disagreements as kids, but I really miss that little bugger."

"Hope he'll be coming by land—and not through the Straits as we did. Florida might be in line for statehood by the time he could get down here."

"Dad didn't look that far ahead, but I already warned him of the southern perils—after our voyage. He does say, though, that he wants me to have the schooner available to take William south when he's ready. Says he can set up his practice in Key West and plan marketing up the coast from there. Suits me, as I'm happy on this end.

"But tell me what other news you're hearing out there. You said there was news on the Seminole movements—but I take it you're not worried, as you said you saw none on your reconnaissance mission."

"Oh, one of our men on recon duty a few months ago reported seeing a large group of Indians near our camp after tattoo. Brooke ordered the troops armed and sent them out to patrol all night. Guess the Seminoles got our message—although it's been reported that they can muster up to seven hundred warriors if needed. Seemed they had planned an attack, but must have thought better of it after our response. As a result, Brooke ordered two six pounders and ammunition from Pensacola. Haven't heard that they've arrived yet, though.

"Made an interesting discovery with some of my buddies a month or so ago. When we were on duty up the beach, we found the remains of three unfortunate souls—who apparently had been attacked on the beach. Shot holes in their hats, and at least one had been burned in a nearby firepit. No sign of a campsite—but then the tides and storms can reduce any evidence after a time."

"My Lord, Lorenzo, how long ago do you think that was? Should I be worried out here?"

"Best we could tell, it was probably before we all arrived here," Lorenzo answered, shaking his head. "Couldn't even tell their nationality. Wasn't much left but bones held together by remaining bits of clothing. With the bullet holes and remains of the firepit, it seemed to have been pirate activity."

"But this far north? I thought . . ."

"I do remember Porter saying that—although most of the activity was in the southern waters, there had still been a few incidents reported up this way. Remember, there were only a few ranchos in this area before we took over the peninsula. Not to worry, though, amigo. Their scalps—as far as we could determine—were still intact, so it obviously wasn't Seminole activity. You've gotta admit that our presence at Cantonment Brooke is now the best deterrent we could have against any further pirate activity. Should make you appreciate our U.S. Army!

"Speaking of which, I can tell by the long shadows out there under your oaks—and the number of happy little bunnies appearing—that it's time I report back to base—before they send the troops out. Sadly, I'm not sure I would be identifiable if my blond scalp were missing," he laughed—standing and putting his cap back on.

"Thanks for the visit," Robert offered—standing and grabbing Lorenzo's hand.

"Always fun, brother. Been a lot of water under the bridge since we started our mutual journey. Hope there'll be many more years to come. Really want to meet that little brother of yours when he gets here."

"Wouldn't recognize him as part of my family," Robert laughed as he followed Lorenzo down the steps. "Dark hair—like his mother. Word is she is descended from Pocahontas. But that's another story."

"And calls for another visit," Lorenzo answered. "Always full of surprises."

· *16* ·

January 1825

"*My* word, Wyatt, you said you were planning a hotel here in Tallahassee, but why did you need one this large—when the only buildings I saw on the way in seem to be that atrocious two-story log cabin across the way on the hill and the nearby small, unpainted log house with the bark roof. With no other buildings or visible settlers, what prompted you to build this monstrous hotel?" Robert asked—dropping a small valise by the desk as he entered the large entryway of the two-story hotel, whose placard by the front door identified it as "The Planters."

"Already had folks sleeping on the floor down here when the legislature met last fall," William Wyatt laughed—emerging from behind the long, wooden desk to shake Robert's hand. "With the clientele I've had during session, I'm already planning to build a second hotel.

"Guess it's been a long time since you've been out this way, Robert, and I'll bet you came straight from St. Marks. Tallahassee is growing by leaps and bounds, I'd say. The log cabin you spied is actually the capitol of this territory—meager though it may seem—although I warrant other new territories haven't seen any better! And the small house nearby is the temporary home of our illustrious governor, William Pope Duval. With the need to provide the governor's immediate residency, the team had no time to import siding and windows from Pensacola—as I did for my hotel. Instead, they just used local oak boards for the construction and cypress bark for the roof. Truth is, though, that Duval has already bought a 160-acre township southeast of here. He has ordered the building supplies from Pensacola and plans to move out there as soon as his new home is finished. Lord knows what the legislature will do with that monstrosity when he moves on—not even big enough for record storage.

"Downtown's going to be beautiful, though. It will have one central square with the new capitol built on it. Now, don't scoff. That cabin will be gone in no time—as they are designing the new building as we speak. There will be four additional squares fanning out from the corner of the main square. All will eventually be part of the territory government."

"So you're happy with your choice to come to Tallahassee at its inception."

"Actually, if you remember, I had originally planned to be the first settler in these parts. I planned this hotel out long before anyone else had settled in the new capital. Sadly, though, one John McIver from Fayetteville, North Carolina, actually beat me to it—settling just out of town as well. He's still finishing his new plantation at the moment. It's going to be lovely."

"So you're saying there are actually only two homes—and a hotel . . ."

"And we also have a printing press—for the legislature. But Judge Jonathan Robinson and Sherrod McCall are already beginning construction on three temporary structures for the Territorial Council. Had their first meeting not long ago. And—for all your good-natured ribbing—we had so many legislators here that we filled my two large upstairs rooms by afternoon, and some late arrivals literally did have to sleep on the floor down here. I started with twelve beds in each room—two to a bed—but my final count was thirty. Got four more beds on order from Pensacola."

"So what's my charge for tonight—and do you have a spare bed?" Robert joked—looking around the empty lobby.

"One dollar is my usual charge—but then you'd be sharing a bed in session. Right now, though, the session's finished before the holidays, so you can have a whole bed to yourself."

"Remind me to come only off session," Robert smiled, taking a pouch from his valise and removing a dollar.

"So how did you get here, and what brings you over this way?" Wyatt questioned—pocketing the bill—and ushering Robert to one of the two ornate Queen Anne chairs positioned by the front window.

"Sailed into St. Marks and left my men to fend for themselves in town, I was lucky enough to convince a carrier bringing supplies from the dock to let me ride out here with him on his wagon. Definitely not the way to entice customers to your lovely establishment, I will remark," he added—faking a bad back as he slid into the chair.

"As to your second question, I got a letter from my father—just before the holidays. Seems the magistrate whom he has chosen to represent our Florida claim wants me to find a lawyer down here and question the validity of the new residences that are springing up—on our land—out by Cantonment Brooke. Word is that they are being allowed to build and settle there if they have any connection with the cantonment. They're calling them tenants of the fort. Our question is, how far does this nomenclature stretch—as to whom is directly connected to the fort. Oh, I can understand the officers wanting to bring in their families, but what about a farmer wanting to sell his crops on the base, a blacksmith offering to shoe the officers' horses, or a merchant bringing in goods by ship? Do you get my drift?"

"Understandable. I never heard it broached over at Fort Barranacas when I was in Pensacola. But then that fort was out on the coast and had been a fort from time immemorial as I understand it. With it housing all of Jackson's men in the Seminole conflict ten years ago, there would have been little room for any civilians. Most of the families I knew lived across the inlet in Pensacola."

"So what I need to do is find a lawyer over here to look into the matter. Seems someone in our new capital should have access to the proper legislation providing for these so-called tenants of our fort. Hoping to save myself another lengthy trip to Pensacola."

"We had the first session here in October. Judge Augustus Woodward presided, but I gather not much got done. Next session is scheduled for April, but I don't know much about it. There was a fellow staying here when he got to town named Benjamin Wright. Told me he was going to represent two different claimants in a lawsuit come April. When I asked how he could represent both, he laughed and replied, 'May the better claimant win.' I could try to get you his information if you'd like."

"Sounds good. I'll take you up on it."

"But now, it's getting close to teatime. So if you've got the time, let me show you to your room and then we can go to the tea room."

Housed in a separate room beyond the main desk, the dining area had a large window on the front wall framed by floor-length beige and rose-patterned drapes—drawn up by tiebacks on each side. The sunny window provided a vision of the open, recently seeded front lawn bordering the dry clay road, which was—conveniently—within walking distance of the proposed town center. As the only attempt at grandeur, however, the window and drapes topped a serviceable rug, which covered the wooden floor from the entrance to the bare back wall—with three dark wooden trestle tables accompanied by six long, wooden benches—designed to hold five or more guests each.

"Seems you are prepared for the crowds you described," Robert remarked as Wyatt led him to the table under the window.

Pouring two cups from a flowered china teapot resting on a silver trivet and placing them on the nearest table, Wyatt shrugged. "So much for gentility when the men all need to race from here to the legislature sessions each morning. Sadly, no time for Southern hospitality out here! Tables and benches are easily replaceable, however, once the town comes into existence and we can house ladies as well as the legislators and even plan proper teatimes. For now, though, expediency is the ground rule out here."

"And well designed," Robert agreed. "I think Cantonment Brooke could take a lesson from you and move the mess hall inside—away from the pesky mosquitoes and flies the men have to endure at each meal.

"But tell me, now that you are ensconced in the former Seminole territory, what are your relations—if any—with the natives? Being out here all alone most of the year, are you at all afraid of the natives? After all, this was one of their largest settlements before the treaty was signed at Moultrie Creek."

"Called it 'Cohowofooche.' Real mouthful, so I'm not sure I'm pronouncing it correctly. Chief is Neamathla—tall, thin, wiry fellow probably over sixty—although it's not easy to assess ages of the Creeks. Angry visage—seems to wear a perpetual scowl—if you know what I mean. I've seen him out here a few times with several of his braves—probably assessing the capitol building. Apparently, he gave permission at the treaty for the area to become the capital—but I hear the natives have all since changed their minds and don't want to leave. Several different groups live out there, Seminoles, Creeks, Mikasukis, and there's even a group of former slaves—hiding out from owners in Alabama and Georgia.

"I heard he's already had it out with Duval. Word from the legislators meeting here was that he allowed no superiority of Duval. Claimed they were two chieftains vying over the same land. The quote one of our guests overheard was, 'This country belongs to the red man.' He said further that if he had the necessary number of warriors, he would not leave a white man on his land."

"But I thought when they signed the treaty the natives had all agreed to move south to the Central Florida area, which being set up. That was one of the reasons the legislature decided to plan the capital here, wasn't it?"

"Until several of Neamathla's men tried it. Said it's too hot and wet down there. Several have already returned stating there's no way they can feed their families in the swamps of Central Florida. Actually, I have to agree with them. So far, this rolling forestland seems to be perfect for crops—cotton for one."

"But with the unrest out there—and Neamathla's threat you all overheard, aren't you and the rest of the new settlers even a little worried?"

"So far, they've posed no real problem, so we're considering it an idle threat. Not sure how many warriors he has out there, but the word is that Duval has ordered all of them down your way where Brooke and his men can curtail them. Not sure how much weight Duval's order holds, but with the land so cheap and productive down here, no one really seems worried. As a matter of fact, I can't believe the number of Southern planters who have recently bought land nearby. I know of fifty families who are already establishing plantations and building their homes. Planning to buy my 160 acres once the hotel proves a success."

"Shouldn't take much effort if they are copying the governor's new home. With all the oak and cypress over here, they should have all the building materials they need," Robert laughed.

"Now, wait a minute," Wyatt interrupted. "That structure was an immediate necessity to house the governor during the first legislative session. These families that are now coming are not backwoodsmen, Robert. All of these new settlers are from the planter class—all the way up the coast. You know, the cotton plantations have almost worn out the land in the South, but their owners still have cash. From the reports I have heard from those coming through here, they are planning to build fairly large plantation homes. Several who were staying here have described their ideas to recreate their present houses—which would seem to be large, lavish brick structures—probably like those you remember from your time in Virginia. St. Marks has really mushroomed lately as they are shipping their supplies, families, and servants down here."

"I was impressed with how busy the port was when I landed yesterday. Only problem I see then would be building a road to get the supplies—and people—up here. Jostling as we did on my journey out here, I can see many loads of siding, windows, and roofing ending up on the side of that makeshift road before they even get to their destination."

"Noted," Wyatt laughed. "Favorite topic of most of the legislators is the lack of roads. They are working on it as we speak. Hoping to have one in the northern area as well to accommodate overland transit for the legislators who are coming across state."

"But back to our former topic. If I remember correctly—isn't that the area where Neamathla's village is located?"

"And don't think Neamathla and his council aren't aware of that. He already filed a complaint with Governor Duval last fall—to no avail, though, I might add. Oh, he was allowed to keep his village up here by the terms of the treaty, but he did give the surrounding area to Florida and now has little recourse. If you remember, one of the provisions of the Moultrie Creek Treaty was that the Seminoles had to allow roads to be built on their properties located outside of the new reservation."

"Having suffered the same loss of territory by Cantonment Brooke usurping my land," Robert nodded, "I can understand."

"But I didn't hear you threatening to 'leave no one on your land.'"

"Well, I don't exactly command several hundred angry natives. But then, the Seminoles are resigned to the buildup in Tallahassee?"

"At the moment there is little they can do. And so far, there are so few of us it hasn't really had much impact—outside of the legislators that were in town last fall. If you're asking me to read these soggy leaves remaining in my teacup, however, it doesn't take much to see that they are only biding their time. Mark my words, Robert, the unrest is already smoldering—both here and in your area—and it won't take much to bring it to full blaze!"

March 1825

$\mathcal{R}$obert smiled at the swarming flock of seagulls—interspersed by large diving pelicans—at the entrance to the Hillsborough River as his sloop made its turn. "Hope Rhodes has sent someone out fishing. Been too long since I've had a snapper or grouper for dinner," he mused. Oh, Tallahassee would be a fine city one day, but until some roads were established, Wyatt had admitted, the long drive from St. Marks would preclude keeping the fish fresh at the hotel.

In addition, it had been too cold over there, Robert considered. Squinting in the bright sunlight reflecting off the river, he removed his heavy jacket—hanging it on the back of his chair as he rose to watch his schooner approach the long wharf his men had built on his initial arrival. Oh, the cantonment had added to its length to accommodate their many ships, but it was still his—and he had every right to land here now when space permitted, he considered—as he watched his crew secure the sails and tie up at the south end of the dock.

"Recognized your ship," Lorenzo called, running down to the wharf as Robert jumped to the dock shouldering his valise. "Hey, I missed you. I'm off duty at the moment, so—need any help?"

"Business trip this time," Robert answered, shaking his head. "Not much to buy in Tallahassee—should I even have needed it. I mainly needed to set up an appointment with a local lawyer in Tallahassee to see about all these new tenants of the fort who are settling on my father's land. But that's a story for another day. If you're free, though, I could use the company heading back to my compound. Would love to hear what's been going on here while I was away."

"The afternoon's well worth a walk, if you ask me. What a beautiful day down here—especially when I remember early March in New York. Saw a doe and her new fawn just this morning, and the small rabbits are lined up on the path to the mess hall every evening. Yesterday, I watched a mother osprey teaching her baby to fly. He was so ungainly I was afraid he would fall, but mama was right there under him. Made me feel sorry for the baby ducks just hatching over by the pond beyond the barracks, though, as I expect mama will teach him to catch one or more of them as soon as he can fly! That's the way with nature my dear grandmother would tell me whenever I complained about finding a dead animal."

"Seen any alligators around? Need to know to look out for them—as my complex backs on one of the sloughs."

"Not too many this time of year," Lorenzo answered, shaking his head. "They prefer warmer temperatures I've been told and seem to stay hidden during the winter months. Heard they can be fierce by May, though. That's when the males all stake out new territory. As if the Seminoles weren't enough to watch out for—I hear the gators can be fierce, especially when defending their young."

"Warning taken. I'll advise Rhodes to keep his men in at night now that spring is coming. Wouldn't want to be dinner for any like the one he and I saw down at Sanybel!"

"Glorious weather all around. Far cry from New York—where we'd still be having ice storms. The oaks are just budding out too," Lorenzo smiled as they made their way up the hill to the dirt path beneath the trees. "Of course the strings of dried blossoms are poor seasoning in our mess hall. As long as we brush them off, though, it's no big problem."

"My friend, Wyatt, has an indoor dining hall at his new hotel. I told him Brooke needed to build one out here for you men. Good weather or not, no one likes sharing his dinner with mosquitoes or whatever else finds its way to the table."

"So how was Tallahassee, amigo? Guess a new hotel would be a great improvement over a tent on the wet forest floor when I was there."

"Not much over there yet. Main accommodations are two pretty large hotels for the representatives when the legislature is in session. New capitol is a joke—two-story cabin fashioned from rough oak planks. And our illustrious governor is staying in what you would consider a hut—roofed with cypress bark—would you believe? Wyatt says the plans are already drawn up for the new capital, though—when they can get supplies in from Pensacola. Says Governor Duval has already purchased property to build his own house and plantation, and over fifty Southern planters have purchased their tracts—saying the area is perfect for growing cotton. So that whole area is bound to build up pretty quickly."

"With the planters moving in, are the Seminoles over there angry at the encroachment on their land? How many do you think are now heading our way? From what I have seen, we can't take many more."

"Not so you could tell it," Robert answered—pausing to lift a long string of ivy out of the way and hold it for Lorenzo. "Surely missed my little hammock," he added, stopping to look at his home on the other side of the trees. You know, it's not what I originally planned, but Rhodes and the rest of my men have made it home. They're all happy in the new bunkhouse as well. And now that I have something to show newcomers, once my father advertises the property, I'm looking forward to a whole village out here before long."

"I can only imagine your shock when Brooke took over that beautiful house I watched you build. I must say, though, that you handled it much better than I would have," Lorenzo added—following Robert's gaze and trailing behind him as he left the hammock, followed his dirt path, and stepped onto the front porch.

"Don't think I had much choice," Robert shrugged. "Now, got time for a visit?" he asked—indicating one of the two chairs on the small front porch.

"Short one. Don't want to miss the meager rations we are now receiving," Lorenzo laughed—taking a seat. "And I'll get a lot of flack when I report that it was your ship at the wharf—and not the naval supply one!"

"To answer your question on Tallahassee: Wyatt says the Seminoles are not happy with the influx of the new settlers, but there's not much they can do about it—as Neamathla gave the area to the U.S. at the treaty. It seems they had no more choice than I did!"

"But I thought the reason we all came over here was to oversee the natives in this new territory."

"And that's the problem. Seems the ones who have come over this way say the land is no good. Most are not happy with Central Florida and—as I hear it—are returning to their village."

"That's news! Couldn't prove it by me! Don't know how many more we can accommodate over here. One of my jobs this morning was to divide rations our government had promised to the relocated Seminoles. After the treaty, many of them actually arrived too late in the area to set up crops for this spring. That—coupled with the drought this past winter—has caused most of them to virtually starve out there. They say they were tricked. The land is no good, and they can't grow any corn—or the arrowroot they rely on. Rations we were given didn't even feed half of the folks who arrived this morning—and I'm not sure when we're getting more provisions. When I saw your ship, I was actually on the lookout for another supply boat. Guess being this late in the day it will now be tomorrow at least."

"I had no idea it was this bad out here."

"Getting worse every week. I hear Brooke was appalled when he returned to bring his family over here. He's taken what he can from our rations and has written the War Department to ask for additional supplies, but you know how slow the mail is out here! To top it all off, besides starving out there, there are reports that several of the Seminoles are suffering from new diseases for which they have no immunity. I'm sure Gadsden had no idea what the decision to move them over here would produce! Only possible saving grace is the growing season is fast approaching. We're clearing every available acre on the base to produce as much as we can.

"As if we don't have enough to do cultivating the new fields and feeding the starving Seminoles, the word just came through this week that our quartermaster on base, Captain Isaac Clark, had received word from Washington that $12,000 has been allocated for us to begin building the Fort King Road from here to Georgia. Washington is looking to provide overland transportation for all the new planters heading our way—as well as for military movements across the territory. Our part is to go northeast from here to Wontons—with an eventual destination to the St. Mary's River. Order came through, I heard, that Brooke was to place all troops that were not needed elsewhere—as well as their officers—on duty to build the road."

"While the weather is beautiful right now," Robert answered, shaking his head, "We both remember the rainy season on our way down here last year. Not much road building through the hammocks and swamps out here when the storms come."

"At any rate, sorry to present you with such a gloomy report on your homecoming," Lorenzo added, rising and grabbing Robert's hand. "Next visit I'll try to bring more pleasant news."

"Just promise to alert me if any of those Seminoles you're feeding begin brandishing their tomahawks and heading out this way."

"You know you're always welcome on base. In fact, Colonel Brooke pulled me aside just the other day to ask me to invite you— should you feel the need. He says now that the officers are bringing their families out here, and several other settlers are moving in, there's a plan in order to house all nonessentials on one of the ships out in the harbor in case of an attack."

"That's if there's sufficient warning. Remembering Jackson's First Seminole War, our new residents are particularly good at hiding and surprise attacks! For now, though, I'm not worried. If they are as undernourished and ill as you say, I don't think there's a problem right now."

· 18 ·

July 1825

$\mathcal{A}$s the door to Colonel Brooke's office flew open, all heads turned at once as the tall, commanding figure emerged in full dress uniform—followed by the thin, worn, Seminole agent who had ridden in to the base from the "Big Swamp" on horseback only moments before demanding an immediate interview with the colonel.

"Get Captain Dade in here—immediately" were the colonel's terse words—as the agent turned and made his way back out the front door—hurrying to his horse at the front porch railing, mounting, and heading back off on the barren sandy road—now designated as the origin of the Fort King Road.

"Not sure where Dade is, Colonel," the sergeant at the front desk called—snapping to attention with a salute.

"Your duty is to find him!" Brooke bellowed—as the sergeant grabbed his hat from the desk and followed the harried agent's path—thundering down the front steps.

Returning to his office, Brooke opened the bottom drawer of his desk and removed a file labeled "Captain Francis Langhorne Dade." The captain had been assigned to the base only a short time ago arriving on one of the supply ships from Pensacola. And to be perfectly honest, Brooke had only interviewed him at his arrival and wasn't even sure he could identify him at this point. Word from Pensacola, however, was that Dade, a thirty-one-year-old captain who hailed from Virginia, had led two successful expeditions in the Twelfth Infantry during the War of 1812 and was—by all accounts—the one to lead any expeditions in the inevitable event of a Seminole conflict.

"Too soon," Brooke muttered, running his fingers through his dark curls. The base had only recently received supplies and permission to begin building the "blockhouses" necessary to house the troops along the proposed Fort King Road. To top that off, there were as yet no stockades around the cantonment and he had only one six pounder to protect the base. With his wife, Lucy, still in rather ill health after the birth of their third child in Pensacola—at the same time he had been establishing Cantonment Brooke over here—he wondered again whether he had made the right decision in building his new house and installing the family on base. Was his desire to have them with him worth the chance of losing them to a Seminole conflict—like the one the agent had just reported at the base on the St. Johns River?

"Captain Dade, sir," the sergeant called—pushing open the office door, saluting, and ushering the tall, dark-haired, bearded man into the room—before vanishing thankfully himself. It was common knowledge that Brooke was not one to be trifled with.

"Sir, you asked to see me?" Dade asked—giving a salute as he entered the room.

"So we meet again. Never thought it would be so soon, but please take a seat," Brooke offered—finally remembering the fit, battle-ready man before him—who had come so highly recommended by Colonel Gadsden.

"I understand you had a visitor today and that it was imperative that I visit you at once," Dade answered—taking the chair. "Luckily, I was only in the mess hall at lunch—or I would have been back out on the god-awful road building project."

"Hoping to have you follow that same trail we've outlined up the state," Brooke nodded. "It seems there have been some hostilities up at St. Johns. An agent arrived from their camp this morning requesting our help. I'm sending two companies for backup. Word from Colonel Gadsden is that you're the man to lead them."

"Better than road building, I can tell you," Dade smiled. "Word from up north, however, is that the roadbed is completely under water due to the recent rains. Not sure our wagons could even get through right now."

"The agent this morning came by horseback, so obviously our pack animals would be able to make it. I'll assign you all the horses and mules you think you would need—as well as provisions for at least twelve days. I don't want to alarm the Seminoles any more than is necessary if it is only a temporal matter—but I trust you will be able to judge the situation when you arrive.

"I will warn you that my instructions from the War Department are 'to act in the most positive manner, to act only on the defensive, unless attacked, and to impart all information of any importance to Washington immediately.' I trust you will follow those directives."

"Understood, Colonel Brooke," Dade replied. "I'll go at once to pick the men—and order the animals and supplies we will need. When would you want the companies to leave?"

"Daybreak," was the curt answer. "I'll order the men myself while you visit supply. I'm putting this in your hands, Dade, but please remember you're still operating under my direction and you might be ordered back at any time—should hostilities occur and your men be needed for protection back here."

"Absolutely," Dade nodded—standing up with a salute and leaving the room.

"Glad I could find your companies," the courier called, jumping off from his horse and slopping across the muddy footpath to the small campsite set in the steamy hammock outside the St. John settlement. "Need to find Captain Dade," he called to the sentry on duty beside the officers' tent.

"He's just inside. Tell me your business, and I'll announce you."

"Message from Colonel Brooke at the cantonment," the soldier responded—flipping open the saddlebag and pulling out a long envelope.

"I'll take it to him," the sentry offered, reaching for the envelope.

"'Hand carry it and wait for the response' was my order," the courier answered, shaking his head and continuing to hold on to the envelope.

"As God is my witness! I mean, we're out here alone in this godawful swamp and you expect me to run off with whatever is in that envelope? Oh, never mind—just wipe your shoes off before you enter. Washing facilities are the nearby pond—and it's full of alligators!" he added as he motioned the courier to the nearest tent and pushed open the flap. "Messenger from Colonel Brooke," the sentry reported with a salute.

"Not sure I could find you," the courier called—saluting as well. "Just followed the proposed roadbed—and hoped for the best. Colonel sent you a message. Said I had to wait for a reply and return immediately," he continued—handing the envelope to the captain.

Reaching across the makeshift desk, Dade opened the envelope and removed the contents—which appeared to be a single handwritten sheet. Perusing the contents, Dade looked up. Signaling to the sentry, he waved a dismissal. "I've got this, John. And you . . ."

"Private Lancaster," the courier answered.

"Might as well take a seat," Dade continued—motioning to the small cot at the side of the desk. "Seems Brooke wants an answer in writing."

"Asked me to bring it back immediately," Lancaster nodded.

"So he wants us to return, does he?" Dade asked—receiving no response from his visitor. "He thinks since little has happened since we got here, we are needed more back at the fort—should hostilities occur. Well, I am of a different mind, Lancaster," Dade answered, pulling out a pen, pulling over his ink well, and writing a hasty response at the bottom of the letter.

Finally, replacing the note in the envelope and resealing it, he handed it back to the courier. "Watch out for alligators on your way back. Seen a lot out here," he added.

"You made good time, Lancaster," Colonel Brooke called as Private Lancaster was announced two days later. "Are Dade and his men following you?"

"Captain Dade wrote his response to you. He didn't confide in me more than to say he was 'of a different mind' after reading your letter."

Ripping the letter open and quickly scanning Dade's response, Brooke slammed his fist on the desk—signaling the sergeant on duty at the first desk to run into the room.

"Problem, sir?" he asked timidly.

"With no stockades arriving here yet and none of the ammunition I have ordered, Dade says 'the difficulty with the Indians still has not been settled' out there and he needs to remain a while longer. Furthermore, he has requested that more provisions be sent to him out there—when things are still so uncertain over here.

"Please be sure to let me know of any Seminole problems you hear of—immediately. With depleted support while Dade and his men are gone—and women and children now on the base, we'll be hard pressed to fend off any attack."

"Begging your pardon, sir," the desk sergeant announced on July 27—appearing at Brooke's open door. "One of our scouts just arrived. Seems pretty agitated and needs to see you."

"Hope it's not Indian trouble," Brooke answered—pushing aside his paperwork. "Show him in immediately. Good Lord, with Dade and his men gone over three weeks right now, we've been lucky things have stayed quiet so far."

Entering in a rush, the scout stopped at Brooke's desk and affected a hasty salute.

"Tell me you're not here to report new Seminole activity," Brooke began.

"The word from Moultrie Creek is that many of the chiefs of the different tribes have joined together and settled a new Indian village about forty miles east of here. Their purpose, we were informed, is to wage an attack on this post," he answered—out of breath.

"Where did you hear this?" Brooke interrupted.

"Luckily, our military has a few Seminoles with mixed loyal ties," the scout nodded. "I heard this from one who has proven invaluable in alerting our troops to action in the various settlements. But frankly, the news seems to have spread throughout the several tribes assembled in the new territory. Seems they feel they were given a raw deal by being ordered to this swampy area where they find they can grow nothing. Indians are starving, and they want their former lands back. Cantonment Brooke is their target—as it stands in the way of any movement back west. Somehow, they know you are understaffed at the moment—probably hearing of Captain Dade's companies from the local tribes at St. Johns. Word is that an attack is imminent."

"How long?" Brooke asked, jumping up and pushing his chair back. "How long do you think we have?"

"It took me two days to ride over here, so—even if they started immediately, I would say they would need at least four days to mobilize and move."

"So you're saying we have only two days?" Brooke thundered.

"I rode as fast as I could," the messenger apologized.

"Then ride back the way you came—and ask that troops be sent immediately to reinforce us here—as we are short two companies."

"Done, Colonel Brooke," the scout added—as he saluted and hurried back out the door. Another ride back through the swamps and hammocks was a welcome diversion from the activity that was about to explode at Cantonment Brooke!

"Attention," Brooke yelled—racing from his door a few minutes later into the large front office—and causing all of the men seated at their desks to jump to their feet and offer a salute.

"Word needs to be heard by all of you. The courier who just arrived has reported from the eastern front that the Seminoles out there have joined to form a reservation about forty miles east of here. Attack is imminent. Now, here's what we need to do—immediately.

"John," he called to the desk sergeant, "is the *Florida* still at the wharf?"

"Unloading those stockades you ordered," the sergeant nodded.

"Hold him in port right now, and deliver this message to Captain Brown," he added—handing John a small envelope. "Just so the rest of you know as well, I am ordering the captain to remain in port for now until we can get all of the women and children on base to the ship. I have also asked him to lend us three of his guns—with as much ammunition as he can spare. Take three men with you and bring the guns back as soon as you can. While you are at the ship, alert the men unloading the stockade material that they are to get it up as soon as possible. Tell the foreman to send someone out to find Captain Clark at the road site and bring those men in to help. Protecting this fort is of far more importance than building a road.

"Now, any of you who have wives and children on the base, consider you are relieved of duty while you ready them for moving to the *Florida*. Once hostilities begin, I will have Captain Brown move the ship into the bay until I give the 'all clear.' Now, is there anyone who doesn't have a job?" he continued—looking around the room until he saw two hands meekly raise.

"Steven, you are a good seaman, so take one of the boats and row across the river to alert the Collers. Tell them they are welcome on the *Florida*. I have alerted Captain Brown to them.

"And, Louis, go find Hackley's friend, Lorenzo. I think he is on the road crew. Order him to go to Robert Hackley's plantation immediately, let him know of the imminent attack, and invite him and his men into the compound for safety. As the materials for two additional blockhouses arrived yesterday, I'm hoping we will have them ready in time.

"At ease, men," Brooke ordered at last. "The sooner we can get everyone safe we can begin to mobilize our own forces. Any questions?" Seeing none, he raised his hand in dismissal, raced back into his own office for his hat, and thundered down the front steps for his house. Oh, what folly had ever convinced him to bring Lucy and the children over here!

· 19 ·

August 1825

"Colonel Brooke, are you up for some good news?" the desk sergeant asked—throwing open the office door.

"The Lord knows I could surely use some of that right now. Lucy has reported from the ship that after a week in the bay, the children are all restless and the women just want to get back home. With Captain Dade and his men still out of the area, however, I just don't want to chance bringing anyone back right now—lest we see the ambush we have been promised."

"But that's just it," the sergeant smiled. "Word is that Dade and his men are just now returning. Private at the stockade entrance reported they and their animals were so mud caked he could barely recognize them. Said he told Dade you had said to send him in whenever he got back, but Dade responded they all needed to wash off a month of dirt before they would be fit company for anyone. He also asked if you would send permission for his men to get a decent meal as soon as they were washed up—as the provisions you sent a few weeks ago had run out before they left their makeshift camp at St. Johns. Besides some berries they found along the road—and some rabbits the men were able to shoot, they were all just short of starving."

"Permission granted!" Brooke answered. "But tell Dade I want him in here immediately upon leaving the mess tent."

Looking out of the long window a half hour or so later, Brooke was pleased to see the tall Captain Dade—looking very much unlike the muscular fellow who had ridden out of here a month ago. His uniform now hung on an emaciated body, and a mop of long, brown hair still wet from his shower protruded from a cap placed haphazardly on the back of his head. Nodding to several men as he passed, he quickly saluted and ran up the front steps.

"Captain Dade," the sergeant announced—smiling as he led the forlorn figure into the room.

"Do you have any idea how glad we all are to see you and your men?" Brooke asked, returning the salute and walking around his desk to shake Dade's hand.

"First, I must apologize for disobeying your request to return," Dade answered—shaking his head. "Sadly, we had just received word of another incident with the Indians and really didn't feel we could leave the settlement unprotected."

"I had trust that you were operating as you saw fit," Brooke nodded—directing Dade to a nearby chair and leaving the desk area to take the companion chair. "But I'm sure you know by now that we have had some unsettling news of an imminent attack by a new force established about forty miles east of us."

"I'm so very sorry. The truth is, though, that I didn't know about it until we got back to the fort," Dade answered, shaking his head. "Only news we got was from St. Johns, and they are so outnumbered up there we couldn't in good conscience leave until the conflict was settled."

"At any rate, you are here now."

"And a little the worse for our adventure, but I assure you, my men will be on the alert again—once we have had a good night's sleep."

"The new blockhouses are up," Brooke nodded, "and I'll see that you get your pick. For now, I would like you to impart my congratulations to your men for a job well done—as you have all affected the object of your visit in a manner highly creditable to yourselves and important to our government. By your presence you have shown the Indians that we are at all times on the alert and that acts of hostility on their part will be immediately punished.

"And, now I must ask you if you had any indication of movement from the east on your way back here—as we had been warned of an imminent attack over a week ago."

"Not a word on our way over here," Dade answered, shaking his head. "Did meet up with a scout about twenty miles back who reported they had received word of a new reservation and planned attack a few weeks ago—however, the scout reported that his captain later determined that the news had turned out to be a false report from an Indian in whom the command had previously placed the highest confidence. Whether the Indian was operating on false information imparted to him or seeking to cause trouble is another question. At any rate, it does seem—for now at least—that the base is safe."

"News I'm sure everyone at the fort—and out on the *Florida*—will be glad to hear!" Brooke announced. "Still, the scare has taught us much and put us in better readiness than we were a month ago. In view of trouble now on several different fronts, I am considering that the best safeguards we can erect right now are a series of blockhouses spaced between the St. Johns and the Suwannee River. With a company stationed at each blockhouse, we can be much better prepared when we hear of a disturbance—and avoid the panic we have been experiencing around here the past month.

"As I've heard from Captain Clark that the roadbed designated for the Fort King Road is now under water after the recent rains . . ."

"As my men and I will attest," Dade nodded.

"I'm thinking I should cease construction until the rains subside and get those blockhouses built and staffed. If nothing else, it will be a line of communication from one company to another so we are not so uninformed over here."

"Sounds like a good idea to me," Dade answered.

"And another even better idea is for you to head out to the wharf with me and let me introduce you to the many folks who have been waiting in safety out there for the past week or so. Once we get them back in port and on shore, I propose we hold a gathering to affirm your safe return and the report of the false attack—so we can all rest peacefully in our own beds—for tonight at least," Brooke laughed as he rose and gestured for Dade to precede him out of the office.

Although the feared Seminole attack proved to be false, the plight of the Amerindians on the reservation closest to Cantonment Brooke worsened daily. By the end of the month, over 1,600 malnourished Indians surrounded the fort—asking for the promised rations. Responding to the humanitarian need, Colonel Brooke ordered the fort's commissary to increase the rations from approximately eight hundred to one thousand—but still the need continued.

Returning to his office one fall afternoon—after watching the unending line of starving Seminoles file past the commissary—Brooke sighed and reluctantly took a sheet of paper and a pen from his desk. His place was not to question the army's authority or decision. The War Department had made the arrangements for the necessary rations and had entrusted him with their dispersal. Yet he was certain no one seated in an office in Washington had any idea of the suffering the Indian removal was causing. Running his fingers through his hair and taking up the pen, he began the necessary letter to the War Department: "It is impossible for me or any other officer who possesses the smallest feelings of humanity to resist affording some relief to men, women, and children who are actually dying for want of something to eat. I can assure you they are in the most miserable condition and unless the government assists them, many of them must starve."

Shaking his head, Brooke reread his request and pulled an envelope to him. Carefully copying the War Department's address on the envelope, he sealed it and headed to the door. "John," he called, motioning to his sergeant. "Is the *Florida* still in port?"

"Yes, sir, but I think the mailbag just came up, so they should be ready to move on with the tide."

"Good, glad I could catch it. Might change my mind about my missive if I have to wait until next week," Brooke responded—taking one last look at the envelope in his hand. Insubordination was not a quality tolerated by the army. Still—with winter on the horizon and few crops to speak of—conditions were only bound to get worse. There was no way Washington would be aware of the intolerable conditions they were imposing on the Indians without a direct report from one designated to tend to their needs, he mused—still holding the envelope.

"Sir," the sergeant asked—unsure of Brooke's hesitation—"did you want me to mail that envelope?"

"Before Captain Brown pulls anchor," Brooke nodded—finally handing the envelope to John. "Please tell him to treat this with the utmost importance and deliver it to the base at Pensacola for direct transport to Washington."

"At once," the sergeant nodded—taking a quick glance at the address before donning his hat and running out the main door.

Hearing the thunder of footsteps vanish as John made his way down the front steps, Brooke silently returned to his office—with no response to the questioning looks from the other officers in the main room. Closing his door behind him, he sat once again at his desk—his head in his hands. "Insubordination!" He knew the charge, but imagining those emaciated bodies by his commissary, what other choice did a God-fearing man have?

• 20 •

January 1826

"Visitor, Colonel Brooke," the desk sergeant called—pushing open the office door and saluting.

"Please ask him to wait until I finish this new ration order for the commissary. I'll need you to . . . ," Brooke began without looking up.

"Sir, begging your pardon, but I think you'll want to see this visitor," the sergeant replied—looking nervously back at the tall, clean-shaven man—his gray, receding hairline giving him an aristocratic look as he perused the office and the dark-haired man with the mussed curls who was bent over the desk.

"Very well," Brooke answered—sighing as he pushed the paper aside and laid his pen on it—before looking at the visitor.

"Governor Duval, sir," John reported nervously.

"Who?" Brooke asked—finally paying attention as the man walked to the desk and extended his hand.

"Governor William Duval," the man smiled. "I caught a ride with Captain Brown on the *Florida* when it left St. Marks. I hope I haven't come at a bad time."

"My Lord, why didn't you tell me, John?" Brooke stammered, getting to his feet and grabbing the offered hand. "To what do I owe this visit, sir?" he asked—motioning to one of the chairs against the wall—as the sergeant retreated and closed the door.

"Responding to a letter I recently received—from President Adams," Duval answered—pulling aside his topcoat and removing a large envelope.

"Adams, but I don't know why he . . ."

"It seems he is as concerned as you about the Indian problem down here. Told me he had passed your request for additional rations and better living conditions for the Seminoles on to Congress several months ago when the War Department delivered your letter. Sadly, however, it seems Congress is still arguing about funding for the starving Indians."

"I wondered why we hadn't heard anything. My God, it's been five months—with me still trying to divide the minuscule rations we're having delivered. In fact, I was just composing a note asking for the men to harvest the new orange crop as soon as possible. Heaven knows there's not much more we can do over here!"

"And that's exactly why I came. Thought before the legislature gets back in session I would just take a little vacation to your cantonment and check things out for myself."

"I hate to be a bother when you have much more important things to consider."

"None more important that our Indian problem. You know we've already seen a lot of unrest up our way. Several of the natives up there have returned to their old reservation saying the land over here is the poorest and most miserable region they have ever seen."

"Don't think I haven't heard the same thing myself from those starving Amerindians who wait in line each week for whatever morsels we can throw them."

"Apparently, the sentiment is the same throughout this new Seminole territory our government created at Moultrie Creek. In fact, the Indian agent, Gad Humphreys, stationed over near Ocala, has used almost the same words you did in your letter. In his words, he says, 'The condition of the Indians of this nation is one of great suffering from hunger,' and that—in his estimation—their situation is wretched and 'almost beyond description.' Since it is his duty—as it is yours—to prevent conflicts between the settlers and the Indians, I felt it was imperative to sort out this problem before it becomes worse. Our new territory surely can't afford another conflict like the one Jackson fought not so long ago."

"If you'd like to see firsthand what I have to witness each day, why don't I take you down to the gate and watch the afternoon crowd of starving Seminoles—who will prove my point much better than any letter I may have written," Brooke offered, standing, retrieving his hat, and ushering Duval to the door.

"My Lord, Brooke," Duval announced—shaking his head as they reentered the office later that afternoon, "I'd heard from the returning Indians at Tallahassee that the land at their new reservation was worthless—at least for their lifestyle and the crops they prefer—but I had no idea until I was able to see it for myself and hear the agents' translations from the Seminoles at your gates. In my estimation, I have never seen a more wretched tract. And from what I heard from the Indians and our agents, there is no land within the Indian settlement near the Hillsborough River that is even worth cultivating.

"I am just beginning a three-month tour of Central Florida, and I can tell you I am surely hoping to find better conditions as I make my way east. When I return to Tallahassee, I intend to report to President Adams that the Seminole land out here is 'wretched, almost beyond description.'

"And now—on another note, I would be remiss if I didn't ask you how your own men—as well as the many families they are bringing in—are responding to this gosh-awful remote location."

"Interesting you should ask that, Governor. As I have reported regularly, desertion has been a problem, and with expiring enlistments fast approaching, I'm not sure how many will decide to stay. One of our men has deserted three times, and another adventurous soul has been absent for over a year now. Lord knows why he thought existing in the conditions you have seen would be preferable to living on the base! Fortunately, though, I might add—after reports from Cantonment Clinch—we have had much less sickness than other areas of the territory.

"On a more positive note, I have given Captain Clark over half my men in building the road to Wantons. As the designated area was almost completely under water until November, little progress could be made until that time. Just this week, however, I received word from Clark, which I am sending on to the quartermaster general with today's mail shipment on the *Florida*, that—after three months of very hard work—the road is now completed and the men will be heading back to the base.

"In Clark's own words," Brooke continued—retrieving the folded letter from his desk file and running his finger down the page, "'it will be pronounced by judges to be the best road which has yet been opened in Florida.' Although we cannot seem to solve the Seminole problem, at least we should receive high marks from Washington for our road construction," he laughed—replacing the letter.

"Well done," Duval remarked. "I have actually been receiving reports from Clark myself. Said in the fall rains he and his men almost drowned out there. I must tell you, however, that recent word is that Washington is hoping to extend the road on beyond Wantons. Because of his excellent work so far, it is most probable that Clark and his crew will be called on to continue the route."

"I've not had any indication of the road's continuation as yet. If word doesn't come until spring, though, we would again face the same problems of flooding once the rains begin—which delayed last year's work until November."

"Of course, we won't have orders until the quartermaster general makes his determination on the present completion, but I will surely keep that in mind when I return to Tallahassee and make my report. Being short over half your force, I am sure you will be happy to have Clark and his men return—for the time being."

"Several of the men stationed in the compound are actually planning a little celebration—to keep up the morale on base," Brooke nodded. "Now that we have families as well as enlisted men, they were looking for something that would be enjoyed by all our residents on the base—and also include locals. If you can arrange transportation on your way back from your tour, we would be thrilled to host you for our first Cantonment Brooke Derby, which will be a three-day race featuring many of the horses on base. I actually have my two oldest children already engaged in making banners for the event. We are also inviting our neighbors, Levi Coller and his family, across the river, and Robert Hackley, who actually built this wonderful home we are using for our offices."

"I heard of his dilemma from William Wyatt, the owner of our local Planters Hotel, when I mentioned I was taking a visit over here," Duval laughed. "It must have been quite a rude awakening to build your dream home and come back to find it taken over by the military. Pays to keep him happy, I'm sure."

"Actually, one of our men booked passage with Hackley from New York when he came down this way. They struck up quite a friendship—which has been of value to us in keeping the peace."

"Your derby sounds like a wonderful idea all around. Tough keeping up morale in such a desolate area, I'm sure," Duval answered. "While I'd love to attend, our legislature will be meeting about the time I finish my tour of the reservation lands. Be sure to send me word on the derby's success. Good news in the territory is hard to come by at the moment.

"And now, I'm sure Captain Brown has finished loading and would be happy to see me step back on board. Keep up the good work out here, Brooke. I understand it isn't easy," he added, rising, and offering his hand before heading to the door.

· *21* ·

July 1826

"*C*aptain Dade and Lieutenant McCall, sir," the desk sergeant called—pushing open the door to Colonel Brooke's office, saluting, and ushering the two officers into the room.

"Happy to see you both," Brooke smiled, standing from his desk and offering a salute to each.

"I understand you have a new assignment for us," Dade began—locking eyes with the younger McCall, who stood stoically awaiting whatever Brooke had in mind.

"At ease, men," Brooke smiled—motioning each to a chair in front of his desk. "Fun assignment this time, I believe—and a chance to see a new part of our territory. Truth is I received a message this morning from Colonel Gad Humphreys, Florida's Indian agent. I know you've met him, Dade, but this will be your first encounter, McCall. I'm sure you will find him a most personable and fair man in his post to create peace between our new residents and the various tribes with which we must deal," he stopped—waiting for Dade's nod before continuing.

"At any rate, to avoid any recurrence of the problems Jackson dealt with in our First Seminole War, Humphreys has set up his Indian agency east of here at Silver Springs—not far from Moultrie Creek— where the treaty was signed. He has now decided that the best action in dealing with the many tribes of Miccosukees, Tallahassees, and Alach-uan Seminoles would be to call an assembly of those three major tribes to elect one man as the Supreme Chief of the Seminole Indian Nation. It will be the chief's job to head up negotiations with Humphreys and our various bases to avoid the conflicts that are bound to occur as more settlers move down here. He has proposed that each of the tribes present two major candidates for an official federal–state election to be held at the assembly later this month."

"Colonel Brooke, begging your pardon, sir, but what about the Red Stick Creeks up near Tallahassee?" Dade interrupted. "I've heard they are a formidable tribe as well that are still giving the new settlers at our capital a lot of trouble."

"And you are right. Their leader, Neamathla, made threats years ago during the First Seminole War that he would kill General Gaines if he crossed the Flint River. Governor Duval has already had meetings with Neamathla and had pronounced him dangerous. As a result, Humphreys has ruled him out of contention for chief—for fear that he would only foment discontent and be unwilling to work with our government.

"The Tallahassees and Miccosukees are both supporting Tukose Emathla. Humphreys says he's known by our men as John Hicks. He's a tall, handsome man I am told—probably about fifty years old, so he claims respect from his tribe. Mild temperament and seems to be a fair man with whom to deal.

"The Miccosukees, on the other hand, have nominated Micanopy—a solid, quiet man. Seems to be fair-minded, Humphreys says, but his second in command, called Jumper, is a rather cunning individual, and has Humphreys worried should Micanopy be elected."

"I've heard about Jumper," McCall nodded. "And you're right, his reputation precedes him. So what do you want Dade and me to do?"

"No more than watch the proceedings, I hope. Humphreys has asked me to send two companies over to the conference—mainly to keep order should any unpleasantness break out—with the Indians or with our forces. With your former involvement with the Seminoles, Dade, I thought your company would be the best to send. But, McCall, you and your company have come highly recommended as well. I trust the two of you will not only present the aspect of military honor but also enjoy the festivities at the convocation," Brooke smiled.

"So when is the conference to take place?" Dade asked.

"Middle of the month," Brooke answered. "It should take you about five days to get there, by my reckoning. But once you get your men lined up, you may proceed. I hear the area near those beautiful springs is well worth the trip, and the men who've witnessed one of the Seminole ceremonies say they are a spectacular experience. Wish I could go as well! I'll want to hear a full account on your return."

"My Lord, the springs are every bit as beautiful as you said!" Lieutenant McCall announced as he followed Agent Humphreys down the hill to a small canoe perched on the sandy shore of the Silver Run River—which emptied into the area called Silver Springs. Stopping a moment at the beach, he looked out across the wide river, which disappeared under a canopy of large oak trees. Three squirrels played up and down the trunks—oblivious to the caws of a group of disgruntled crows perched above them. Low-hanging branches dipped gray Spanish moss into the clear water at the feet of a lone white egret—eyeing his lunch below.

Ushering McCall into the boat, Humphreys pushed it into the clear river and jumped in behind him. "We couldn't have picked a choicer location for our agency! I am constantly amazed at all the beauty I am witnessing in this new area," Humphreys nodded. "Pity the Seminoles do not see it that way."

"It seems the starving Indians we see daily at Cantonment Brooke are looking at the water-logged soil—while missing the beauty of their new land."

"Mark my words. Though few have yet had this opportunity, someday this pristine natural wonder will be hailed as a natural treasure."

"We can only hope the Seminoles eventually see it that way! It's unbelievable how the land and water almost seem to merge at the horizon," McCall observed as Humphreys rowed into the center of the open springs. "With the sky perfectly reflected in the water, the canoe seems perched in thin air!"

"After seeing the pollution in our rivers and streams up north, it's the clarity that impressed me most the first time I came out here," Humphreys nodded. "Want to know how clear this water is, watch this," he called. Laying aside his oar, he pulled a small button from his shirt sleeve and dropped it into the clear water beside the canoe.

As McCall watched the button descend almost forty feet to the sandy bottom, he called out, "The water is so clear I can still see the buttonholes! I'm sure no one at home would even believe me if I told them. You need to bring Captain Dade out here as well."

"I've scheduled a trip for him tomorrow—once he has had time to brief his men on the election proceedings."

"I'm scheduled to meet John Hicks tomorrow—rather Tukose Emathla. Which name do you prefer?"

"He's a smart fellow—adopting an Anglicized name, which makes him seem more approachable to our men, but he answers to either. His Indian name means 'Ant-chief.'" At McCall's laugh, Humphreys shook his head. "As tall as he is, that's hardly the meaning. I'm told the title refers to his determination to promote the welfare of his people—as an ant leader would do. I found him quite agreeable in our meetings, but I'm told he can be most forceful if threatened.

"Micanopy seems another threat altogether. His men call him Governor—denoting his position of authority over them. I've met with him several times as well. He's quite heavyset with a broad face. He appears rather indolent when you first meet him, but a lot of anger seems to be locked inside his sleepy eyes. I've also been warned to beware of his man Jumper, who is second in command and wields a lot of power.

"But now—beautiful as this river is—I guess we both have more important things to take care of today," Humphreys sighed, dragging his oar in the water to turn the canoe back around.

"Here's hoping the tribes have all voted for Hicks," Dade confided as he and McCall waited for Humphreys and his men to convene at the small Indian agency office to record the election results.

"Actually, I was most impressed with him," McCall nodded. "Seemed to want the best for the Seminoles, but he wanted to be fair to our settlers as well. I think he will be one we can work with. And believe me, when our companies are being sent all over the territory now to keep the peace, it would be good to know he's one who will look at both sides."

"I don't know about you, but after meeting Micanopy, I was rather leery of making him the chief—as his attitude toward our delegation seemed quite negative. I'm not sure he would ever be amenable to a fair settlement of any issues."

"I'll tell you I wouldn't want to meet either him or his man Jumper in the wild. Over the years I have grown rather fond of my scalp," McCall replied—running his fingers through his dark hair.

"Let's hope we never have to," Dade nodded—as Humphreys and his men entered carrying the ballot boxes from the various tribes.

"As we had hoped," Humphreys announced after checking the many ballots from the assembled tribes, "Hicks is the clear winner," as a sigh went up from all those assembled. Grabbing a pen from the desk in front of him, he dipped it in the inkwell and placed a large check beside Hicks's name on the mock ballots in front of him—signing, folding, and sealing each one. Handing the stack to the sergeant by the door, he returned to his seat and breathed a sigh of relief. "Now we will wait until the news has reached each of the tribal leaders."

"So now that the election has ended peacefully, our presence is no longer needed," Dade observed. "Guess our companies will be relieved there have been no problems, but I'm not sure any of them want to head back to Brooke—where they will most likely be reassigned to building the Wantons Road."

"I'd rather like you to stay in place—at least for the foreseeable future. Brooke did say you were to stay until we saw this election through."

"But the election is finished—is it not?" McCall asked.

"Once the news has reached each village, the Miccosukees have planned an inauguration ceremony for the new leader. They tell me we are likely to have over 3,000 warriors present. I don't expect trouble, but with that many Indians present, who knows what might happen. At any rate, Silver Springs is a much more tempting spot than the swamp where your roadbed is located," Humphreys laughed, "and I can make my canoe available for a few fishing trips until the ceremony."

"Would you believe there was nothing in this glade two weeks ago?" McCall asked—as he and Dade were escorted to their reserved seats by Miccosukee ushers dressed in full warrior mode.

"I can't believe how quickly they built this beautiful amphitheater," Dade observed—looking around the large nearly fifty-foot-wide structure, which was set up under a tree-covered arbor composed of local oak boughs interspersed with palmetto fronds.

Festivities began at seven o'clock and were destined to last until sunset. As the event began, over a hundred Miccosukee men entered in full regalia. "That's the rattlesnake dance," McCall whispered. "They've been practicing all week out here when I led my men by. It's in honor of Tukose Emathla, Humphreys told me."

As the men exited the central stage, several more men ran into the ring—followed by a group of Miccosukee women—their colorful layered skirts swirling to the beat of drummers situated on each side of the stage.

Finally—as sunlight bounced from the tranquil springs beyond the seating area and flooded the stage with a fiery sunset—a herald entered waving a small American flag and calling slowly, "Tukose Emathla!" On the third call, the chief appeared to cheers from those assembled. As he walked into the center ring, the herald reached out and grabbed the chief's scalp lock—to which he attached a small, carved war club—as a deafening chant of "Tukose Emathla" erupted from the crowd.

As the shouts finally subsided, the chief gave a rousing speech—much of it in English—and ended with his promise to enforce the laws without favor to any individual tribe—respecting them each as an equal entity. Ending with a solemn prayer spoken in his own dialect, he left the stage—to the chants and cheers of the many assembled.

"I don't know about you, Dade," Mc Call began as they were led from their seats by the same ushers who had earlier directed them, "but I feel we have just heard from a great, eloquent man who is possessed of good sense and will be ready to lead his people. I can only pray that his reign will mean peace for all of us for the time being."

"We can only offer our own prayer to answer his—that Washington will respect him and his Seminole brethren, honor our treaties, and ease up the pressure to remove his people from the territory—as has been rumored," Dade answered as the two made their way back to their secluded campground—past the steady drone of the bullfrogs now taking up their nightly conversation beside the tranquil waters of Silver Springs.

• 22 •

December 1826

"Hey, Hackley," Lorenzo called, running after Robert as he was approaching his ship, which was pulled up at the wharf. "What, you don't even tell a bro you are leaving—or wish him goodbye?"

"Heading to see another bro," Robert smiled—laying down his valise and offering a hug as Lorenzo approached. "Little brother, William, is now in Tallahassee. He got his degree at William and Mary and is now determined to get a license to practice law in Florida—when things heat back up in the capital in January. I think he has an idea of building a settlement on Dad's property down near Sanybel."

"Good luck with that," Lorenzo laughed. "I can still picture you and Rhodes running back to the ship—ahead of that lumbering alligator!"

"Obviously, he hasn't seen the area. I think William was afraid I wouldn't want to share the southern property, but I actually have enough to do up here, so more power to him. I thought I'd head up to Tallahassee and see him for Christmas. He's staying at my friend Wyatt's hotel. At this time of year—once the legislators leave—there should be plenty of room for one more, and I'm thinking Tallahassee might be more fun than the cantonment over the holidays."

"But you'll miss all the celebration."

"So what are you all celebrating—another section of road completed?"

"The new baby!" Lorenzo answered. "First U.S. citizen to be born out here. Colonel Brooke and his wife are expecting their fourth just before Christmas. We've all planned a big celebration to honor the new little Brooke. The colonel asked me to invite you, but I haven't had a chance to get over your way."

"I thought Lucy had been pretty sick—at least that was the word I heard the last time I was on base."

"She's been sick for a while," Lorenzo nodded sadly. "It's no secret the colonel's worried about her. He was planning to take her back to Pensacola for the birth—until Governor Duval sent a letter on the last boat warning of a new conflict with the Indians. He's sending two additional companies to Cantonment Brooke and has asked the colonel to ready our local men as well. Obviously, he can't leave now, so we thought we'd try to provide a little happiness for the family as they welcome their new addition. Actually, I was watching for the troop arrival when I spotted you heading this way."

"Any idea what the conflict is about?" Robert asked. "Should I be worried about leaving my place?"

"My guess is it's over in the agency's area—as I heard Dade discussing problems he had heard about. We've heard nothing locally, and I know Rhodes and your men are pretty dependable—so I wouldn't worry. But although I'd like to visit further, I guess with the new ship heading our way, you probably will want to get your schooner out before they arrive. When do you expect to come back?"

"That depends on William. I promised to have the ship available to take him south whenever he wants. He's been asking about starting at Key West, so who knows? That town certainly has a lot more going for it at the moment than Tallahassee, so perhaps he could practice law down there while he decides what to do with the Sanybel property. Will keep you posted!

"Thanks for caring, bro!" Robert called—reaching out to hug Lorenzo. Then, picking up his valise, he turned and ran to the wharf—giving a nod to the crew as he jumped on board.

"Robert! It's great to see you," William Wyatt called, running around the desk to grab Robert's hand. "Your brother told me you were coming, but I didn't know when. You should have let me know, and I could have sent someone for you."

"Can anyone predict how long a trip over here takes?" Robert laughed—dropping his valise by the desk. "At any rate, I figured as fast as Tallahassee is growing there would be sure to be someone heading this way from St. Marks—although the traffic all seemed to be heading the other way today after the legislature closed!"

"We had a full house," Wyatt nodded. "But as soon as we can get to it, there will be a clean bed for you—unless you want to share with your brother."

"Being used to having a bed all to myself, I definitely prefer my own, thank you! But tell me, do you have any idea where I might find William?"

"Studious young man I've observed. Spends each day at a back table in the dining room poring over all those books he's brought in. I'm sure you'd like to see him. I think you know the way. If you just want to leave your things here, I'll take them up when the room is ready."

Crossing the hall and stopping at the door, Robert smiled at the studious young man bent over the far dining table. His prematurely balding head was balanced by a bushy dark beard hiding his face as he hastily took notes from a large leather volume propped beside him.

"Making up for the loss on top, or did you forget to pack a razor?" Robert called—approaching silently and clapping his brother on the back.

"Robert! My Lord, I didn't know you would be here today!" William called—laying his papers inside the book to mark his place and jumping up to hug his brother.

"Travel is an adventure down here," Robert laughed. "Never know what a ship's voyage will bring. But now that I'm here, let me take a look at you," he added—holding the young man at arm's length. "Guess they didn't feed you at William and Mary. As your mother would say, you are skin and bones. Never mind, I've been on the receiving end of Wyatt's hospitality more than once. Stick around and he'll fatten you up in no time."

"Looks like you're doing all right," William responded. "Dad said you had established several orchards, vegetable gardens, and a vineyard and that the fish over your way just jump into the net. Can't wait to see it all."

"I'll take you there—as soon as you take your bar exam. Any idea when that will be?"

"Not until the session restarts in January. As much as I learned in college, though, there is still so much to memorize. As happy as I am to see you, I'll be a pretty lame companion while you're here."

"Been there, done that," Robert smiled—clapping his brother on the back—"although I suspect the bar exam down here will be quite different from when I took it in New York."

"All the same if it means I can practice law in Florida. I'm hoping to head on down to Key West, which is a little more developed than Tallahassee right now. Dad thinks it's a good place to start while we look at developing his property at Sanybel and Charlotte Harbor. You did say you'd take me on down there when I'm ready?"

"Ready when you are," Robert nodded. "After all, Dad bought the schooner for both of us. Got a contact you might enjoy meeting in Key West named Bunce—burly, red-headed guy who is bigger than life. He was building a general store when I was down there, but he seemed to be in touch with everyone. I'd enjoy seeing him again, and I'd be happy to turn you over when I head back."

"So you're still set on being out there by Fort Brooke? No hard feelings about the army taking over your house and land? Mother was furious when Dad told her about it—said they had no right—and I know he's still working overtime trying to get his claim recognized."

"As a matter of fact, with the Seminole skirmishes nearby and over at Silver Springs, I'm really relieved Colonel Brooke and the troops are there to handle the problems. Leaves me time to clear the rest of our land. Hoping to build and sell some property once Dad gets the word out up north."

"But how much of it can you sell with the base encompassing so much space?"

"'Tenants of the fort' is the term for new residents. Won't take much to talk them into building a store, a blacksmith shop, or a stable. It will ensure a livelihood in their new home as well."

"Now that you two have had a chance to catch up," Wyatt called from the doorway, "who's ready for afternoon tea?"

"Something a little stronger sounds better right now," Robert laughed. "I've had a long trip."

"I'm saving that for tonight," Wyatt answered. "Thought you two would like to meet some of our new locals, so—now that the legislators are all gone—I've got a reception planned for later. It should be interesting for you to meet all those new plantation owners. I've built my own place out northeast of the city. The word from our Georgia transplants is that this heavy red clay we have to move to build our new homes is the best they've seen for raising cotton. Although my wife, Nancy Catherine, says it's turning all the children's playclothes orange! With the complaints we've heard from down your way though, Robert, I told her every stain is money in our pockets once the cotton is ready for harvesting!"

"No wonder the Indians didn't want to leave," Robert smiled. "I've heard their complaints that the sand down our way is worthless."

"It will remain to be seen," Wyatt nodded—pulling three mugs from the long, wooden counter beside the wall.

"Welcome to The Planters," the tiny dark-haired woman smiled—extending her hand in welcome as Robert and William descended the stairs at the inn. "I'm Nancy Catherine Wyatt, William's wife, and those two little girls by the refreshment table and the boy who just raced by as you came downstairs are our brood."

"Robert Hackley. I first met your husband in Pensacola—when this establishment was only a dream. This young, hopeful scholar is my brother, William, who's planning to take the law board here in Tallahassee—sometime in the near future," he added.

"My husband told me he had both of the sons of Richard Hackley staying here at the moment," Nancy Catherine nodded—her piercing blue eyes engaging each one. "I must admit I was astounded at the story of your father purchasing all that land from Spain."

"At least Father thought he had purchased the land," Robert answered. "The truth is that we are still awaiting clarification on his claim before we can offer our tracts for sale. We thought with three lawyers in the family we might be able to figure out our approach."

"Then, I suppose you two will be interested in meeting our local judge. Perhaps he can help the two of you with your claim. As a matter of fact, he's just across the room—if you'll follow me," she offered, turning and directing the two men to the refreshment table set up under the large front window.

"Excuse me, Judge Woodward, but I would like to introduce you to Robert and William Hackley. They are the sons of Spanish consul, Richard Hackley, the man who bought all of Southwest Florida from Spain.

"Augustus Woodward is our local judge and head of our court system over here . . ."

"Despite our lack of legal incidents down here right now," Woodward laughed—extending his hand to each of the brothers. "Wyatt told us of your friendship. Happy to meet both of you—and to have you in our local law ranks, William."

"I think I will have to pass the bar exam first," William answered, embarrassed.

"Not a problem—if you're prepared. Wyatt tells me you just graduated from William and Mary. I expect you've had the training you will need. Not much action over here, however, but I expect all that will change once the area builds up with more residents."

"Actually, I'm hoping to move down to Key West eventually—to help maintain my father's claims down south."

"Lots more action down there, I hear. Probably needs a younger man. Piracy, contraband, and slave trading—much more exciting than the few legal claims and disputes we are seeing up here—right, Ambrose?" he asked—addressing the young, slim, dark-haired man who had just approached the table.

"Where's that?" the newcomer asked.

"These gentlemen are Robert and William Hackley . . ."

"The sons of Consul Hackley, who owns our coast?" Ambrose laughed.

"I'm surprised our father's purchase is so well known over here," Robert began.

"Not so surprising when you hear that Ambrose Crane is the editor of our local newspaper, the *Tallahassee Florida Intelligencer*. Not a piece of news he doesn't miss. I've also been lucky enough to have him chosen as Leon County's new clerk of court, so we'll be spending a lot of time together."

"And I've heard of both of you—you especially, Robert. Such a shame you spent so much money and time on your home on Hillsborough Bay. Seeing how much time and money I'm spending on my own home, I can certainly sympathize," Crane added—extending his hand.

"Brought the brood, I see," Woodward called—as a young boy ran up beside Crane and reached for a cookie.

"I was bringing refreshments for all of you," Crane answered as the child scampered off. "Hoping he'll learn some manners when Wyatt's new academy starts in January," he continued. "Nice to have met you both," he answered, filling a plate and heading back across the room to a blond woman surrounded by several children.

"I'm counting on that new academy as well," a well-dressed, bearded man announced—approaching Woodward. "Too easy to let them run wild over here," he continued, shaking his head. "Now, who might these two gentlemen be?"

"Robert and William Hackley, meet Mr. Benjamin Chaires, who designed Jacksonville's layout and is planning to start our first bank in Tallahassee."

"Pleased to meet you," Robert answered. "I'd really love to find a bank closer than Pensacola, which is too far by ship from Cantonment Brooke."

"So that's who you are!" Chaires answered. "Heard about you from Wyatt. Rotten luck Gadsden chose your property for the fort! I can only hope I have no problem—as I'm planning my own home I'm calling 'Verdura,' just outside of town—near the former reservation."

"Don't let him kid you," Woodward smiled. "I've seen the plans. Williamsburg would be better suited to them than our Tallahassee frontier!"

"Just left Williamsburg myself," William smiled, "and I love the Virginia tidewater architecture. I'd love to take a look at your plans while I am here. Both Robert and I are planning to build several developments up and down the coast. It would be interesting to see what's feasible in our new territory."

"Glad to oblige," Chaires smiled. "We've encountered several topographical problems I might help you avoid. Although the land down your way is rather different, we do still face similar problems with the heat and humidity."

"I'm sorry to interrupt," Woodward whispered—turning to an entourage just entering the front doors, "but our local royalty has arrived."

"Should have guessed he'd make an appearance," Chaires laughed. "Stick with me, you two, and meet Tallahassee's most illustrious citizen," he smiled—taking a chocolate cookie from the plate behind him and propelling Robert and William toward the entryway.

Looking at his brother, William shrugged as he caught sight of the disheveled newcomer dressed in buckskins with a worn, wide-brimmed felt hat perched atop a mop of unkempt, stringy brown hair. Followed in the door by several well-dressed men and a bevy of young women decked out in the latest fashion, the man was definitely memorable—he had to admit.

William Wyatt and Nancy Catherine had quickly formed a receiving line at the door—which Ambrose Crane and his young wife joined. "Prince Murat, welcome to The Planters," Wyatt called—reaching out to take the man's hand.

"Prince Charles Louis Achille Murat—nephew of Napoleon Bonaparte," Chaires whispered as the men joined the throng welcoming the newcomer. Has a new plantation called 'Lipona,' just outside of town—not anything like Williamsburg, I'm afraid, though. All I have seen so far is a one-room log cabin. He's the only royalty Tallahassee possesses at the moment, however, so we all pay homage!"

· 23 ·

May 1827

"*H*ackley, welcome back to Cantonment Brooke," Colonel Brooke called from the front porch of the headquarters building as Robert headed up the path from the wharf—where his ship had just docked. "It's good to see you. If you have a moment, I need to talk to you."

"To me?" Robert asked—shielding his eyes from the blinding noonday sun as he stopped at the bottom of the hill. "I hope nothing has happened to my home since I was in Tallahassee."

"No. As far as I know your home and plantation are fine, but there have been some new activities out here since you left of which you need to be aware. If you don't have to rush off right away, how about coming up here to your very own front porch—where you and I can hold a very much delayed visit?"

Shouldering his valise, Robert crossed the path and ran up the steps. "So I understand congratulations are in order for the new little one!" he offered—extending his hand. "Lorenzo told me your fourth offspring was due after I left in December. Sorry I missed the festivities. Boy or girl?"

"Boy, named John Mercer Brooke, Jr."

"Mother and baby doing well, I hope."

"That's part of what I want to talk to you about. Why not take a seat out here. Beautiful spot you chose," he sighed—looking down the hill to the newly green live oaks and the flock of white ibis pecking diligently beneath long tendrils of Spanish moss. "I'm sure you have missed it—as will I."

"What? Are you being reassigned?" Robert asked—dropping his bag and taking the chair beside Brooke.

"Taking a leave of absence," Brooke answered, shaking his head. "Actually, the baby is fine, but Lucy did not fare well. I wanted to take her back to Pensacola for the birth, but with the new Seminole uprising in December, it was up to me to outfit and assign two new companies of soldiers sent by Governor Duval. I couldn't leave—and she didn't want to go without me.

"Then in January, Florida's Legislative Council passed an act to prevent the Indians from roaming throughout the territory—ordering any citizen who found an Indian 'roaming at large' to take him captive and bring him in to the closest justice."

"I did hear about that in Tallahassee. Seems the new residents there were in favor of the act—to protect their property since they are building on the site of Neamathla's former reservation."

"It's one thing when the justice is just across town. However, can you imagine the impossibility of taking charge of a wandering Indian and attempting to find a justice way out here? The logical conclusion of that act, I'm afraid, is to encourage citizens to take the law into their own hands. As hard as we have worked at Cantonment Brooke to keep the Indians happy and well fed, I would hate to see one episode cause unrest in their midst—as you can understand. Living outside the fort, you would be particularly vulnerable to following the new law."

"Don't see many out near my place, and I've been inclined to let them wander about without incident. They just seem to be hunting. I had heard of the new act, but I'll admit, it never occurred to me that I would be responsible for turning one of them in!"

"As far as Cantonment Brooke is concerned, as of January, Washington has reacted to growing tension with the Indians by centering military authority in Florida under one officer, Colonel Clinch. His regiment is housed in Pensacola, and he has the option of commanding a battalion of the First Infantry, which is also in Pensacola. An additional company of the Fourth Artillery in St. Augustine will also be under him—if there is activity out near Fort King.

"As you can imagine, things were fairly uncertain during the winter. Finally, when things blew over, I was able to secure leave in February to take both Lucy and the children back to Pensacola."

"So they are all there now? I'm sure you must be worried."

"As any husband and father would be," Brooke nodded. "As a matter of fact, I am due to head back to Pensacola momentarily—once the mail ship gets in. Now that things are quiet for the moment, General Gaines has granted me sixty days' leave. Guess it's about time—as I told him I actually haven't had a furlough for the past ten years."

"How sad that it must be for a health concern," Robert answered. "So is Lucy improving in Pensacola?"

"Not much," Brooke answered—shaking his head. "She hasn't been well for some time, and with four children to take care of alone, I'm afraid there's no time for her to recover. I'm hoping I can take a lot of the day-to-day work off her shoulders while I am there."

"And you think things will stay quiet over here while you are away?"

"That's uncertain—to be honest. While I was in Pensacola in February, I was able to get an audience with Colonel Clinch. He said Jacob Brown, the army's commanding general, had cautioned him that the public mind—as more and more residents now move down—is becoming inflamed. General Brown cautioned Clinch as he took command to be extremely careful in dispensing justice—so as not to cause further friction. His assessment was that with Clinch's new power the Indians would understand our country's attempt at justice and their chieftains would manage to keep the peace."

"What is your interpretation?" Robert asked. "In Tallahassee the citizens I met were all worried about a group of Seminoles who had—reportedly—been murdering Americans in both northern Florida and Georgia last winter. I heard Colonel Clinch had been in command to deal with those hostilities as well. Judging by the further pronouncements, however, it seems things are no better at present."

"I fear you are right. In March—just after I got back here, Clinch sent two companies to us—under Lieutenant Glassell—with instructions for them to report to Agent Humphreys at the Indian agency—over near Silver Springs. Their responsibility over there was to build a new fort and stockade—with a two-story building in the center manned by armed sentry. They're calling it Cantonment King—in honor of Colonel William King, who preceded Clinch in the Fourth Infantry."

"So have there been new uprisings over there? I heard nothing while I was in Tallahassee."

"Mainly, I think Humphreys had heard rumors from the Creeks. The Seminoles are really pretty peaceful at the moment, but their representatives have reported a lot of unrest with the Creek settlements about our government's restrictions on their travel outside of their reservations. Last I heard, our territorial delegate, Joseph White, has called a group of chiefs to meet on May 20 at the new fort to try to sell them on migrating west. From what we've seen earlier, however, I think any requests we make may fall on deaf ears."

"What's the next step if they refuse?"

"That remains to be seen," Brooke answered, shaking his head. "At any rate, it does seem like things are coming to a head. According to Clinch, White seems to feel the answer will be this new attempt by Washington to move the Indians west where they can farm at will and be protected from unruly citizens—thereby preventing a recurrence of Jackson's war when Spain was in charge down here.

"I am leaving the base in good hands, and things here at Cantonment Brooke are peaceful at the moment—as long as we continue to deliver the allotted provisions to our local tribes. I can only hope they will remain that way for the next sixty days. With the meeting coming up, it also provides a breather for us here—as the various tribes will be waiting for their chieftains to hear and consider our proposals."

"And it gives you a chance to look after your family. Please know that you and Lucy will be in my prayers," Robert answered—standing and reaching for Brooke's hand as he rose.

"I'm so glad I got to see you in person before I leave. I've also informed the Collers. Living outside the base as the two of you do, you need to be aware of any meetings with the chiefs. As I told Levi, you are all welcome at the cantonment any time you feel unsafe. I am sure my men will arrange housing on base—should the need arise."

Sadly, he had been unaware of the present unrest between Fort Brooke and the new Fort King while he was in Tallahassee, Robert mused as he made his way beyond the base fencing and headed onto the narrow path through the dense pine forest—which separated his property from the base. Should he have been worried, he would have returned—since he had not conceived of any need for fortification with the few Indians he had observed during his time in the area. The new residents and legislators at the capital—having quickly outnumbered the Indian remnants at Neamathla's old reservation—had presented a firm conviction that Colonel Clinch and his regiments in Pensacola had everything under control.

At any rate, he had missed his home and had been anxious to bid farewell to William once he had passed his bar exam. Over the past four years, he had observed that May was definitely the prettiest month in the Hillsborough area, and he hadn't wanted to miss it. He smiled as he looked across the vast vista of waist-high palmettos that extended to the banks of the nearby creek. Wouldn't his stepmother be amazed at the beauty of the yellow jessamine vines suspended from pine boughs in the sunny areas—where zebra striped Monarch butterflies now flitted. Oh, the Virginia azaleas were lovely—but cultivated into the bordered paths leading up to his family home—they lacked the spontaneity of Florida's beauty.

Catching sight of a distant mother doe introducing her new off-spring to the beauty of the pine forest, he stopped a moment—unwilling to scare her away—while frightening a raccoon, which ran past with a small, cherished fish he had captured in the distant creek. As long as I don't meet any alligators, Robert considered—with a wary look at the creek bed—as he knew male gators were said to be especially active in seeking new territory in May.

Suddenly hearing hoof beats behind him, he turned. Since he had been away, had the Indians become more brazen near his home?

"Robert," Lorenzo called—stopping the wagon on the path behind Robert. "Didn't mean to scare you," he laughed. "On my way off the base, I saw your ship out there and thought you might need a ride to your place. I'm heading out that way anyway taking supplies to the Seminoles out at Thonotosassa.

"How was little brother, William? Wondered about you the whole time you were gone."

"William is doing well, Lorenzo, but I missed you as well," Robert called—relieved at seeing his friend. Throwing his valise into the back of the wagon, he thankfully climbed on board. "He passed his law exam and is now qualified to practice in Tallahassee, I'm happy to say."

"Is he staying there, then? I had rather hoped he would be joining you over here. Would love to meet my new bro at last."

"At the moment he's laying the groundwork for a move to Key West—just waiting for word from our father on our claim down south.

Since I've heard nothing on this end of the claim, he was hoping to have better results getting things moving at the capital on the area from Charlotte Harbor and Sanybel. Once he gets the go-ahead, I'm to pick him up and take him down to Key West. Thought he'd like to meet up with our buddy, Bunce."

"Just the man," Lorenzo laughed. "I remember he wanted to get back at sea on his boat."

"Better him than me. While I'll be happy to take little bro down south, after Sanybel, I've no intention of trying to develop that area, thank you. I'm happy to deal with our property up here.

"Since you're heading out to the reservation, what's the word on hostilities out there?"

"I think they're waiting to hear the results from the meeting at Fort King—although from what I'm hearing, they want no part of moving out west. I can't really blame them—as this has been their home for so long.

"They're chafing under the new restrictions that prevent them from traveling out of their territorial boundaries. The new law is an attempt to keep them from buying rum or contraband from Cuban sailors at the coast—but it's also limiting their fishing spots. The drought we've experienced this past winter and spring has dried up many of the smaller creeks and lakes, which makes things even worse. At the base, we're all just praying that the summer rains begin early—to fill their fishing spots near their reservation again. As long as I'm bringing food," he continued—motioning to the boxes in the back of the wagon, "they're congenial, but I'm afraid it won't last for long."

• *24* •

December 1828

"*S*o you decided to head south for the winter," Robert laughed—watching his brother pull his cap down farther and jam his hands in his jacket pocket as they stood on deck watching the St. Marks harbor disappear beneath a cloud of steam emanating from the warm Gulf waters into the frigid morning air.

"I thought Florida was tropical!" William spat out. "Couldn't prove it by me! Even the gulls are complaining," he added—motioning to a flock of noisy seagulls following the boat's wake and hopeful of a handout.

"Just wait until we get to Key West, and I promise you will see the difference. Why the legislators ever decided to make Tallahassee the territory's capital has always escaped me. Might as well be Georgia or Alabama—as it's so far north. Why, even the Hillsborough area is preferable weather wise.

"I can tell you, however, that you may regret your decision by August. I remember so well the inescapable heat and the summer storm we experienced when we came through there. And Commodore Porter also warned us of the yellow fever epidemic that had sent a full load of sick sailors back to Hampton Roads. If you settle there, you may just decide to head back to Virginia yourself by summer."

"It's a start, though, in a brand-new town. When we heard in Tallahassee that the Florida territory had incorporated Key West as a city this year and that it was also now considered as a port of entry, I decided it was time to set up my law practice down there—where I could also pursue developing Dad's west coast lands."

132

"More power to you," Robert nodded. "It sounds like you have it all thought out."

"But are you sure you don't want to develop the Sanybel area yourself?"

"I have enough on my plate in the Hillsborough area for now. With the several new Indian incidents nearby and a new commander at the base . . ."

"What do you mean—new commander? What happened to Brooke?"

"Sad story," Robert answered—shaking his head. "When his wife didn't recover her health, Brooke asked for another furlough to join her and the family. While he was with them, my friend Lorenzo told me, the family all caught a very serious fever in October—from which his daughter and oldest son died. His wife shortly afterward delivered a stillborn son. I don't know how much more Brooke can take. The army has been good to give him the time he needs, but it's clear neither he nor his wife want to return to the fort. Lorenzo says he will be reassigned once they all recover. They really just want to return north—where his wife has family."

"I can certainly understand their grief—as I still remember hearing the loss Dad felt when your mom died. Mom told me she doesn't think he has ever really gotten over it—although she doesn't doubt his love for her or the rest of us!"

"My heart really goes out to Brooke and his family, yet the future of the base is unclear right now. The Seminoles rejected the proposed treaty last year, and there has been a lot of unrest in all of the tribes. With Brooke now gone, Colonel Clinch has decided to move the Fourth Infantry headquarters from Pensacola to Fort Brooke—bringing his companies with him."

"I did hear about Clinch moving when Wyatt housed him and several of his men on their way through St. Marks, but I hadn't heard about Brooke," William added, shaking his head. "I just thought it was to shore up the facilities nearer Fort King."

"Nothing is settled right now. In October, I understand, five of the chiefs told the Indian agent, Gad Humphreys, they would agree to send a delegation to look at the western lands, but I haven't heard that they've gone yet. And now with Jackson due to be sworn in as president in March—with all of the hatred the Seminoles have for him after the first Seminole War, I'm afraid there is bound to be turmoil. That's why I agreed to take you to Key West now—as promised," Robert smiled. "But I really will have to just introduce you to the men I met there and leave you on your own—assuming you will let me know what you decide to do with the Sanybel property."

"I appreciate your agreeing to take me down to Key West—at such an uneasy time."

"What are brothers for? Besides it gives us a quiet vacation—together—which we have never really had."

"I promise to keep you informed on my plans—once I settle in Key West and determine the lay of the land down there—if you're sure you don't want to join me in this new venture."

"The only thing I'm sure of at the moment," Robert added—pulling his coat together more tightly—"is that I want to head below deck—before my skin matches that perfect blue sky out there. I also expect George might want a cup of coffee. I left some on in the galley if you'd like to join me."

As the sun suddenly rose above the dark islands, William stood fascinated at the port railing—watching as the light filtered through the distant mangroves—to illuminate the shallow, algae-covered water—where sporadic silver fish nipped at the large dragonflies as they touched down gently in the piles of seaweed beneath the mangrove roots—a far cry from the Atlantic side of the country—where he had grown up—with its pounding waves and broad sandy beaches. And it was actually warm enough now to go swimming—should he want to, he admitted as he pulled off his heavy jacket and threw it on the deck.

"Finally made it to the tropics!" Robert called, emerging from the cabin below.

"Considering an early morning swim. Want to join me?"

"Not sure you'd appreciate your companions down here. As long as we're in the bay side of the coastal islands, you'd find the 'gators more than ready to join you. Rhodes and I left one at Sanybel you may meet when you get over there! Better to wait until we get to the beach at Key West before you do any swimming," Robert laughed.

"Do you think we'll get there today? I'd really like to find a room to let and an office and get set up sometime early in the New Year."

"We should make it to port either today—or tomorrow—can't be too sure down here. The Florida Straits can be deceiving—and often deadly. I remember Porter's tales of the many shipwrecks out here.

"But don't worry, little brother," he added after seeing William's expression. "No storms this time of year, so it will just depend on the tides."

Rounding the tip of the island in late afternoon, Robert was surprised to see mainly personal watercraft in the harbor—where the Mosquito Fleet had been stationed on his last trip.

"Wow! Who would have suspected a real city—way down here," William called from the port side of the deck as Robert emerged—sheltering his eyes from the glare of the setting sun.

"Far cry from what the town looked like when I was here. That's for sure," Robert remarked. "And I guess the holidays have brought more than the usual down here. Just hope there's room for one more ship. Stay here on deck to help the men lower the sails and tie her up if George and I can find a berth," he added—vanishing into the cabin.

"Bit of a feat—both finding a spot and getting into it," Robert called several minutes later—as he ran back on deck.

Carefully securing his rope to a back post, William turned to Robert. "I've never seen so many crafts in Florida waters. Even beats Pensacola when I came down initially. Guess I'm glad we have beds on board, or you and George and I and the crew might all be sleeping on the dock!"

"Just lucky we found a berth. Why not stay here and help George close up while I go sign us in? If all goes well, I'll treat you and George to a big bowl of conch chowder—assuming we can find a restaurant, that is. I can't believe how much the town has grown," Robert remarked.

Leading the way down the main street, he paused to take in the new, small two-story wooden dwellings, whose elevated porches festooned with wooden rockers were now edged in between several new shops.

"Let's see, my friend Bunce had his shop right over there," he pointed—stopping as two men emerged from the door. A burly Irishman sporting a bushy red beard waited for a slender, bearded, dark-haired man to follow as he turned and locked the door.

"Bunce! Just the man I wanted to see," Robert called—crossing the street.

"I'm sorry," Bunce answered. "Do I know you?"

"Robert Hackley. I know that it's been awhile . . ."

"Aha! The owner of Southwest Florida. I recognize you now," Bunce called with a boisterous laugh—crossing the street with his hand extended. "And to what do we owe the honor of your visit to our fair town?"

"Brought my little brother down. He's hoping to set up a law practice and develop the southern end of our dad's property—over at Sanybel. William Hackley, meet William Bunce," he offered—as William extended his hand. "And this is my second in command, George Brady," he continued with the introduction. "Sorry to bother you, but we just arrived from Fort Brooke, and I promised them a large bowl of the conch chowder I enjoyed so much the last time I was here."

"Then, you've come to the right spot," Bunce smiled. "This is my friend, Frenchie, who is better known as Fred Tresca," he continued as the men shook hands all around. "We were just on our way to greet the sunset and take in a bowl or two of the chowder ourselves. Why don't you three join us?"

"We'd be delighted. Nothing like locals to show us the ropes," Robert nodded.

"Now that you've seen your first sunset, you've officially established residency," Bunce announced—slapping William on the back as he sidestepped a wandering chicken and ushered the others to an outdoor table in the plaza. "Got the best ale in town," he offered—motioning a waitress over.

"Brought you a new resident who wants to try your best brew—straight from Havana. You'll love it," he added, turning to Robert.

"Not like that vile coffee everyone tried to offer me on my last visit, I hope," Robert answered.

"Oh, I remember now. Porter loved that stuff. Luckily, I was able to import some domestic brands for those of us from northern climes. It's taken Fred, here, quite a while to get used to both cuisines—from Havana or America. No French delicacies down here yet. Been trying to talk him into opening a Parisian café—even have a space for one next door to my shop," Bunce laughed.

"Got enough on my plate," Fred Tresca answered, shaking his head. "And who do you think would keep a café staffed while I'm away?"

"Oh, are you leaving town?" William asked.

"Sporadically," Tresca nodded. "Actually, I'm employed over at the base—where my job is to ferry mail and army or navy members from Key West to Fort Brooke, St. Marks, Pensacola, and even to New Orleans occasionally."

"Not sure I'd want to do that much sailing," Robert said. "How about you, George?"

"Not a bad life," George answered. "Ever need a co-captain?"

"Hey, wait a minute, you have a job," Robert cut in. "But, Tresca, do you ever take civilians on those runs?"

"Often take dependents to join some of the officers. If I have room on board, I have taken others on occasion as well."

"So, William, if you should want to go back to either St. Marks or to visit me at Fort Brooke, there's your ticket."

"Fort Brooke, so that's where I've heard of you," Tresca interrupted. "Now I remember, you're the man who built that beautiful home on the bluff up there and had the army take it away. I never owned any property myself, but I can't imagine what it must have felt like to build it and have it confiscated almost immediately. Just saving up myself now to buy my own boat. That's enough property for me."

"Tresca has quite a tale," Bunce offered—nodding as the waitress set the pitcher and five mugs on the table and began to fill them. "He came down here about the same time I did—as a cabin boy on a French ship. . . . But go ahead, Tresca, and fill them in."

"Actually, I had served for several years—starting as a young boy on a ship that was carrying Napoleon. Rotten job, but at least it got me out in the world and on shipboard—which I loved—still do. Didn't have much family, and there wasn't much other work in my small town in France.

"Somehow, though, when we pulled into port here, I took one look at the new territory and decided this was where I wanted to live. Actually, I jumped ship and looked for a place to hide out until the ship left without me. I met Bunce shortly afterward, and he gave me a job sorting stock in his shop—until I was finally able to secure a spot on base.

"It's been a few years now, and I was able to get on with the navy ferrying all their men and supplies up and down the coast. I was so sorry to hear of Brooke leaving, Robert. I actually took his wife and kids over to Pensacola—and then took him to follow them. Wasn't so sure I wanted the whole lot on board, but those kids were so well behaved. The boys even offered to help with the sails. Older one even helped tie us up in St. Marks. I was so sorry to hear of the tragedies. I've been warned down here of all the yellow fever. Seems you can't get away from it."

"If it's not fever, it's hurricanes—or Seminoles," Robert added.

"Speaking of which," Bunce remarked, "did you know Major Dade is now on base down here? I know he has led at least two companies up your way to Fort King. He has a new wife—very lovely lady. Hope he gets to stay down here. I think I'd rather face a bout of the fever than either Micanopy or his second, Jumper. I heard from some of the men on base that they may have it in for Dade after their last two encounters."

"I met Dade only once—at Brooke. Heck of a warrior I understand—and the one they want in charge if things get out of hand again."

"Then I sincerely hope you folks up there get things quieted down between Fort Brooke and Fort King. I'd hate to see his wife become a widow."

"Now," Bunce continued, "you say you are planning to set up a law practice in town—and develop your father's property up the way in Sanybel. Got any idea how you will accomplish both?"

"Just got my Florida license in Tallahassee. And with Key West being a new port of entry, I thought I'd start here, establish my practice, and visit Sanybel when I have time—and can find a ship to take me up there."

"Got the ship," Bunce interrupted. "My *Associate* is just gathering barnacles over at the port, and it—just like its owner—is itching for an adventure. Just say the word, and I'm at your disposal," he continued—moving the candle as two waitresses arrived with five steaming bowls of conch chowder.

September 1830

"So how's my favorite Key West councilman?" Fred Tresca called—throwing his battered hat on the hat rack and running his fingers through his long, dark hair as he sauntered through the open office door.

"My God, Tresca, have you ever heard of knocking?" William Hackley laughed—laying his pen on the desk and sorting the papers before him into a stack. "Glad to see you, though, and—if truth be known—I'm more than glad to put these shipwreck reports aside for the moment. Frankly, I had no idea what I was getting into by running for councilman while establishing a new law practice. It's unbelievable how much red tape there is in dealing with all the new shipping and salvage laws. But don't get me started—for I'm sure you'll hear more than enough from our pal, Bunce. With the recent recession in our country, there seems to be an increased influx of trading with Cuba. As the new U.S. customs inspector, he says he hasn't even had time for lunch in weeks."

"Hasn't hurt him, I'll bet," Tresca interrupted. "Last I saw of him, the many bowls of crab Rangoon had done a job on his waistline."

"Be that as it may, I had hoped to take him up on his offer to take me exploring the many keys down this way before the storms arrive."

"Wrong time of year," Tresca added—shaking his head. "Never know what to expect in the fall—with storms and yellow fever competing. And the heat's pretty unbearable this time of year as well. By the time I got my ship anchored out at the base, I was drenched from head to toe."

"So you came in here before even washing off? Thanks a lot," William teased—holding his nose. "At least you did wait until the yellow fever got under control down here before returning."

"We heard how bad it was when I was in St. Marks. I saw several ships heading north with sickened soldiers from the base out here."

"It's been a real concern. You were lucky to have been gone. New fellow, Benjamin Strobel, with his medical degree pitched in right away, though. Probably saved many locals. Good to have all the new talent we're finding down here.

"But how about some limeade? I'll be happy to take a break and hear what's happening in Seminole land," William continued—closing the logbook on his desk and leading the way back out the open door to a side table with two wooden chairs set on the small wooden porch, which fronted the street. Nodding to a woman toting a market basket, he poured two glasses from a small pitcher and ushered Fred Tresca into one of the chairs.

"Thanks. I needed this. Deck's still rolling for me, but I wanted to see you as soon as I got in. Got several epistles I think you'll want to see," Tresca continued—reaching into his inside coat pocket and removing two letters addressed to William.

"Good to see big brother Robert is still alive and kicking," William added—looking at the first envelope—as he laid the two on the table beside him. "You'll excuse me if I save these for my evening's entertainment, though. Despite my crowded day job, the nights can get pretty long down here."

"Things are heating up at Fort Brooke right now," Tresca remarked. "The army closed Fort King last year, you know, so all of the Indian trouble is being handled by Clinch at Brooke. And now that Congress passed Jackson's Indian Removal Act in May to remove the Indians to Oklahoma within the next three years, there's bound to be trouble.

"I was able to see Robert for a short visit just before I left the fort. He says he's still not worried about the status at Fort Brooke, and there are actually several new residents who have set up homes and businesses on the base. A fellow named William Saunders has even started a general store just off the base, and there are plans for a harness repair and shoe shop, a laundry, and even a ship repair yard. Actually, the latter one couldn't come at a better time—as there is no other repair yard all the way up to St. Marks.

"At any rate, your brother is convinced they are encroaching on your father's land and has spoken to Clinch about allowing the new residents to settle there. Clinch's only response, he said, was that they are all allowed to settle nearby as long as they are providing services for Fort Brooke, and he has assured all of them that there will be room on base should things get dicey.

"Robert also says your father is now pushing to get the lot sales underway as soon as possible, though—before there's more Seminole trouble."

"As this second letter is from Dad, I expect he wants me to get the keys and the Sanybel properties off and running as well."

"What do you think? The keys up the east side of the territory are still pretty much uninhabited. But—as you know only too well—they are a shipping nightmare with the tidal variations that can strand a loaded sloop. Won't see me heading east and risking my *Margaret Ann*, I can tell you."

"Somebody should have warned each of the ship owners I've been dealing with," William laughed. "Can't tell you how much cargo has been lost in the wrecks out there. But on the other hand, it's a boon for all the salvage operators who are setting up shop down here."

"As for Sanybel and the western keys, you know I pass by there on each of my trips. The ranchos are once again up and running this month. If you're planning a trip up there, though, I would advise you to wait until winter—as the unpredictable storms and hurricanes can produce havoc on shipping. Taking my life in my hands each time I set out from here to Pensacola."

"I'll talk to Bunce when he gets home. I need some supplies from his store anyway. Maybe we can both take some time off and check out my dad's holdings. After all, he did promise—oh, when was it? The day Robert and I arrived, wasn't it? Want to come along? I could use your knowledge of all those ranchos and their owners."

"While I'd love to be with you two, my regular army trips up the coast are quite enough travel for me for the time being, thank you. Between sun, mosquitoes, and storms, I've had enough of extra travel in either way for the moment."

"Well, if it isn't two of my favorite conch buddies!" William Bunce called—shading his eyes as he stopped at the foot of the porch stairs. "Didn't know you were back in town, Tresca."

"Just got in. Had some mail for William and decided to deliver it on my way home."

"How about coming up for a visit and sharing a glass of limeade?" William asked. "I was planning to go see you when I finished work."

"Looks like you've already done that," Bunce laughed—a wide grin spreading across his ruddy face as he headed up the steps to join them. "But I had something a little stronger in mind. Anybody ready for a pitcher or two of Cuban ale and some conch chowder? Sunset's a little too late this time of year, but I warrant we can talk Rosie into finding us a table early."

"Since I came straight from the ship, I'll need to go home and change first," Tresca answered. "I'm just lucky William didn't throw me out of the door."

"Figured the porch at least provided some ventilation," William added—wrinkling his nose.

"I just need to head over to close up the shop, and then I'm done for the day—thank the Lord," Bunce replied. "Will an hour do it, Tresca?"

"Meet you at the dock, then?" Tresca nodded—rising and heading down the stairs.

"Does that work for you?" Bunce asked—turning to William.

"Perfect," William answered. "That'll give me time to read both my dad's and brother's letters and see what they have to say."

Finding a table under a trio of towering palm trees and dislodging two small chickens that were picking at crumbs under a nearby chair, Bunce removed his hat, ran his fingers through his shock of red hair, and signaled to a waitress leaning on the nearby bar. "Hey, Rosie, gonna need a pitcher of your best brew and three mugs—and a promise to keep it coming. Been a long day!"

Pouring his own mug, Bunce noticed William heading toward him—shading his eyes against the blinding sun to the west of the dock area. Motioning him over, he pulled another mug over and began filling it.

"My Lord, Bunce, did you have to find the hottest spot on the coast?" William called—removing his suit coat and hanging it on the chair as he took a seat.

"Like me, you chose Key West," Bunce laughed.

"You chose it. My residence here was chosen by my father—which is exactly what I need to talk to you about. Glad Tresca isn't here yet."

"So what is it that is so all-fired important that you can't just enjoy a mug before talking business?"

"Sorry. I'll keep it short, but Tresca's already heard part of my dilemma. He brought me two letters today—neither of which is good news. Although he didn't say anything about it to Tresca—as far as I heard—Robert has now decided to leave the Fort Brooke area and move to Tallahassee by the end of the year. Says he's found a good agent in Fort Brooke to handle land sales outside the base, but he's still worried about my dad's claim to the area and wants to be in the capital to pursue our legal claims.

"Then, there's Dad's letter," he paused—taking a sip from his mug and sighing as he put it down. "Remember when I arrived in town and told you about my dad's purchase of most of Southwest Florida . . ."

"Which you have yet to explore down here," Bunce nodded.

"Well, now my dad is pushing both of us to move forward in developing the land. Robert has already sold lots up his way, but Dad wants to get enough lots sold not only at Fort Brooke but over east in the keys and over at Sanybel."

"Good idea to get them all underway—before news of the Indian stalemate gets up north and scares off buyers."

"Which is obviously worrying Robert as well—as he is much closer to the action up there.

"So you once offered to take me exploring in your *Associate*. I'll admit I've been too busy setting up my law practice and now settling my councilman duties to even consider a trip—anywhere. But I think with Dad's letter Tresca just brought me," he continued—removing an envelope from his shirt pocket and placing it on the table—"I'd better make some headway before he gets too impatient. Believe me I don't need him breathing down my back for lack of duty!"

"So what is it your dad wants?"

"It seems he now has a project underway to sell lots over at Sanybel to a New York group of investors, who are calling themselves the Florida Peninsula Land Company. I'll admit that—as a lawyer—it seems very suspect to me—as the government has yet to affirm Dad's title from the Alagon purchase.

"Be that as it may, according to Dad, once the sale goes through, the investors are planning to create fifty shares of stock—each one equaling 1,800 acres and extending from the Gulf to the bay with a lot in town thrown in."

"Hold on a minute," Bunce interrupted. "I haven't even finished my first mug yet, so I've still got my faculties intact. So tell me, what town are we talking about? No one other than a rancho owner or two has even tried to settle on Sanybel."

"That's my dilemma. While I don't want to throw a wet blanket on Dad's plan, I still see flags going up in several directions. All I know is that Robert reported the east side of the island was almost all mangrove—and alligators—and pretty much impassable. Gonna take a lot of time and money to clear homesteads there. Although he didn't explore the Gulf side, you and I both know—from all our work with shipping down here—that it's only a prayer away from total devastation should one of those hurricanes decide to land on Sanybel.

"First of all, I expect—despite what Robert thinks he can do in Tallahassee—once the word gets out the government will start legal proceedings about Dad's title to the land—in which I don't want to be involved, to say the least. Second, I actually don't see any buyer being naive enough to buy a lot sight unseen—so it all may turn into a financial loss for both Dad and the investors. As I've heard from my mother about several of his former dealings, I really don't want to be responsible for another disappointment.

"The gist of his letter," William continued—throwing it down on the table beside him—"is that because he asked me to look after things on this end, I am involved."

"So how is it I can help you, buddy?"

"Dad has planned a trip to both Fort Brooke and Key West next year—once the sale gets underway. So I was wondering, since you offered your *Associate*, whether you would be available to take me to explore both sides of Dad's South Florida land. "I'm prepared to pay whatever a trip might cost—with your expertise thrown in. I venture to say that—with all my respect for Tresca—you probably have more knowledge of this part of the territory than anyone else."

"And I'm sure Tresca would turn you down if you approach him—as his regular trips for the army would probably preclude him from an extended trip at this time," Bunce laughed. "So you need a boat and a guide. Did I get that right?"

"I guess that really sums it up."

"Only problem is that—although today promises a clear sunset out there," he added—pointing to the point, "storm season is right now upon us—probably until the end of the year. While I dearly love our coastal area, I also love my *Associate* and my work down here, so I don't really think I can chance getting wrecked or stranded until the season ends. If you can wait until the first of next year, I'm your man. If not, I can recommend another more risky captain."

"It will take until next year to get Dad's legal status on the deed certified, and he isn't planning to come down until after the holidays— as Mom insists on Christmas in Virginia every year. So, yes, let's plan on early 1831."

"Sounds good to me," Bunce answered. "And—if the truth be known—I've actually got my eye on buying a rancho at a place called Shaw's Point, which is all the way up the coast near the Manatee River—not far from Fort Brooke. In my position as customs inspector, I hear a lot of talk. Latest rumor is that a tariff war is looming between our country and Spain by next year, which may adversely affect the Spanish fishermen. The trader I talked to up at Shaw seems ready to move out and has offered it for sale. If you wouldn't mind a longer voyage, I'll be more than happy to take you to Sanybel on my way."

"To the new year!" William answered, reaching across the table to grab Bunce's hand.

"So what are we toasting?" Fred Tresca called, throwing his hat on the table, turning a chair backward, sitting down, and holding the empty mug over to Bunce.

"Might have known our Frenchman would arrive in time for a toast," Bunce laughed. "Be careful, or William here will put you on the passenger list as well!"

· 26 ·

February 1831

"Glad to see we can finally explore Dad's property," William Hackley called—running up the plank on Bunce's sloop, *Aristocrat*, as the first hints of sunrise filled the eastern sky.

"Not so sure," Bunce answered—holding on to his hat and bracing his feet as a swift northwest wind rattled the sails, which were already set. "Captain Rooke is a little nervous," he added—looking at the blowing palm branches on the beach to the west as the first raindrops began to fall. "As it's from the northwest, we should be okay once we round the point and head up the east side, though. Why not come below until he gives the go-ahead? Got some coffee brewing—not that Cuban kind your brother hates," he laughed as he led the way down the steps into the cabin.

"Now, how far are you determined to go on this trip?" Bunce asked when they were both seated with a full mug of steaming coffee.

"According to Dad's map," William answered—pulling a crumpled paper from his pocket, "the land he purchased from Alagon goes all the way around the tip of the territory and up the east coast past all those islands—or keys. Seems to include all the area up to the Miami River on the mainland."

"Not much on those keys, you know—unless your legal expertise wants you to examine all the wrecks out there! Land is mostly rock—limestone, I think. It's far from the sand we see on the west coast. Would be pretty difficult to dig foundations in it—from what I've seen. Not sure the cost of building out there would be worth it. The tidal action is also much greater on the Atlantic side. I've actually seen some of those keys inundated after a storm—and the reefs out there can play havoc with any ships approaching—as we have both seen in the reports we are filing daily.

"Still if the weather cooperates—and Rooke is willing to take us over, I'm ready for the adventure. Really glad to get away from the paperwork for a bit."

"I heard from Dad during the holidays, and he is really pushing me to explore both sides of the coast for possible development. Thought we'd start on the east side. If what you have told me is true, we can then concentrate on Sanybel—as originally planned."

"Storm has passed," Rooke called as he headed into the room. "Ready when you are, Bunce."

"Then, let's go. Heading up to Key Vacas first, right, Tom? Said you'd show us how to catch a key deer out there—by moonlight."

"What is this?" William interrupted, "an exploration or a hunting trip?"

"Deep passage at Vacas, but it's not safe to travel farther after dark. And you've never lived until you've tasted key deer!" Bunce laughed— as he nodded and saluted his captain.

"So where are we headed today?" William asked the following morning—heading up to the deck and squinting as the full sunrise suddenly burst from the starboard side of the ship.

"Heading up to Lignum Vitae Key. Worth looking into for your development—as it is one of the few where I would agree to build. Captain Rooke actually has already built a home there. Thought the crew and I might offer to help him thatch it while you take a walk around."

"Hadn't planned on building a home at this point!" William answered.

"Oh, come on. You want to look around—which leaves the rest of us to either fish for those pike the Bahamians love or go crabbing. Got enough fish on our last stop, so what's the harm in helping Tom thatch his house while we're here? He still needs to cut palmetto leaves for the roof, and the rest of the men have offered to help him."

"As long as we can leave before evening. I'd really like to get on to the Florida Reef tomorrow."

"East wind doesn't promise an easy trip," Bunce announced—shaking his head, "I've had to deal with too many wrecks on the reef, thank you!"

"Oh, my Lord, Bunce, I see what you mean," William called two days later as Captain Rooke rounded the long reef in a blinding rainstorm. "I had no idea how many ships actually come up this way."

"And wreck on the reef," Bunce nodded—pointing to a ship lying on its side in the shallow harbor. Through the blinding rain, the men could make out a wrecking vessel anchored nearby—its crew busily attempting to load the cargo from the ship's bilge into several rowboats pulled up alongside. "My God, it's the *Amulet* out of Boston. That ship goes regularly to New Orleans. Have to check it in when it comes through the port. It draws about thirteen feet—more if it's loaded. Doesn't look like more than eight to ten feet to me out here right now," he continued—looking over the deck at the swirling water below. "The tides in the last storm must have drained the port."

"Looks like it was heading back," William remarked—shielding his eyes from the steady rain. "Seems to be cotton bales they are loading off."

"They're going to need help transferring the bales to port," Captain Rooke called—approaching the men on deck. "Got any problem with me offering to take some of them back to Key West with us? They pay up to two dollars a bale—and our lower deck is free of cargo."

"Whatever," William shrugged. "As long as it can wait until our return trip—as we still need to get on up to Bear Cut."

"Ain't nobody going anywhere today," the captain announced. "Got at least seven other wrecking vessels lined up in port. I'll check with the *Amulet* captain and see where the wrecker will be off-loading the cotton. Maybe at Bear Cut—as that's as good a port as any. Save us a trip—and make some money for you at the same time," he smiled—heading over to the small lifeboat on the side of the ship, taking it down, and jumping in.

"He knows these waters," Bunce shrugged—as he watched him row off. "Me, although I love the sea, I prefer a more solid craft under my feet in weather like this. What do you say, William, coffee in the dining room?"

"Best idea I've heard all day," William answered—following Bunce down the steps. "Can't wait to tell my dad he can forget the east coast. I, for one, have had enough. And I can't expect any of his prospective buyers will be willing to go through what we have the last few days. So if you're okay with it, let's just head up to the Miami River when the weather clears—so I can give my full report—and then head back to Key West."

"I think you'll find the Gulf a lot friendlier," Bunce laughed—pulling off his jacket and grabbing a mug off the shelf.

• 27 •

June 1832

"*B*rought someone I thought you might like to see," Fred Tresca called out—running up the steps to William Hackley's open front door.

"Who's that?" William asked, turning from his desk to his visitor.

"Just your father!" a well-dressed, rotund man announced—removing his hat and running his fingers through his thinning hair as he approached the desk.

"Dad! I had no idea you would be in today! Actually, I thought I might receive word from Robert with today's mail delivery about your visit at Hillsborough Bay."

"Got things set up pretty quickly up there. Actually, Robert was only waiting for me before moving forward with the land sales before heading back to Tallahassee. With the Seminole situation so tenuous between Fort Brooke and Fort King, I expect he's right to move on—as long as the new residents don't sense a panic.

"Now, thanks to Tresca, who was heading down this way, I made the trip in record time. We're all anxious to start this development over on Sanybel before the weather turns against us. Enough delays—on both areas of the coast."

"But, Dad, where's your luggage?"

"Mr. Tresca was kind enough to wheel it over here for me with his mail cart," Richard Hackley answered. "Hot as Hades out there, son. Couldn't expect me to carry it!"

"If it's okay, I'll bring it right up. Got several important correspondences to deliver—before sunset. Mr. Hackley, be sure William puts down his papers and gets you over to the dock. Can't be a real conch without a sunset under your belt—as well as a mug of Cuban ale!" he answered—disappearing down the front stairs.

"Dad, I would have met you at the dock had I known you were arriving."

"Wanted to see this area you love so much anyway. Amazing town you have here."

"City, Dad. Got incorporated about the time I got here. Not quite up to New York specifications, but it's all I need. You can't imagine the work all these salvage cases have brought. But enough of the law business. Why not come outside where it's cooler, and tell me your plans now that you're here. Who is it we're going to be working with to set up your new settlement on the coastal islands?" he asked as he led his father to the front porch—nodding to Tresca as he took his father's valise from him and set it inside the door.

"I've actually arranged to meet with your local marshal, P. B. Prior, and Colonel George Murray, whom I think you know as well," Richard answered—settling in the wooden rocker. "Murray will be representing the land company for us."

"Dad, are you sure you have checked out this company you're dealing with? This is a very small town, and I need to tell you, there have been several real estate cases I've been involved in recently. Several plaintiffs have accused Murray of reneging on property sales both here in Key West and in Cape Florida."

"Any proof of that?" Richard asked—settling back in his chair.

"Jury seemed to think so," William nodded—leaning forward to assess his father's expression.

"Two sides to every story," Richard responded. "At any rate, I've made the property transfer, and Murray's the local representative we have to deal with."

"We, Dad? You forget I live down here and will have to be responsible long after you are back in your New York manor."

"Easy, son. The Florida Peninsula Land Company owns most of the land title—so whatever the result, we are just setting up the development, and any fallback will be their problem.

"Now, I understood you were setting up a ship and crew to take you to look at the various properties up the coast. Pretty areas—as Tresca pointed them all out to me on our way down. But too much time has passed since I sold the property. With the new meeting

President Jackson called at Payne's Landing last month—when he forced the Seminole leaders to sign a new treaty—the word on base is that they're likely to react once the news reaches the various settlements. All the more reason to start a community and get these anxious northerners buying at Hillsborough and down here—before the news is commonplace or there's some sort of uprising."

"I need to tell you I don't approve of either trying to hoodwink settlers—or of leaving them high and dry with a rotten real estate deal. I've worked hard to build my reputation down here, and I'm not sure I want to rub elbows with any irresponsible representative from the Florida Land Company.

"At any rate, though, I did as you said and contracted with my pal, William Bunce, who owns the *Associate,* to take us to look over the various sites. He's got a five-man crew, and he owns a rancho up the coast near Robert's, so there's no one more experienced to help us ascertain the properties. As soon as I finish the case I'm arguing this week, he's ready to take us over. As it's now summer, we've both got the next three months free. I'm glad to go for you, Dad, but I need to warn you I won't put my name on anything I judge to be fraudulent!"

"Oh, come on, son, I'd never have gotten anywhere if I hadn't taken a few chances in life. Suppose I had told Alagon to peddle his tamales elsewhere!"

"Happy to be away from court for a while?" Bunce asked as he and William stood on the deck of his *Associate* to watch the Key West harbor disappear behind them.

"Mixed feelings—between you and me," William answered, shaking his head. "I have a very comfortable home on the island, and I've built a pretty substantial and honest practice in town. I'm not sure I relish spending the next three months trying to wrest a settlement out of one of those mangrove- and alligator-infested morasses up the coast—nor do I want to jeopardize my reputation by entering into any shady deals—and I'm not sure about this one. But my dad is so insistent.

"There's no way at his age he could withstand the summer down here, and Robert is fully settled in Tallahassee now. He took over a land auction business up there and seems to be doing quite well selling property to all the new settlers. I think auctioneering is in his blood. I still remember as a kid that he could talk me into anything," he laughed.

"It's imperative, though, that one of us survey the area on this end of the territory. I just couldn't let Dad down."

"Guess I should be glad my family is dirt poor," Bunce laughed. "Never thought to be happy about that before. But on another note, what is your take on our companions? I'm familiar with Prior. He's got a good reputation as marshal, but what about Murray? I've heard his name mentioned in a few questionable deals down in Cape Florida . . ."

"Guess that will remain to be seen. I—for one—intend to be sure whatever settlement we decide on will be handled properly and legally for any buyers."

"How long until we get to Charlotte Harbor?" Prior asked coming up on deck. "I think that was to be our first stop—right?"

"Weather's looking good," Bunce answered. "Shouldn't be too long a trip. Question will be how close we can get to the coast this time of year. Summer's been dry so far, so the bay may be pretty shallow. Many a smaller ship has been beached up our coast."

"Costing enough, Bunce. Better make sure we don't run aground," Murray barked as he emerged behind Prior.

"Got a pretty good five-man crew who are used to the conditions down here," Bunce answered—shaking off the slight. "Why not just sit back and enjoy the trip. You'll be swapping my cleared deck for trekking through those cursed mangroves soon enough!"

"Looks like we have a dolphin escort," William called—attempting to diffuse the atmosphere as he leaned over the deck to watch several playful dolphins jumping beside the ship.

"Hey, Bunce, we're wasting a lot of time out here," Murray called—stepping out on deck as the crew pulled anchor and directed the ship southward from the Caloosahatchee. "We wanted to be finished surveying and have the land ready to settle by September. At your direction now, we've looked at all the islands from Charlotte Harbor south. I know the rancho owners have cleared a lot of the land and have made a go of their businesses out here, but I'm not sure any of the places we've explored so far have enough dry land to make our venture profitable. The water supply is also questionable—as the water table is so high getting fresh water for an entire community will be suspect. Do you think Sanybel will be any better, or are we wasting our time there as well? I don't mind telling you I have to make a report to the owners of the

Florida Peninsula Land Company when we get back to Key West, and I'm not accustomed to reneging on a deal."

"Sanybel was my choice from the beginning," Bunce announced noncommittally, giving a signal to dismiss his men and crossing to the starboard side as the island slipped behind them. "I told Richard Hackley that from the beginning, and I think he advised both you and Prior—but the two of you wanted to check out all the barrier islands up here—which we have done at your direction.

"We should be able to anchor at Sanybel tonight—if you still want to check it out. The weather is perfect, and my crew thinks the harbor looked deep enough when we passed a few days ago."

"Time to check out Sanybel," William announced—stepping out on deck. "As I remember, Bunce, it was your choice from the beginning—although I remember my brother's assessment of the island when he passed there a few years ago."

"Not much has changed in the meantime," Bunce laughed. "You may be of your brother's same mind once you try blazing a trail from the east side of the island where we will need to anchor! At any rate, we should be there by sunset. That will leave us a whole day tomorrow to explore. Once you find a place you want to pursue, my men have equipment to build you some palmetto houses to settle in—so you won't have to come back and forth to the ship."

"Good Lord, I think Robert underestimated the jungle out here!" William called—swatting at the many mosquitoes flying around his face as the canoe approached a tiny beach hidden within the mangrove forest on the shore.

"Summer's the worst time," Bunce laughed—swatting at a buzzing insect circling his forehead. "Told your father that, if you remember, but he was insistent. As were his cohorts," Bunce replied—motioning to the following canoe carrying Murray and Prior.

"I'm not sure Dad had much choice once he contracted with them. Although news travels slowly down here, the reports of recent Seminole activities in Florida have still managed to reach New York—where the investors are worried potential purchasers will get cold feet once they realize the dangers they may face."

"Heard a lot more up at my new rancho on Tampa Bay before I left last month. Most of my employees there are worried about the new treaty

President Jackson forced the Seminoles to sign up at Payne's Landing. Word from Fort King is that the government will force the Seminoles to leave Florida—even though most of them have been here for years. Gonna be havoc I can tell you if that goes through. Many of the natives are already planning insurrections. Risky business settling anywhere in the territory right now. But who am I to warn those money-hungry tycoons?" Bunce shrugged as he beached the canoe, jumped out, and directed his crew member to bring Prior and Murray's canoe alongside.

Following Bunce, William alighted in the ankle-deep water and offered a hand to Prior, who was attempting to stand in his canoe. As Murray also shifted in his seat, William followed Bunce's quick action instead and grabbed the canoe's side to steady it and pull it up on the beach until the two men could step onto the soft sand.

"Good God, Bunce, is this the best landing spot you could find?" Murray yelled—brushing sand from his trousers and swatting at the mosquitoes attacking his face at the same time. I can't imagine our New York purchasers submitting to this greeting at their new homestead!"

"Harbor's best out here in the sound," Bunce shrugged. "I promise you'll be pleasantly surprised once you get to the Gulf side, though."

"Can't be soon enough," Prior added. "Is there a path, or do we have to hack our way through these dense mangroves?"

"Not far," Bunce nodded—motioning the men to follow him down the beach—while signaling his crewman back to the ship to bring the rest of his crew. "Just keep a lookout for alligators. They love this side of the island!"

"Now, that's more like it!" Murray called as the foursome at last emerged from the swampy, east side of the island and viewed the flat, grassy, central plain dotted with cabbage palms. "Already cleared and ready for development. And look at that view! What a selling point for new residents with that view of the Gulf! Why didn't you bring us here first, Bunce?"

"Since I value my *Associate*, I take pains to keep it afloat," Bunce replied. "Too shallow on the west side over here—although many of the Cuban ranchos seem to have had no trouble beaching their smaller craft on this side. Closer to the travel lanes to Cuba. They're the ones who cleared the land—years ago—but most of them have long since vanished after the U.S. took possession of Sanybel and the islands over here."

"So it's ours for the taking," Prior remarked heading to the top of the slight rise, "Murray, what do you think about a large hotel—just at the crest of this rise? Although we're looking for permanent settlers, can't overlook the potential buyers who will be coming—as well as those looking for a tropical vacation."

"Our intent is to draw settlers—not vacationers," Murray snorted—while pacing off steps to the distant beach. "Think we can get about fifty lots on this part of the island, which we'll make the town center . . ."

"Hold on," Bunce interrupted. "Are you allowing for tidal actions and—heaven forbid—storm surges that can swamp the island? If you want my opinion, you'll need to portion off lots on the eastern side—over here," he cautioned—walking back toward the area from which they had emerged. "I still think you can get fifty or more lots back here. Then, there's also the option of granting additional land on the mainland side for farms. The ranchos have existed like that for years."

"You've got a point, Bunce," William added. "In my short time in Key West, I've heard too many tales of the islands on Florida's east side being inundated in storms. Although the Gulf side is generally more tranquil, we don't want to sell flood-prone land."

"Time for consideration tomorrow," Bunce announced—looking back as his five crew members approached carrying stacks of wood and large piles of palmetto fronds they had cut on their way across the island. "My advice is that we use this area on the crest for some temporary structures where potential buyers can bed down for the night—without having to head back to the ship—as we will need to do before dark. My men can begin work tomorrow on the five palmetto houses we had planned up here on the rise."

• 28 •

January 1833

"*R*ather chilly for a Florida vacation," Bunce laughed—pulling the hood of his jacket over his mass of red curls as he watched William heading up the plank to his *Associate*. You'll be happy to know that—as cool as it has become, though—the alligators on Sanybel will be hibernating."

"Thank God for that," William called as he stepped onto the deck and held out his hand to help Marshal Prior, who was following him, aboard.

"What's the weather prediction, though, Bunce?" Prior asked looking at the dark clouds hovering above the Gulf.

"Seems to be a cold front on the way," Bunce answered, shaking his head. "Still sure you want to head on up right now?"

"Looks questionable, doesn't it?" Prior answered hesitantly. "All those investors from New York are on a tight shoestring, though—and they'll have much worse problems with winter storms up the Atlantic on their way home."

"Got Dr. Strobel and the other investors squared away on the *Olynthus*," Murray called—running up the plank and dropping his valise on the deck. "Looks like a squall approaching, Bunce, so let's get this ship underway."

"We were just discussing whether or not it's wise to set out right now," William said—gesturing at the approaching clouds.

"Got no choice. You know that, Hackley," Murray yelled. "Your father and the Land Company executives are looking to get these sales underway before the Fort Gibson Treaty takes place next month. Lord knows how the Seminoles will react when they realize they will be given three years before being forced to move from the territory. Once that news reaches New York, no one will want to take a chance on buying land in Florida in the next three years—with the potential for Seminole uprisings."

"Do you see any problem in docking at Sanybel?" William asked Bunce—as he watched him untying the ropes and signaling to a sister schooner tied up at the next pier.

"Been sailing my *Associate* up and down this coast for years, so I see no problem with it. Not sure about the *Olynthus*, however. Bigger ship than mine, but it was the only additional craft I could find right now—when Dr. Strobel returned from New York and told me he had joined the Florida Land Company and had brought all the new investors down for a Florida visit. May see more than they want to if their ship gets marooned!" he shrugged—signaling to the captain.

"Weather seems to be getting worse," William yelled—pulling himself along the starboard railing to find Bunce, who was holding on to the main mast and trying to see through the heavy sheets of rain pummeling the ship.

"Have to hope we can get to Sanybel before dark. Harbor's difficult enough in daylight. Don't want to chance it in this gale. With the tidal surge, it would be easy to run aground before we get close enough to drop anchor."

"Foolhardy trip all the way," William yelled over the whistling wind. "Unbelievable the things my father asks of me—out here at the mercy of the elements when I could be holed up safe in my office or bedroom back at Key West! Makes me wonder if all those investors over there on the *Olynthus* are having the same thoughts. A safe haven—even in a snowstorm—seems preferable at the moment."

"Wonder how many will still purchase lots," Bunce chuckled. "Not sure if we even get to land, they will be any too happy with only our palmetto shelters to keep out the storm."

"Land ho!" suddenly burst from one of the crew stationed at the front of the ship.

"Think it's Sanybel?" William asked.

"Can't tell until I can see the shoreline," Bunce called back grappling his way across deck to the port railing and shielding his eyes to look ahead. "Made it," he sighed. "Gonna drop anchor out here, though. Surf's too choppy to chance running aground if we get any closer."

"What about the *Olynthus?*" William called. "Can you see her?"

"In this storm, I'm lucky to see the bow of my own ship! We'll just have to hope her captain finds his way here as well. He's traveled this route often enough, so we'll have to leave him to it for now. I suggest we go find some dinner below deck and bed down on board for tonight. Tomorrow is soon enough to venture on land."

Early morning brought an eerie dawn—with swirling red clouds behind the ship to the east reflecting in the churning sound, which still imperiled the ship as it rode precariously at anchor. Pulling his hood more firmly over his head and shielding his eyes, Bunce opened the hatch and ventured on deck—to a desperate knocking and yelling beneath him. Carefully making his way to the port side of the ship, he was surprised to see two crew members from the *Olynthus* trying to keep a small canoe afloat—while screaming into the wind. "*Olynthus* ran aground last night," one man yelled. "Strobel says since the rain has stopped for now, you need to rescue the passengers and get them to land—as they're none too happy!"

"Not sure they'll be any happier on Sanybel after the night we just had," Bunce called down—trying to subdue a chuckle. "Tell you what. I'm going to get my passengers ashore first and then head off to find your sloop. How far away is it?" he asked—shielding his eyes and trying to see behind the *Associate*—to the south.

"Down south in the cut," the other man answered. "Not too far, but until the tide shifts, we can't make it off the sandbar. We can take four at a time, but with all those landlubbers, that's all we can hope to get ashore. Sure could use some help," he called—pushing the canoe away from the ship with an oar as the men headed back south.

"Couldn't have had a more unfriendly welcome to Sanybel," William called to Prior as the two made their way up the beach from the mangrove forest—through the piles of washed-up seaweed—littered with dead fish.

"You and I warned against the trip," Prior answered swatting at his face and the many swarming mosquitoes that were attacking both men. "Not sure they'll feel any more welcome once they get over here.

Probably a done deal before we even get to the settlement. But Murray and Strobel were so all-fired anxious to get these investors over here before any Seminole skirmishes. Makes me wonder about my connection in the company, I'll tell you."

"My thoughts are about making them sleep in those five huts Bunce had put up out there on the rise—especially if the rain comes back in," William added—pointing to the west with its ominous black clouds still gathering.

"Not sure the palmetto roofs are waterproof either," Prior added with a smile. "Not the first-class accommodations they are used to in New York."

"Especially if the tide shifts and floods those shell floors! Seeing their faces will be worth the trip."

"My God! Where in heck are you leading us?" one of the investors yelled—attempting to catch up to William and Prior—while tripping over the many submerged mangrove roots at the water's edge. "Where's this beautiful paradise we're investing in?"

"Be patient. I swear it will all be worth it once you see the Gulf from the crest of the development," Dr. Strobel called—catching up to him. "Can't believe the number of birds and other wildlife out there on the prairie. Brought my friend John James Audubon over here several times. Just wait until you catch sight of the roseate spoonbill he's been researching.

"Thinking of setting up my own sanitarium on the rise overlooking the ocean. Might build a hotel there as well. Can't think of a better place for folks to recover."

"Right now, Fifth Avenue seems a better site—for my money," the investor spat out—slapping at the incessant swarm of mosquitoes.

"Raging winter storm, stranded ship, swarming mosquitoes, flooded huts," William chuckled—shaking his head as he and Bunce dropped their luggage beside the table at Key West's small outdoor café, motioned for the waitress, and took their seats facing the spectacular winter sunset.

"Can't believe the Florida Land Company actually managed to sell all the lots over there—despite the investors' inauspicious introduction!" Bunce laughed as well. "Just goes to show what fools money can make of even the most careful of men. With the hurricanes I've heard of both up and down the coast, good luck on having anything left of the development by next fall!"

"Murray says they're going forward with plans to incorporate two towns on the island: Sanybel on the east, where they've located the town center, and Murray—named for him, of course—over on the west side. Now that we're back in Key West, he's going to look at purchasing cattle and setting up the farms on the mainland—as originally promised. Wants me to write Dad and have him arrange transport down here.

"The only good thing at least is that Murray and the Land Company are now in control of Sanybel."

"So no more trips to the promised land?" Bunce laughed.

"Made my choice," William answered, shaking his head. "To Key West," he answered—lifting the mug the waitress had just set down beside him.

"Great town," Bunce nodded—with a salute to the sunset, "but I've made my choice as well—with my new fishing rancho up at the base of Hillsborough Bay. Welcome mat is out if you come up my way."

"And you're always welcome back in Key West—if things get too hectic up near Fort Brooke," William countered—shaking his head. "Just glad Robert saw the light early and moved on to Tallahassee— where it seems to be quiet for the moment."

"I'm not sure anywhere in Florida will stay quiet for long—once the Seminoles realize that the treaty they're heading to Fort Gibson to sign next month will mean they will be forced to move west—like it or not. It all remains to be seen!"

· 29 ·

November 1834

$\mathcal{P}$ulling his coat more tightly about him before securing his freezing hands in his deep pockets, Fred Tresca stepped on deck as his beloved *Margaret Ann*, rounded the point at the end of Hillsborough Bay, and approached the southern mangrove-covered peninsula. "Far cry from Key West," he muttered to himself. "Whatever possessed William Bunce to leave the tropics and move up here?"

The extensive rancho Bunce had bought last year, however, had proven to be quite prosperous his friend had told him and had helped to make up for the financial loss he had incurred while living in Key West. Now, it seemed Bunce had come into his own once again—after having been appointed "justice of the peace" in the new Hillsborough County. Laughing at the thought of the burly, red-headed Irishman presiding over the wedding of an unsuspecting young couple, Tresca found himself looking forward to reconnecting with the genial host of the resurrected Cuban rancho he had visited on his trip north.

Looking forward to seeing an old friend—as well as carrying on a conversation in English, Bunce had issued a long-standing invitation to visit his rancho any time Tresca was in the area on his various jaunts up or down the coast for the U.S. military and had promised him a bed for the night.

Granted, Bunce had erected a house for himself with actual plank floors and paneled doors—similar to the one he had fashioned in Key West—which he had shown off with great gusto on Tresca's last visit. The building was partitioned off for a shop on one side—with sleeping quarters on the other. Remembering the apartment was planned for only one occupant, however, Tresca had to laugh as he remembered the several thatched cottages that served as domiciles for workers and visitors on Bunce's Manatee rancho. A fresh fish dinner he would accept—as well as several goblets of the superb Claret Bunce seemed to bring back on his *Enterprise* after each trip to Havana. The bunk below him on his beloved *Margaret Ann*, however, would serve most nicely for the night—thank you! As daylight was limited this time of year as well, sleeping on board would allow him to get under sail much earlier than if he were on the mainland.

"Had enough winter already?" Bunce yelled—waving as he caught sight of the slim Frenchman huddled in his hooded coat as he tied up at the wharf.

"Just reminds me why I jumped ship all those many years ago in Key West," Tresca yelled back jumping to the dock to accept the welcoming handshake of his friend. "And don't think I don't remember to whom I owe my livelihood in this territory! If you hadn't given me a job in your store down there . . . I'd probably be like so many of those conchs fishing from the docks and peddling my wares."

"But look where it's gotten you," Bunce laughed—leading the way up the dock. "New ship and all! Looks like the good Lord has done all right for both of us. But remember if you ever want another job with me, I could use a captain to run trips from my new Sanybel rancho to Cuba. I'd be willing to work a deal with someone as capable as you."

"Tell me, though, are you still running shipments back and forth to Cuba? We heard in Key West about the cholera epidemic in Havana. Seems most of the southern ranchos have suspended trips until it's under control."

"My men are careful—loading and unloading only from shipboard. I've prohibited them from spending time in port. So far, we're doing all right. I think only Caldez and I are running at the moment, though—more business for us, I say! So I can always use another ship, amigo!"

"I may seriously be interested by the new year," Tresca answered, shaking his head. "The Florida Straits may have been dangerous in the piracy era, but I suspect the new Seminole problem may prove even more dangerous up this side of the territory."

"Why, what have you heard?" Bunce asked—pushing open the door of the small enclosure at the end of the dock and ushering Tresca inside. "Got a new shipment of Claret inside if it's a long tale!"

"How large is your goblet?"

"Wait—you're serious, aren't you?"

"Just got back from Fort Brooke, and I can tell you, events are about to explode over by Fort King."

"They've just reopened that base, haven't they?"

"And are in the process of resupplying troops for both bases," Tresca nodded. "As a matter of fact, I'm on the way back to Key West now to bring in more troops for Fort Brooke and then will be heading on to Pensacola to secure additional men from Barrancas."

"My Lord, what's going on?" Bunce asked—setting a full goblet of red wine in front of his friend and sitting opposite him with an identical glass. "I thought the chiefs had all signed the treaty at Payne's Landing and then approved moving west to the Creek territory with the treaty at Fort Gibson. Don't tell me they've changed their minds now."

"My only job was to deliver the mail and some supplies Clinch had ordered from the base at Pensacola. As I gathered the packages to take them to Clinch at headquarters, a fairly large contingency on horseback came roaring onto the base—yelling for Clinch."

"Were they coming from Fort King?" Bunce asked.

"The new Indian agent, Wiley Thompson, was leading the delegation," Tresca nodded. "Quite a powerful figure, I will tell you—even when worn out from five days of travel. Don't think I'd want to be on Thompson's enemy list. On the other hand, if he comes across as strong as he did with Clinch, I'm afraid he's likely to turn even the most agreeable Seminole into an opponent.

"While I was sitting there at the base office waiting for Clinch to check over my supply list, Thompson ran in and erupted saying the Indians all swore they had never signed the Gibson treaty and would not agree to move. He said he had been proven right when he proposed that the Seminoles would not take kindly to Jackson's order that they be removed to the west by the end of next year.

"Although Thompson had been on friendly terms earlier with that new fellow, Osceola, from the Red Stick Creeks, it seems he confronted Thompson on the spot—declaring, as Thompson said, 'This is our land. We do not need an Indian agent.' Seems he ended by threatening to fight 'until the last drop of our blood moistens the earth,'" Tresca concluded—shaking his head.

"Thompson ended by telling Clinch that he had heard from several sources that the Seminoles have been using the annuities our government has given them to buy both powder and lead—so he has no doubt they are preparing for war if Jackson persists with trying to remove them."

"So what's next? I mean, most of my workers out here—as well as on Sanybel—are considered natives by our government, although they don't have an allegiance to the Seminoles—nor have any of them ever been in the center of the state. If there's a renewed conflict, though, is Thompson going to order them to move west as well?"

"I'm sure I can't pretend to know what will happen next. My only job is with the U.S. Army to bring the recruits to Brooke as soon as possible—where they will eventually be stationed at King to protect against any future uprisings. Not going to be easy, I can tell you, convincing all those men to not only head into the illnesses that have been reported at King but also to possibly be scalped by a group of uncontrolled Seminoles!"

"I'd planned a winter trip back to Sanybel and Key West," Bunce answered, shaking his head. "At dinner, I'd like to have you tell my associate, Fielding Browne, what you have heard—as I will be leaving him in charge while I'm gone. Make sure to get him alone, though, as I surely don't want any of my workers to get wind of the unrest over by Fort King—or—heaven forbid—decide to take sides with the Seminoles!"

· 30 ·

May 1835

"*H*ey, bro," William Hackley called—looking around as he entered the large, cavernous wooden building that served as Tallahassee's auction house. "Quite an establishment you have here!"

Hurrying from his office when he heard the footsteps on the bare wooden floor and then rushing to embrace his brother, Robert Hackley answered proudly, "Pretty lucrative business as well. I'd offer you a tour—but what you see is pretty much the extent of the property," he offered—waving a hand to encompass the darkened interior. "Benches and podium are for conducting the weekly auctions. Items for sale are stored out back. But frankly, most of the trades are land deals. Keep me in the business as I continue to sell Dad's property in the Tampa and Sarazota areas.

"Come on in the office. Got a cup of coffee if you'd like it," he added—ushering his brother into his large, open office lined with file cabinets. Pulling a chair up to the long mahogany desk, he pushed aside the large stack of papers and offered William a seat as he poured two mugs of coffee from the nearby carafe. "Pretty long trip from Key West. What brings you up here? Didn't know you were coming," he continued—setting the mugs down and taking his own seat.

"Hitched a ride with Fred Tresca who was heading to Barrancas to bring more troops to Fort Brooke. Set me down at St. Marks when he put in for the afternoon. I'll meet up with him on his way back to Fort Brooke and Key West. Got a room at the hotel until his return.

"Actually, on Dad's last trip to Key West to check on the Florida Peninsula Land Company sales at Sanybel, he asked me to check with you on the status of our case claiming possession of his property. I thought a trip up to see my favorite sibling was preferable to just sending a letter and then waiting for Tresca to bring your answer back—whenever that might be. So what progress have you made?"

"Still in the courts," Robert answered, shaking his head. "Did get a statement from my old friend, Lorenzo—you remember the young West Point grad I brought down to Florida. At any rate, he swore in court that he had seen the copy of Dad's deed that I had with me on our arrival. And then—would you believe it—Colonel Brooke actually sent in a sworn statement from Fort Mackinac in the Michigan territory, where he's now stationed, testifying that my house and plantation were already standing when he and his troops arrived to start his Cantonment Brooke. Said he had no choice but to occupy it—as the area had already been designated as government property. Our final proof of ownership, though, actually came last August from Judge Augustus Steele himself when he swore that he knew that I had built a house and cultivated the land—before Brooke and his troops arrived."

"So it seems Dad is right to go ahead with lot sales in both the Tampa and Sanybel areas. Since we've now sold over fifty lots at Sanybel and have established two towns over there, as a lawyer, I don't mind telling you I've had many sleepless nights wondering if it's all legitimate."

"We have to hope our documentation is all we need and it will just take time to work its way through the courts. Since Fort Brooke has been pretty much closed down the last few years, I've had a lot of interest in the lots over there as well. Seems the settlers are actually setting up a town around the base."

"Isn't that what you wanted in the first place—a plantation home with lots of new settlers? I mean . . . what I want to know is whatever persuaded you to give up both your legal career and your Hillsborough property and move all the way over here? I thought you hated Tallahassee when you first came."

"A lot has changed in the last ten years," Robert laughed—"here as well as at Tampa Bay. Actually, while selling Dad's property was enticing at first, somehow, I really wanted to carve my own career. When I heard on a trip over here that the auction house was going up for sale, it seemed like the perfect opportunity to make something of myself—and to continue selling our land deals as the auctioneer. As the capital,

Tallahassee has become the focal point for new settlers looking to put down roots in Florida. If native uprisings stay quiet, I'll stand to make a killing as the area becomes populated."

"Guess you haven't heard the news," William interrupted—shaking his head.

"Being located on the main street, I'm usually one of the first to hear news here in the capital. So tell me—what have I missed?"

"When we stopped in St. Marks, the town was abuzz with news one of the captains had brought in and was heading up here to relay. Seems word had gotten to Washington that the Seminoles had been dragging their feet in moving from the reservation. So in March the Indian agent, Wiley Thompson, called the Seminole chiefs to Fort King to read a rather forceful message from President Jackson himself. The gist of it was—if I remember correctly—'Should you refuse to move, I have then directed the Commanding Officer to remove you by force!'"

"Quite a burden to put on both Thompson at King and Clinch at Brooke—especially as both bases have been operating at reduced staff for the last several years. No wonder Tresca has been sent for more troops."

"It seems that after reading Jackson's proclamation, Thompson went even further in ordering the various tribes that they must dispose of their cattle before moving—by the end of the year."

"Hope whatever action the Seminoles take stays over by Fort King—and stays out of national news," Robert sighed. "If northern prospects get wind of any uprisings, it will really hurt business—at both Brooke and Sanybel. I can only imagine Dad's reaction when you tell him the news."

"Oh, so it has to be me?" William laughed—downing his coffee. "I thought he liked you best!"

St. Marks was abuzz with activity when William arrived back to meet with Fred Tresca on his beloved *Margaret Ann*. Finding the captain alone on deck, William ran up the plank carrying his small valise. "Got here as fast as I could," he apologized. "Didn't want to keep you waiting."

"Just got into port," Tresca answered—greeting William with a pat on the back as he dropped his case on the deck. "Told the recruits to find lunch and meet me back here in an hour. Sadly, it may be the last liberty they are likely to get—if events play out the way they are looking. I waited around to find you. Up for a bowl of chowder down the pier? I've just heard lots of news in which you might be interested."

"You mean there's something worse than Jackson's warning?"

"Being a ship captain, I find that folks are all ready to share whatever news they have once they get into port. And I just heard plenty while I was watching for you. Come on, I'll take you to my favorite spot in St. Marks—my treat," Tresca answered—leading the way off the ship.

Waving to several shop keepers standing by their door at the noon hour—trying to entice the several sailors on the pier to buy a souvenir or two to take back home—Tresca eventually pushed open a swinging door and motioned William into a darkened bar—peopled by two disparate groups: the hardened seamen with their long, disheveled hair and beards in a variety of jackets and trousers, who contrasted greatly with the few army recruits with their fresh haircuts and starched blue uniforms. Stifling a laugh at the contrast, Tresca led William to a table where he was quickly approached by a young woman, who obviously recognized him.

"Your usual, Captain Tresca?" she asked.

"Marie, please tell your father his chowder rivals anything I ever had in France, and I—for one—should know," Fred Tresca smiled.

"And now," he continued—turning to William, "I've kept you in suspense long enough."

"And I'm all ears—after Jackson's ultimatum we heard when we docked."

"You know the chiefs asked for a month to consider Jackson's order."

"I can only imagine their answer—as I know what I would have said if told I had to leave my home within only nine months!"

"And you would be right. But apparently eight of the chiefs agreed to move west if Thompson would delay their departure to the end of the year."

"Did he agree?"

"Seems he was hoping to defuse the issue—at least until he got all the new recruits he's been waiting for," Tresca nodded.

"So we have a reprieve for the time being. My father and his partners will be relieved—as they are hoping to sell some new plots at

Sanybel by summer and certainly don't want potential buyers to fear a Seminole uprising,"

"But there's more," Tresca interrupted—shaking his head. "Just before you got here, I met a captain who was bringing a messenger from Fort King in to Tallahassee to see Governor Eaton. Seems after he made the agreement, Thompson got wind of some gun and ammunition purchases several of the Seminoles were making. Being worried about renewed skirmishes, he then forbade the sale of either to the Seminoles. That young brave, Osceola, we are hearing so much about took particular offense to the ban and proclaimed to Thompson that he would 'make the white man red with blood, blacken him in the sun and rain, and leave him for the buzzard to live upon his flesh!' as the courier reported."

"Wow!" William answered. "I can only imagine how that went over with Thompson."

"He's a pretty hotheaded man, I've heard. General Clinch has already had to intervene to prevent bloodshed with the chiefs' first refusal. At any rate, Osceola's statement was enough to send Thompson completely out of control, and he had Osceola arrested and locked up for the night at Fort King."

"And what was the outcome of that encounter?"

"In order to receive his release, Osceola apparently agreed to honor the Treaty of Payne's Landing and to bring in his followers. General Clinch, however, is—rightly—worried about reprisal, which is why he sent the courier over here from Brooke. As the weather heats up for the summer and their December deadline draws closer, Clinch is worried more of the Seminoles will react—especially counseled by Osceola—as no Seminole can ever forget an affront to his honor."

"My Lord, Tresca," William Hackley yelled—running into the cabin as the *Margaret Ann* rounded the turn from Hillsborough Bay and headed east toward Fort Brooke. "Looks like the whole west bank of the river is on fire!"

Setting the wheel, Tresca turned to the port side of the ship—where the sixteen recruits he had brought from Pensacola were anxiously watching as both smoke and flames leapt from the vegetation on shore and blackened branches from nearby oaks dropped with a sizzle into the bay. "That's Levi Coller's plantation," Tresca called. "He's one of my customers. I take hogs and cattle down to Key West for him several times a year. Has a very accommodating wife, who kindly feeds me when I'm over here, and a passel of really cute children. Wonder what started the fire and if the family has gotten out. As large as the fire seems to be, though, I don't think it's safe to try to go over there. Just hope we can make it across the bay ourselves," he called—reversing the wheel to head east.

"Seems to be a crowd on the wharf over at Brooke," William observed as they moved closer shielding his eyes and peering through the smoke, which now enveloped the ship's starboard side.

"Will need to guide us over there before visibility is totally gone," Tresca called. "Can you act as lookout as I try to pull into port over there? Heaven forbid one of those branches should hit my ship. Much as I love her, I'm still paying for dear *Margaret Ann* and can't afford to lose her!"

"Some of the men at the wharf are gesturing for us to pull in at the south dock—the one my brother built," William called—motioning to a small wooden pier jutting into the water several yards below the larger base establishment.

"Think it's safe?" Tresca asked.

"Fire seems to be contained on the west shore. Smoke makes it hard to see much, but I don't see any flames to the starboard."

"Then we don't have much choice," Tresca called. "Trying to steer back out of the river's mouth right now would be foolhardy— lots of shoals out there. And I'd have to come back at any rate to deposit my recruits. Have the men sit down on deck. It might be a hard landing."

As his *Margaret Ann* came in hard on the dock, Tresca set the wheel and ran to check for any damage before attaching to a piling. Finding none, he continued to set the other lines and extend the plank. Calling to the recruits to get their belongings and leave the ship, he turned to William. "Guess we'd better go find out what happened."

"Hope it hasn't damaged any of Dad's property over here," William called—waiting until the last recruit had left the ship before following Tresca up the beach to the main wharf—crowded with both settlers and base members. "Foolhardy of Robert to leave the area when Dad is counting on him to look after affairs at Brooke."

"I need to look for the Collers," Tresca called over his shoulder. "Sure hope they got out!"

"Captain Tresca! So glad to see you got your ship in. I was worried about you trying to navigate through that conflagration," Levi Coller called as the skinny man in soot-blackened overalls ran to take Tresca's hand.

"Not as glad as I am to see you are all right," Fred Tresca called. "And your wife and family?"

"All accounted for—thanks to Colonel Clinch and the men at the fort. Sorry, I won't have any stock to send back with you this trip, though—unless my customers prefer it 'precooked.'"

"But what caused the fire? I know you and your wife are always so careful in both your kitchen and blacksmith shop . . ."

"Cursed Seminoles," Coller hissed. "Seems at least there was one decent member of the tribe who overheard a plan to start a local warpath by burning us out—before attacking the fort. Think he was one I helped out a few years ago when he was injured out behind our property. At any rate, once he heard the plan that was to take place in three days, he left three sticks carefully arranged on our doorstep. Scared the wife when she saw him leaving, but I didn't know what it meant. Luckily, our older son had heard of the signal and filled us in. Fearing an attack on the base as well, he took the boat and went over to let Clinch know.

"As things have been heating up with Osceola fomenting discontent over near King, Clinch was worried as well and sent two soldiers by boat to help us move over to the base. With their help, we were able to move what we needed over here. The base has always been so good to us and has afforded us one of the abandoned homes nearby for as long as we need it.

"At any rate, just as we got across the bay, we saw the first flames appear behind the distant oaks—in the area by our house. Luckily, we were far enough away to be safe, but I'm afraid Nancy is disconsolate at the loss of everything we had worked for all these years."

"Understandable," Tresca offered. "What do you think you will do now?"

"Too soon to tell. Obviously, we can't rebuild on the blackened land—and with the extent of the fire we can see from here, I expect it's covered all of our property. I guess time will tell. We could always go back to the St. John's area where we started and where Nancy has family. Sadly, however, I'm not sure anywhere in Florida is safe right now. I expect—although we are the first—we certainly won't be the last to reap the Seminoles' wrath. Mark my words: I believe this is just the beginning of a sad tale of our settlers' futile attempt to coexist."

• 31 •

October 1835

"Good Lord, I for one will be so glad to leave this past fall to the history books," William Hackley announced as he pulled up a chair at the small outdoor cafe near the Key West dock and threw his hat onto the table. Shielding his eyes against the brilliant glow of the bright orange sunset, he continued. "Never thought I'd see a clear sunset again—or you two vagabonds as well! So glad to see you and Bunce both back in Key West for the moment. Being the only landlubber of our trio, I miss you when you're at sea. So thankful you're both safe."

"I'm just thankful I was able to save my *Margaret Ann*," Fred Tresca offered—pouring his friend a fresh mug from the pitcher on the table. "She never would have made it through the September hurricane if she'd been at dock down here. Thank God I was up at Brooke—although the base did suffer a lot of damage when the storm came into the bay."

"Couldn't have been as bad as when it roared through here. As you can see, we're still picking up the pieces," William added—motioning toward the nearby streets that extended from the waterfront—where huge piles of debris were still visible. "And you won't believe Sanybel! Haven't even calculated Dad's company's losses over there! Now, he wants me to handle all the lawsuits coming from the local settlers claiming damages to both their homes and the civic structures that were lost when that tidal wave swept through!"

"Assessing damages does no good," William Bunce called—turning a chair backward and hanging his hat from the side rung as he took a seat. "Heard something at the dock about the hurricane being caused by the current appearance of Halley's Comet. But come on. I've learned from past experience that it is what it is. Doesn't help to go placing blame. Wiped out all my fish tanks at my Manatee rancho. Darn fish and manatees all escaped when the walls collapsed and let them swim back to sea. To top it off, one of my best schooners was wrecked on the way back from Havana, and another was sunk at my dock. Gonna have to start over up there. Came down here to see about hiring another captain and ship. Sorry you're not available, Tresca. I could make it worth your while—once I catch enough fish to make a renewed run to Cuba profitable."

"With all the military activity up at Brooke—and the recent storm damage—I don't think I'll have any time for the foreseeable future," Tresca answered—shaking his head.

"But what happened at Brooke?" William asked. "I hadn't heard that the storm traveled that far up the coast. How extensive was the damage up there? Expect with Robert in Tallahassee Dad will want to send me back up to Brooke to assess losses there."

"Nearly destroyed the wharf, I can tell you that," Tresca answered. "Huge wave just swept the oak flooring your brother and his men had put up right out into the river—where it washed down into the bay. Luckily, I was tied up at the smaller dock, which was lower in the water and managed to withstand the waves until the winds had died down. Rather puts Brooke at a disadvantage right now, though, as Clinch is still calling for recruits after all the recent incidents—and only the smaller ships can now dock up there."

"So what else have we missed down here?" William asked. "With no recent shipping or mail delivery since the storm, the news has been nil."

"Just before I left Manatee, I heard of that confrontation over at Hickory Sink near Gainesville," Bunce replied. "What did you hear about that?"

"Happened in June," Tresca nodded. "Seems a group of young settlers were searching for lost cattle when they came upon a group of Indians sitting around a campfire roasting what appeared to be one of their cows. Things escalated—as you can imagine—and the result was a skirmish with three of the cattlemen injured, one Seminole dead, and another injured.

"Word at Brooke was that the Seminoles complained to Thompson about the attack and the loss of their comrade. Sadly, they thought he had dismissed their complaint, so they were waiting for a chance to settle the score."

"So have there been any more episodes?" William asked. "I'll admit I hadn't heard of that—or anything else for that matter since the storm."

"Worst reprisal was just before the storm hit—sometime in August," said Tresca. "Clinch had sent a courier, Private Kinsey Dalton, to carry the mail from Fort Brooke to Fort King. Nice fellow—young man who had recently arrived on base. I met him when I delivered several packets from Pensacola addressed to Fort King. At any rate, he was all alone on that godforsaken swampy road when a group of Seminoles attacked and killed him. Took several days to find his body.

"Suspicion is on Osceola—or his sidekick Harry from the Red Stick Creeks over at the Peace River Minatti settlement, but neither Thompson nor Clinch have formally charged either of them as yet—waiting for more information. Their chief, Holato Micco, however, has been taking every chance to try to unite all the tribes in resistance to Jackson's evacuation orders."

"Although the storm and aftermath have consumed all our activities on this coast," Bunce answered—shaking his head, "I assume the reservation area down by Fort King has been pretty much spared and it's been business as usual with the tribes' unrest. I know my crew out at Manatee had heard of several attempts to waylay settlers. They've been hoping things will settle down and the various tribes will just adhere to their promise to move west. If things stay peaceful, they're hoping the rancho workers will be able to avoid the orders. You know most of their families have been here since Spain was in control—and they actually have no contacts with the Creeks or Seminoles—nor do they want to move."

"Not sure that holds any water with Thompson—or Jackson for that matter," Tresca answered, shaking his head. "The order I heard was 'all Indians.' All I can tell you from what I've been hearing is that Dalton's murder has alarmed all the settlers from Brooke to King. Word at Brooke is that local towns are already organizing armed militia groups to confront any uprisings. I'm afraid it won't take much of a spark to set off a confrontation from which we can't back down."

"So what do you think will be next—anything likely out my way?" Bunce asked—pouring another mug from the pitcher. "On my way down here, I stopped at Antonio Pacheco's rancho on Sarazota Bay—where he told me that several months ago he had sent a petition to the Secretary of War asking him to reinforce the troops at Fort Brooke 'in order to keep the Indians in check' as he put it. He said the local tribes seemed to think the fishery families were part of the band seeking to drive them out. As the ranchos were isolated, they had become prey to the marauding bands that had been killing his cattle, scattering them in the forest or driving them off. Although I haven't had any recent incidents, I need to prepare my workers for any reprisals—as my rancho's pretty accessible from the Manatee River. It wouldn't take much to set the Indians on a raid or two out my way. Lord knows I've lost enough from the recent storm!"

"So Pacheco is the reason I've been ferrying troops from Key West and Barrancas since late summer," Tresca smiled. "Didn't know who set the ball rolling at Brooke! I've met Pacheco. Forceful fellow whose word wields a lot of clout with Clinch. Guess his petition actually got some attention—although more troops at distant Fort Brooke does little to manage things in the rest of the territory. Biggest problem is likely to be centered at Fort King—where the Indian agency is located, and the next big milestone is December 1—as I see it," Tresca answered, shaking his head.

"What's happening then?" William asked. "I'll need to know if Dad wants me to head up to Brooke to check on the hurricane damage. Don't want to enter a hornet's nest!"

"That's the final date Thompson has given the various chiefs for selling their cattle before they move west. Then, according to the Treaty of Payne's Landing, the tribes are all supposed to gather outside of Fort Brooke to begin their relocation west by the first of January. On my last trip, I heard that Clinch is making preparation for over five hundred Indians to camp outside Brooke until they can be moved by ship to New Orleans and then on to the new reservation—west of the Mississippi.

"Word is, though, that Holato Micco and Osceola have told the tribes to resist Thompson's order, to not sell their cattle, and to refuse to move west. Apparently, many of the Seminoles are holding to the original twenty-year date for their migration that was agreed on at Payne's Landing as 1843. I feel sorry for Thompson, whose orders are coming from Washington and leave him no recourse," Tresca continued—as a wild chorus of whoops filled the air behind him. Turning at the sound, he stopped to watch in awe as the large, fiery globe disappeared into the Gulf.

"Never gets old, does it?" William smiled. "Did you see the 'green flash'? Not often we can see it—even out here. Means good luck I've heard. Hopefully, it's a new beginning for our storm-torn city."

"We can only hope," Bunce answered—shaking his head.

"Not sure any hope we might have will hold water up there," Tresca replied—gesturing to the northern coast. "As things stand, I can tell you that there's a lot of fear at Brooke that Osceola could not only enact a reprisal against Thompson and the Indian agency—but against any chief and his tribe if they follow the orders. Green flash—or not—could be a bloodbath before the end of the year!"

· *32* ·

December 14–15, 1835

*A*fter the clamor of the waterfront—where horns, bells, shouts, and pounding waves all vied for attention from both newly arrived and departing seamen—the halls of the army headquarters seemed ghostly quiet as Fred Tresca removed his rain-soaked jacket, let the door close quietly behind him, and headed down the whitewashed halls to the commander's office. The plaque on the door of the last room read Major Francis L. Dade.

Having known Dade many years ago when—while stationed at Fort Brooke—Dade had led two successful raids to quell Seminole uprisings, Tresca was nonetheless aware that Osceola had not forgotten either episode and had sworn revenge on the major. Tresca had been relieved when Dade had been established last year as the army commander at Key West, which was removed by its island position from any Seminole activity. With his wife, Amanda, and young daughter, Fannie, in tow, the major had now become a well-known figure in the local area and participated in many of the local festivities.

It was with much trepidation that Tresca approached the door to deliver the missives he had had in his possession for the past three days—after receiving them on his mail route at Fort Brooke. The return addresses from General Roger Jones, the U.S. Army's adjutant general in Washington, and General Duncan Clinch, the army's head of Florida operations, could only spell renewed unrest—as well as a possible return to active service. Delivering either—and especially both—was a duty he wished he could have pawned off on a crew member. As important as they both seemed, however, entrusting them to someone else was not in the cards,

His heavy knock engendered a quick "Enter," as he found the major seated at his desk—highlighted by a sliver of the setting sun beneath a black cloud in the window behind him. The formidable, dark-bearded man was dressed in a full, dark blue uniform, which included a pair of knee-high leather boots—one of which projected from the side of the desk. While maintaining his stiff army posture, Dade smiled at Tresca in recognition and gestured for him to approach the desk. "I saw your *Margaret Ann* as you arrived, Tresca," he smiled, "and wondered if you would be bringing mail. Lots going on up the coast, I hear."

"Two letters I thought were important enough to bring in myself," Tresca nodded—handing the two envelopes to Dade.

"Limeade on the bookcase and a plate of cookies," Dade gestured. "Amanda keeps me supplied, but I keep telling her that now that I'm off the trails I can't afford to outgrow my uniforms. Got time for me to look at these? May need to send a reply. When do you head off again?"

"I'm going back to Brooke day after tomorrow—on the sixteenth, which should get me back here in time for Christmas. Happy to take you with me—if you need transport. I promised William Hackley a spot as well since his father wants a report on the recent incidents at Brooke. Seems just before I arrived on my last visit, the Indians had burned down the Sutler's store. Captain Saunders barely escaped with his life, I was told. Don't think William will be any too happy to hear that—since the area surrounding the base is part of the Hackley tract."

"I just recently returned from Pensacola. Quick trip, so I didn't take time to stop in Fort Brooke. Could have picked these up then and saved you the visit, but I'm glad I missed your news. As we left Pensacola, however, we heard of Osceola's murder of Chief Charley Emathla late last month—as Emathla was following Clinch's orders and had sold his cattle. Osceola had warned in the Seminole council that any Seminole who followed the order and sold his cattle would be signing his death sentence. In the report I heard, Osceola followed Emathla back to his village and killed him on the spot—scattering the money he had received from the cattle sale to prove the reason was not robbery!

"Wrong to misjudge Osceola in any way! Knowing the man, he never makes a threat he doesn't carry out. After our last two encounters, I wouldn't be surprised if his tomahawk has a notch reserved for me."

"So you're not anxious to head back on the trail, I assume."

"Not on your life! Key West suits me fine for the time being. Thanks for the transport offer, but I hope to settle in here for the winter. Activity on base keeps me busy enough—and it's safe for my family as well. Surely hope neither of these has another trip in store for me," he added—looking at the postmarks as he picked up his letter opener. "I've promised Amanda and Fannie a real Christmas this year—as we spent most of last year's holiday getting our home settled here."

"Well, the offer is still open after you read the letters," Tresca offered—taking a cookie from the plate and heading to the door. "I'll stop back tomorrow. I've got several more missives to deliver right now and really want a bowl of conch chowder and a good night's sleep—uninterrupted by the heavy seas out there."

Hurrying to the waterfront, Fred Tresca arrived just as the final shouts died down from the few assembled on the cold, rain-drenched dock. Hailing William Hackley, who was seated under an umbrella with a pitcher of ale, he waved a hand at the blood-red sunset remnant. "Sorry, tried to make it, but I had some letters for Major Dade to deliver. Too important to leave at the front desk."

"More going on at Brooke?" William asked. "Wait, don't tell me until I've had my second mug!" he added, picking up the cup and draining it. Exhaling at last, he continued, "Okay, what is it I need to know, and does it affect our planned outing in two days?"

"The Sutler's store was burned down just before I got there. Indians are getting bold—operating near the base."

"Oh, my God, Saunders's store is on our property! Can't remember what arrangement Robert had with him, but it's sure to cause havoc when I get there. Curses on my brother for moving up to Tallahassee and leaving the Hackley tract at Brooke for me. As if I don't have enough looking after the Sanybel development and the damage the hurricane caused there."

"May have another shipmate as well—as one of Dade's letters was from General Clinch. Dade said he'd promised to have Christmas here in Key West with his wife and daughter, but Osceola and the rest of the Seminoles don't celebrate Christmas—so it will probably only give them a new opportunity for an attack while the rest of us are celebrating. I promised to check back with Dade tomorrow to get either a letter—or a passenger."

"Hard to say whether family or professional requirements are harder to ignore. At least, though, I doubt Dad would court martial me if I refused to head to Brooke!"

"And—as the saying goes—the mail must go through, so I'm locked in as well. My motto is live one day at a time. And—at the moment—I just want to down a bowl of chowder and to find a bed that isn't rocking!"

After enjoying a full night's sleep, Fred Tresca settled into his usual seat at the café on the corner from his house—ready to order his favorite, eggs and bacon—as William Bunce entered the restaurant, waved, and headed to Tresca's table. "Surprised to find you in here," he called. "Lots of activity at the docks. Thought you might be part of it."

"No, I got in yesterday. Why, what's going on over there?"

"The *Motto* is tied up at the dock—with a full contingent of uniformed men waiting in line. Don't know where they are heading, but it's going to be a full crew."

"Oh, my God, I promised to meet with Dade this morning to see if he had any letters I needed to take north. Sit down, enjoy the coffee I just ordered, and I'll see you later. Need to make it over to the base. Although I offered him a ride when I leave tomorrow, Dade said he planned to stay in town for Christmas."

"Well, something has changed at the base," Bunce added—shaking his head as William rose, donned his hat, and headed for the door. "Nice of you to order me a pot," he called after the fleeing figure.

As Bunce had said, the dock was alive with activity—with the large naval ship *Motto* occupying the berth nearest to the base headquarters. Hurrying past the line of uniformed soldiers—each shouldering a valise—Tresca headed to headquarters, entered, and continued to the end of the hall. Dade's office door was ajar—with Dade, himself, in full uniform busily rifling through papers on his desk and shoving several papers and letters into a satchel.

"Glad I found you," Tresca called. "I promised to be back for any correspondence you needed me to take to Fort Brooke. Saw your men out there, but you said you were not leaving. Have things changed?"

"Letter from Clinch was bad news," Dade nodded—while continuing to shuffle through his in-box. "Looks like I'm heading up to Brooke anyway."

"Now? But I thought . . ."

"So did I," Dade sighed—looking over his shoulder as he opened his top drawer and removed another set of papers. "Seems the Seminoles don't observe our holidays, though, and things are heating up. Clinch has ordered me to embark immediately—leaving only one non-commissioned officer and three privates down here—as the island is safe from Indian attack at the moment.

"My first assignment is to visit the chief at Charlotte Harbor and give a warning to him to remain on his base there, although I'm not sure what good it will do when we won't have any men down here to respond if there is an incident near Sanybel. From there, we are to embark for Brooke immediately. Clinch is worried that since the removal date at Fort King is set for January 1, there might be increased resistance at the reservation. Right now, so many of the men from Fort King have been reassigned to the new stockade called Fort Drane—about twenty miles northwest of King—that there is only a meager force left at King.

"As a result, Clinch has ordered me to bring two companies to Brooke to march to King before the first of the year. On such short notice, I could dispatch only thirty-eight men at present, but I've left instructions for more to follow as soon as they can be assembled. Knowing the number of Osceola's men, it seems like a death trap—even when I can assemble the one hundred or so men I can produce!

"Since I hadn't seen you this morning, I was going to leave a message for you at the desk—as I think by leaving today, I will beat you to Brooke myself."

"I'm so sorry you have to leave. I don't have anyone to leave behind when I travel—and I like it that way, but I can understand your family's disappointment."

"Fannie's just four and is so excited about Christmas. We had planned to celebrate it as a family," Dade answered—shaking his head. "But maybe next year—once the Seminoles are resettled out west! I tell you; it can't come soon enough!

"Many days I wonder about my decision to join the U.S. Army. Despite all my years of service and the many campaigns in which I have participated, I still can't lose the 'Brevet Major' title, which has frozen my salary. The other letter I received yesterday was from General Roger Jones, whom I had written earlier in the year approving his plan to increase the pay of the army field officers. The army needs to make it worth a recruit's while to plan for a lifetime of commitment—not penalize him for staying in the service.

"I don't think any of us realize when we enlist that we are giving up not only our personal freedoms for our career—but often our beliefs as well. When the brass in Washington make a decision, our military are sworn to carry out the necessary details—without question.

"For my part, I can understand the Seminoles' reluctance to leave their home and the resistance they are showing. One can surely recognize Osceola as a respected leader—and Jackson's ultimatum was bound to push him and the rest of the Seminoles to the limit. I certainly don't understand or support, however, the new attacks he has instigated—against innocent settlers—or even one of his own! Despite my military career, I don't—and never have supported—killing for any reason. Yet here I am about to embark on another assignment that will surely cause one—or many of us—to lose his life.

"Amanda wants me to retire, as I already have over twenty years in the U.S. Army. With what lays ahead of me, I may wish I'd taken her suggestion earlier. Right now, though, I am sworn to obey Clinch's order and hoping it won't be my last assignment!" he concluded—straightening his blotter, slamming his drawer closed, and sliding his chair into place.

"And I pray you will make it back to Amanda and Fannie. Having lost my father as a lad, I can feel for your little daughter. I've seen how much she adores you."

"Happy travels. I may see you at Brooke before we head off," Dade sighed as he shouldered his pack, motioned to Tresca, and followed him to the door—turning the lock and closing it with a final click.

"Whatever lies ahead, you are in my prayers."

• 33 •

December 21, 1835

*H*eavy clouds blocked what little sun the early morning was attempting to offer. Storm-weathered oak trees festooned with sodden, green Spanish moss bent their branches low over the wet, leaf-strewn path leading to the officers' quarters at Fort Brooke as Fred Tresca and William Hackley exited the *Margaret Ann* and headed to the base officers' quarters. "Not quite our sun-drenched Key West," William observed—sticking both hands into the sleeves of his heavy jacket and shivering involuntarily.

"And I, for one, will be happy to get back there," Tresca observed—pulling his hat down over his disheveled dark locks. "How long do you think it will take for you to interview Saunders and get a report to send to your father?"

"Knowing my dad, he will want a concise monetary assessment—in writing. Despite my legal degree, I will probably need one of the Brooke lawyers to sign onto the loss. Hope with the holiday upon us, there are still some legal brains among the infantry! Won't know until we check in at headquarters."

"Really thought to be here and on the way home by now. Had planned to spend Christmas in my own bed—not the rolling one we have experienced for the past five days. December storms are rare out here, but—as you said—it's not Key West!

"Actually, expected to see the *Motto* out there," he continued—pointing to the large, empty wharf to the north of the smaller dock where he had tied up. "Dade and his contingent left two days before us. He said he was heading to Charlotte Harbor for a quick visit. Hope he didn't have trouble over there!"

"If the Seminoles out there caused any uprisings, I may have a problem back at Sanybel on the way home. Sorry, Tresca. I'd hoped for a quick trip as well.

"Just imagine what life would have been like if this gorgeous plantation house had remained in the family," William sighed—as they made their way to the veranda of the lovely Southern mansion—where a large placard at the base of the wide, white wooden veranda steps announced "Fort Brooke Headquarters."

"Amazing how much things have changed since I first came up here," Tresca nodded. "Forgotten rancho, a few Seminole remnants, and a transfer station for illegal goods from Cuba. Big lore at the time was about a pirate named Gaspar, who had frequented the area. Despicable fellow I heard. Once captured a group of novices headed to a convent in Mexico. Took a liking to the young princess, Useppa, who was in charge. When she rebuffed his advances, however, story is he beheaded her down south of here—and buried her on the island that now bears her name."

"So that's where the island gets its unusual name. It's part of Father's property as well. Actually thought of marketing it, but it's not as approachable as Sanybel, and we couldn't find a real water source. Now that I know the tale, though, the story might provide enough interest to sell lots there as well."

"While you may have problems dealing with your father's property, never let it be said that you don't look for a way to make a dollar out of the most tragic situations!" Fred Tresca laughed as they ascended the steps and made their way to the front door.

Heavy footfalls on the steps behind them caused both men to stop and back away as a uniformed sentry ran past them, pushed open the main door, saluted, and announced to the front desk sergeant, "Just spotted the *Motto*—heading upriver. Should be here in a few minutes. Please alert Captain Belton. He asked me to watch for it. Captains Gardiner and Fraser will want to be advised as well."

"So Dade made it at last," Fred Tresca smiled. "I could have gotten him here at the same time, and he would have had two extra days at home!"

"Just as well," William laughed. "Wouldn't have wanted to share my bunk with all those recruits he was bringing with him. Hope they brought enough warm clothes if Belton has a march in mind. Far cry from the Caribbean up here."

As Tresca and William were seated in the office reception room waiting for William's interview with the army lawyer on duty, a thunder of footsteps sounded on the front veranda—as the sentry opened the door, saluted, and announced "Major Francis Dade."

Following the man into the room, the formidable Dade's face registered an immediate smile as he recognized his Key West friends. "So you actually beat me here!"

"Tough trip for both of us. December weather is not always predictable," Tresca added—rising to shake Dade's hand.

"Nor warm," Dade offered—shivering involuntarily. "Worried about my men out there. Many of them have not known winter recently—if ever."

"Troubles down in Sanybel?" William asked—rising and extending his hand as well. "Tresca tells me you were visiting one of the local chieftains . . ."

"Sadly, he'd heard about the unrest up here—as well as Osceola's murder of Emathla—from one of his men who had come back from the Peace River area. His tribe is a small one, though, and I don't really think he wants to get into the fray at the moment—or risk his own life if he complies with Clinch's order. For the moment then, he seems to be hoping the turmoil will pass him by."

"As do I," William sighed. "Don't need an incident down at Sanybel when I'm dealing with the destruction of Saunders's store and the unrest on our Hillsborough properties up here."

"Major Dade, Captain Belton will see you, sir," the sentry who had led Dade in called—walking back from the office wing.

"Good to see you both," Dade called—affecting a salute as he turned. Then, turning back, he called, "Tresca, when you get back home, would you please visit Amanda and tell her we got here safely? She always worries when I'm on a ship!" he added as he headed down the hall.

"If what I think is about to transpire down that hall, I think poor Amanda has a lot more to worry about on land!" Fred Tresca said sadly as he and William took their seats again.

Within moments, a second sentry arrived—escorting a small-statured man in his early forties dressed in a blue wool overcoat.

Removing his black leather cap, the officer shook the raindrops from his dark hair and attempted to dry his beard with his gloved hand as he announced "Captain Upton Fraser. I believe Captain Belton is expecting me."

"My Lord, Fraser, so you got the call as well!" called a second officer—also dressed in the same blue overcoat, which—unlike Fraser's—was stretched over a rather wide frame, which exhibited a middle-aged spread. "Captain George Gardiner," he announced to the desk clerk, who saluted and headed off down the hall.

"I saw the *Motto* at the dock as I came up. Guess this means our Key West reinforcements have finally arrived. Ready to get this assignment underway—as soon as Belton approves it—although I find it hard to leave right now."

"Always hard to leave at Christmas," Fraser nodded.

"Not the holiday," Gardiner answered—removing his leather cap as well and running his fingers through a shock of white hair. "Frances is pretty sick, and I really hate to leave her right now. So the sooner we get this assignment underway the quicker I can get back to her."

"Not sure how many men Dade was able to bring," Fraser added—shaking his head. "Saw the men filing off the *Motto*. Unless he has hidden several more away, though, it didn't look like more than forty or so. Last I heard, the Mikasuki have already amassed over 250 at the Withlacoochee. Seems like certain suicide with the one hundred or so we can muster on the Fort King march."

"What else is new, Fraser? I've been around long enough to learn our army big wigs are quick to sign and send orders to those of us in the field—while they throw another log on their fire."

"Still, I'd rather have a physical assignment any day—than to try to plan attacks from a desktop."

"You may think differently when you reach my age," Gardiner answered—shaking his head. "Freezing, soaking, fording rivers, jumping palmettos, felling trees—while keeping a constant lookout for the natives! I've been there one too many times, I tell you. Only wish there were another go-getter like you who was eager to take my place."

"Sirs, the captain will see both of you now," the clerk announced—saluting and waving the two men down the hall.

"Oh, my God," Fred Tresca whispered to William after the men had left, "it sounds like Dade is marching his men into the Seminoles' trap. I wonder if Clinch knew the extent of the buildup when he sent that letter I delivered to Dade."

"Jackson's order for the Seminoles to move by January 1 certainly seems to have set the powder keg," William answered.

• *34* •

December 23, 1835

"*W*eather's getting worse," William Hackley called—shivering as he wiped the intermittent raindrops from his face, shoved his gloved hands farther into his overcoat, and joined Fred Tresca on deck.

Attempting to unfurl one of the sails into the oncoming gale, Tresca shook his head. "Had hoped to head home today and—hopefully—get there by Christmas. Looks like the powers that be have other ideas, however. Not worth the risk with wind like this," he continued—rerolling the sail and securing it in place. "Seems the *Motto* crew is of the same mind—as they haven't yet raised their sails," he observed—pointing up the beach to the larger naval vessel that had brought Dade and his men from Key West. "Looks like we'll all have to spend the next day or two in port."

"Better than spending it in Davy Jones' Locker," William remarked. "Sorry it took me so long to settle Saunders's claim, but at least it's done and I won't need to come back up here. With all that's about to happen from here to Fort King, I'll be glad to get back to Key West."

"My sentiments exactly; however, I don't have that luxury. Dade gave me a letter to take back to the base, and I expect his replacement there will have a reply I'll have to bring back up here for him when he returns. While there's nothing better than a sunny day of sailing, it can prove pretty harrowing on days like this one!

"Hey, got some coffee in the cabin," he added—retying the sail. "What do you say we go grab a mug? We can even sing a carol or two if you'd like! Don't think either of us wants to go even as far as the mess hall on base today. Expect the planned march will be delayed as well."

"Not on your life," William called out—pointing toward the large lawn in front of the base headquarters. "Unless I miss my guess, that's Gardiner out there—with the roan horse. Can't miss his silhouette. Seems to be mustering his troops," he added—watching as a crowd of men in sky-blue uniforms—highlighted with white cross-belts—suddenly materialized on the field in front of base headquarters. Quickly donning a blue wool cape and pulling a black leather cap farther down as the relentless rain pounded the front lawn, each man secured his knapsack, placed his musket across his chest, and turned to Gardiner, who seemed to be lining them up two by two.

"Where? What foolhardy move is it to send the men out on a march in this deluge?"

"I'm sure I don't know, but the shorter officer in the blue coat looks a lot like Captain Fraser. One of his men just brought his horse, and he seems to be organizing his company as well."

"Do you see Dade? I'm sure Amanda will want to know he got off safely," Tresca asked—turning to the railing himself.

"Don't see him yet. Oh, wait, there he is. Just rode up and dismounted—over there with Gardiner. They seem to be having some sort of conversation. Lots of hand gesturing," William laughed. "Probably trying to decide who gets to lead the brigade and who has to handle the cannon. Think I'd prefer to bring up the rear—even with having to pull the cannon—if the Seminoles are waiting en route."

"Looks like Dade won out—whatever the question was—as Gardiner just remounted and seems to be leaving," Tresca noted.

"Strange. Yet what do I know? I never had any interest in joining the military."

"Probably most of those men out there wish they had never joined as well. Looks like they have no choice right now," Tresca called as a shrill horn suddenly sounded. The men quickly saluted, turned, and began their trek—following Dade as he rode to the base perimeter. At Dade's approach, the gates of the fort suddenly parted. Positioned two by two and followed by a horse-drawn supply wagon and four oxen pulling the cannon, the column quickly advanced up the muddy Fort King Road—as the gate swung closed behind them.

As hoof beats muffled on the wet, sandy path, protesting horses whinnied their discomfort, freezing soldiers pulled their overcoats tighter, and the plodding oxen hauling the creaking cannon reluctantly brought up the rear, Major Francis Dade's B and C Companies marched to their destiny.

Watching the gate swing shut with a final click echoing in the damp morning air, Fred Tresca—a loyal Frenchman—effected a salute and then crossed his chest with the sign of the cross. Looking upward, he called, "God be with you, my friend."

January 1, 1836

A smoky, gray fog hung over the white-capped Hillsborough River as William Bunce guided his *Associate* toward Brooke. Rounding the point, he raised his telescope—smiling as he glimpsed Tresca's mail boat, the *Margaret Ann,* anchored at the dock. "Luck is on my side," he called. "Just hope he doesn't leave before I get there."

Quickly heading upriver, Bunce pulled his small schooner in behind the *Margaret Ann,* and tied up at the dock. Running into the cabin, he picked up a large envelope and slid it inside his jacket to protect it from the damp weather, slammed his leather cap over a shock of unruly red curls, returned to the deck, and lowered the plank.

Hurrying up the dock to the *Margaret Ann,* but seeing no one on board, he looked across the wide front lawn of the Fort Brooke officers' quarters to see Fred Tresca heading down the steps with a full mailbag.

"Glad I caught you," Bunce called out—running up the walk to meet him. "Afraid you might have left already. Waited for the celebrations here last night, I suppose. I had a small gathering at my rancho, but nothing much with the inclement weather. I, for one, am more than glad to see 1835 ended. Guess the sentiment on base was the same."

"Bunce, sorry, William and I planned to stop at your place on our way up here, but Key West had some important messages that needed to reach Captain Belton before the end of the year. Was hoping that was the end of it and I could return home, but that wasn't to be. Had to send William and a letter from Dade back on the *Motto* because—wouldn't you know it—Belton asked me to wait for news on Dade and take it on to Tallahassee. Since we've heard nothing yet, though, he wants me to take a new message on to Tallahassee."

"As do I," Bunce interrupted—holding out his letter. "January first was the time for the Indian removal—right? That's what my letter is about. My ranch hands want to be immune to the order—as their ancestry predates the present tribes in the territory and they don't really hold with the Seminoles—or any of their chiefs. Frankly, though, whatever the decision, I need them through the season and am asking for at least a temporary reprieve from Tallahassee."

"Seems things are pretty much up in the air right now—if what I've heard is true," Tresca answered—shaking his head as he slipped the envelope into the mailbag.

"You say there's been no news yet on Dade's campaign? Heard it was understaffed when further recruits didn't show. The *Motto* stopped on its way back to Key West, and William was able to give me the early details," Bunce nodded. "Seems Gardiner was able to put his wife on board as well and then traveled on to join Dade's group. Brave souls— all of them. Not sure I would have agreed to march into the bloodbath Osceola had promised."

"They are soldiers," Tresca sighed, "and sworn to obey orders—no matter the danger involved. As a youngster, I heard enough of the Napoleonic wars to determine I never wanted to let another man make a decision for me. Master of my own ship—and my own destiny—suits me just fine. As far as I've heard, though, there has still been no news of their arrival at Fort King—or any further entanglements with the Seminoles."

"I gathered things had slowed when I passed Egmont Key. Seminoles were supposed to depart from there yesterday on their way to New Orleans and their new home, but several ships were still in port and there didn't seem to be any action," Bunce continued—as a sentry suddenly thundered up the steps to the officers' quarters and flung open the front door.

"Looks like some kind of action here, though," Tresca called— turning with Bunce to head down the walk. Within a few minutes, the sentry returned—followed by two medics with a stretcher who ran across the lawn and disappeared on the way to the back gate.

"Wonder if some of Dade's forces have returned?" Bunce asked. "Worth waiting for the news," he continued as he took a seat on one of the benches under the nearby mess tent.

"I'll just throw my bag on board and join you. Governor Eaton will want to know whatever news there is, and I'll be at St. Marks by tomorrow—weather permitting."

Within minutes, the medics ran up the walk carrying the stretcher containing a young man in a disheveled blue uniform—the white cross on his chest smeared with both mud and what looked like dried blood.

"One of Dade's men?" Bunce asked.

"That's their uniform," Tresca nodded as the men made their way up the steps and into the office compound. "Not sure anyone could recognize him in his present condition, though."

Within minutes, one of the sentries ran down the steps—headed toward Tresca's schooner. Seeing Fred Tresca under the tent, however, he turned and ran over to him. "So glad you're still here. Captain Belton wants you to wait. Says he needs to send another letter to Governor Eaton."

"Was that one of Dade's men that was carried in just now?"

"The only one—if what he said is correct," the sentry answered—shaking his head. "Private Ransom Clark. Young kid, but one of our intrepid mail carriers to Fort King. Actually asked to go on the march, he said."

"Passed a mail-bag for Fort King off to him one day last fall," Tresca nodded. "Quick to tell me he's had several encounters with the Seminoles on his various trips. Did he say what happened?"

"Only that Dade's companies were apparently followed from the time they left Brooke. Said he'd heard them in the palmettos at night and had reported it to Dade, who told him not to worry. Said—despite the rotten weather—Dade had determined they were safe when they crossed into open ground over near Bushnell. They'd no sooner entered the pine barren when a shot rang out—knocking Dade from his horse and killing him instantly. The Seminoles under Micanopy and Alligator proceeded to wipe out all but two of the company by nightfall. Although severely wounded, Clark was able to find one other survivor, and the two decided to head back to Brooke together until his friend, DeCourcy, was met by a lone Seminole.

"Couldn't tell us much else—as he's too badly injured. Medics got him in to Captain Belton immediately to get the full story. Guess we'll find out more once Belton has finished with him. I'm supposed to make sure you don't leave until Captain Belton finishes his interview and writes his summary to Governor Eaton."

"Sadly, all the strides our territory has made since the Adams-Onis Treaty will now become a part of 'Forgotten Florida' as we struggle once again to make this land safe for our citizens. Of course, I'll wait for the epistle—and—most likely bring back word from Tallahassee that our Second Seminole War is now underway!"

Afterword

$\mathcal{M}$ajor Francis Dade had taken command—to allow Captain George Gardiner to return to his seriously ill wife. When Gardiner discovered, however, that the *Motto* was still in port and could take her back to Key West—where she had family—he rethought his decision and rode out to join the march several days later.

On the morning of December 28, 1835, Major Francis Dade's force of 110 men of Companies B and C was met in an ambush staged by over 180 Seminole warriors—led by Micanopy and Alligator—at a pine barren near Bushnell. Chief Micanopy, who recognized Dade from one of his earlier encounters, fired the first shot—knocking Dade from his horse with a fatal shot through his heart. Hostilities continued throughout the day—leaving only three survivors.

The guide, Louis Pacheco, was taken prisoner by the Seminoles and led away by sundown. Nineteen-year-old Private Ransom Clark and Private Edwin DeCourcy were left for dead, but—although severely wounded—managed to find each other after dark and decided to find their way back to Fort Brooke.

A mounted Seminole scout found the two the following day—shooting and killing DeCourcy. Clark, however, eluded the scout and proceeded to follow the road back to Fort Brooke for the next three days—where he was able to report the massacre. One additional survivor, Private Joseph Sprague, wandered into the fort the following day—where the two survivors related the incident.

Also, on the afternoon of December 28, Indian agent, Wiley Thompson, and Lieutenant Constantine Smith were ambushed and killed by a contingent led by Osceola outside the walls of Fort King—as they strolled after dinner. These two concurrent incidents were the impetus for Florida's Second Seminole War—which lasted until 1842.

Sadly, Dade's battle site, abandoned equipment, and the 107 bodies of the loyal soldiers were left undisturbed for over six weeks as the various battles erupted throughout the interior of the territory. Finally, on February 13, 1836, General Gaines led a thousand-man brigade into Seminole territory en route to Fort King—where they at last discovered the site of Dade's battle. Burying the 107 bodies, they played the funeral march—posthumously honoring the many brave men whose memory is still alive at the Dade Massacre site at Bushnell—as well as in the southern county of "Dade," which bears the major's name.

Further Reading

Anholt, Betty, and Charles LeBuff, *Protecting Sanibel and Captiva Islands, The Conservation Story*, The History Press, Charleston, SC, December 10, 2018.

Bair, Cinnamon, "How Fort Brooke Came to Be," *The Ledger*, Lakeland, FL, November 15, 2011.

Bickel, Karl A., *The Mangrove Coast*, Omni Print Media, Inc., 1989.

Brooke, George Mercer, Jr., *Early Days of Fort Brooke*, Vol. 1, Scholar Commons—University of South Florida, 1974.

Burnett, Gene M., "Of Red Hopes and White Politics," *Florida's Past*, Vol. 3, Pineapple Press, Inc., Sarasota, Florida, 1991.

Conrad, Gibby, "The Cracker Prince," *Tallahassee Magazine,* June 28, 2012.

Covington, James W., ed., "The Establishment of Fort Brooke—The Beginning of Tampa," *Florida Historical Quarterly*, Vol. 31, No. 4 (Apr. 1953), pp. 273–278.

Delle, James, ed., *The Limits of Tyranny*, p. 220, University of Tennessee Press, 2015.

Gannon, Michael, *Florida: A Short History*, University Press of Florida, 1993.

Grismer, Karl, *A History of Tampa and the Tampa Bay Region of Florida*, Library Press @ University of Florida, 1950.

Hambright, Tom, "Commodore David Porter Arrives at Key West," *Florida Keys Sea Heritage Journal*, Vol. 22, No. 3, Spring 2012.

Hammond, E. A., "The Spanish Fisheries of Charlotte Harbor," *Florida Historical Quarterly*, Vol. 51, No. 4, April 1973.

Liles, Harriet Stiger, "A Gallant Soldier," *The Historical Association of Southern Florida*, Vol. 13, No. 1, 1986.

Magg, Jeri, *Remarkable Women of Sanibel and Captiva*, The History Press, Charleston, SC, 2016.

Mahan, John K., *History of the Second Seminole War 1835-1842*, Library Press @ University of Florida, George A. Smathers Libraries, pp. 51–68.

Matthews, Janet Snyder, *Edge of Wilderness*, Caprine Press, 1981.

Maynard, Jackson Wilder, Jr., "According to Their Capacities and Talents," *Frontier Attorneys in Tallahassee During the Territorial Period*, Florida State University Libraries, 2004.

McIver, Stuart, "Riding the Seminole Trail," *Sun Sentinel*, Deerfield Beach, FL, July 23, 1989.

Paisley, Clifton, *The Red Hills of Florida, 1528-1865*, University of Alabama Press, 1989.

Pizzo, Tony, *Fort Brooke: The First Ten Years*, Sunland Tribune, Vol. 14, Art. 4, Scholar Commons, University of South Florida, 1988.

Roberts, Donald J., II, "The Seminole Indian War," Warfare History Network, McLean, VA, November 26, 2015.

Sivilich, Michelle, Norman Sean, and Jonathan Dean, *Fort King Road: Battlefields and Baggage Trains*, Gulf Archeology Research Institute, 2017.